Praise for *The Me I Used to Be*

"Jennifer Ryan takes family drama to a new level in this tangled emotional web of a novel. Secrets come to light, love is rekindled, and redemption is found—all in the glorious golden sunshine of the Napa Valley. I loved it!"

—Susan Wiggs, *New York Times* bestselling author

"*The Me I Used to Be* is Jennifer Ryan at the height of her storytelling best. Page-turning, powerful, with high-stakes drama and unforgettable romance. I couldn't put it down!"

—Jill Shalvis, *New York Times* bestselling author

"Gripping and emotionally compelling, *The Me I Used to Be* is a beautiful story of losing yourself, starting over against all odds, and coming out triumphant. I was hooked from page one!"

—Lori Foster, *New York Times* bestselling author

"Ryan (*Dirty Little Secret*) delivers an intoxicating blend of hair-raising suspense, betrayal, and true love with this gripping contemporary set in the rich vineyards of Napa Valley. . . . Ryan's fans will devour this outstanding tale, as will the many new readers she's bound to win."

—*Publishers Weekly* (starred review)

Praise for *Sisters and Secrets*

"Jennifer Ryan's *Sisters and Secrets* should win an award for being the most unputdownable book of the whole year. The drama will keep you on the edge of your seat, and the emotional roller coaster will touch every emotion."

—Carolyn Brown, *New York Times* and *USA Today* bestselling author

"Sibling rivalry comes to a head in a masterpiece of family and secrets."

—Fresh Fiction

Praise for *Lost and Found Family*

"Ryan is a master of the dysfunctional family unit, creating characters that draw you in and keep you engaged while immersing the reader in twisty stories that are overflowing with secrets and betrayals. *Lost and Found Family* is a complex, deeply emotional, and satisfying story that reinforces Jennifer Ryan's immense storytelling skill and a book I recommend."

—The Romance Dish

"*Lost and Found Family* is a rags-to-riches story in a totally unique package. . . . Sarah just may be Jennifer Ryan's most complex character to date. . . . Ryan masterfully sets the scene for Sarah's new world with grace, heart, and integrity."

—Fresh Fiction

The One You Want

Also by Jennifer Ryan

STAND-ALONE NOVELS
Lost and Found Family • *Sisters and Secrets*
The Me I Used to Be

THE WYOMING WILDE SERIES
Chase Wilde Comes Home

THE MCGRATH SERIES
True Love Cowboy • *Love of a Cowboy* • *Waiting on a Cowboy*

WILD ROSE RANCH SERIES
Tough Talking Cowboy • *Restless Rancher* • *Dirty Little Secret*

MONTANA HEAT SERIES
Tempted by Love • *True to You*
Escape to You • *Protected by Love*

MONTANA MEN SERIES
His Cowboy Heart • *Her Renegade Rancher*
Stone Cold Cowboy • *Her Lucky Cowboy*
When It's Right • *At Wolf Ranch*

THE MCBRIDES SERIES
Dylan's Redemption • *Falling for Owen*
The Return of Brody McBride

THE HUNTED SERIES
Everything She Wanted • *Chasing Morgan*
The Right Bride • *Lucky Like Us* • *Saved by the Rancher*

SHORT STORIES
"Close to Perfect" (appears in *Snowbound at Christmas*)
"Can't Wait" (appears in *All I Want for Christmas Is a Cowboy*)
"Waiting for You" (appears in *Confessions of a Secret Admirer*)

The
One You Want

A Novel

JENNIFER
RYAN

AVON

An Imprint of HarperCollinsPublishers

This is a work of fiction. Names, characters, places, and incidents are products of the author's imagination or are used fictitiously and are not to be construed as real. Any resemblance to actual events, locales, organizations, or persons, living or dead, is entirely coincidental.

THE ONE YOU WANT. Copyright © 2022 by Jennifer Ryan. All rights reserved. Printed in the United States of America. No part of this book may be used or reproduced in any manner whatsoever without written permission except in the case of brief quotations embodied in critical articles and reviews. For information, address HarperCollins Publishers, 195 Broadway, New York, NY 10007.

HarperCollins books may be purchased for educational, business, or sales promotional use. For information, please email the Special Markets Department at SPsales@harpercollins.com.

FIRST EDITION

Designed by Diahann Sturge

Title page and chapter opener image © satit sewtiw / Shutterstock, Inc.

Library of Congress Cataloging-in-Publication Data has been applied for.

ISBN 978-0-06-309411-6

22 23 24 25 26   LSC   10 9 8 7 6 5 4 3 2 1

For all the fearless hearts out there who dive into love with the expectation they will find a soft, safe place to land.

Chapter One

8 days to Maggie's wedding . . .

Rose Howell stared out the car windshield at the two-story clapboard house painted in three different shades of beige. Cheerful flowering bushes lined the path to the porch and front door. The house she grew up in. It looked plain. Ordinary. Nothing special. A family's house. The picture of normal. No one outside those walls knew the secrets this house held. How those four walls and a roof made a house, but not a home.

Outside was the image of middle-class success.

Inside, a nightmare played out of a family ruined by alcoholism, anger, abuse, unfulfilled dreams and promises, and a gnawing desire to escape even though you had nowhere to go.

Trapped in that house as a child, Rose had felt the walls closing in, but the windows had given her a glimpse of the outside world that seemed vast and peaceful. The tension had suffocated her. And her father's presence loomed large and scary, a threat waiting to happen.

Rose escaped this particular circle of hell on earth by taking the one opportunity she had worked hard for because it offered her a better life. College.

Her father drilled into her that the only way to succeed was to be better than everyone else. As a child, that meant getting the best grades in school. She did so easily. School was never that hard for her. It was a sanctuary even in the worst of times, though school could be its own social challenge. She graduated third in her class.

Most parents would have been ecstatic. Not her father. She wasn't number one. In his eyes, she'd failed miserably.

Strange he thought so, since he hadn't even graduated in the top ten percent of his class.

Her mom revealed that little secret to cheer her up after a particularly blistering setdown by her dad for the B+ she received on an AP geometry test.

Logic didn't often play into his outbursts and demands for his daughters.

He wanted Rose and her younger sister, Poppy, to be the best at everything, so they wouldn't be held back the way her father seemed to believe everyone held him back from achieving greatness.

He didn't get the promotion because someone less productive, less deserving, somehow stole it from him. The boss had it in for him. Someone didn't like him. They never gave him credit for all his hard work. They didn't see his potential.

At first as a young girl, she'd thought it terribly unfair that people treated her father so badly. As she got older, she realized the truth. He hadn't been overlooked or underestimated. He'd simply expected to be given what he thought he deserved even if he hadn't earned it.

But the hardest thing to accept and understand was that nothing she did would ever be good enough. She'd never win his approval or praise.

She left for college with one intent in mind. To never go home again. To build a life free of her father, this place, and its dark memories.

She'd been gone eight years.

Not nearly long enough to forget.

She stared at the house, her roiling emotions a swirl of anger, resentment, hate, and deep sadness.

I will never forget.

But she'd learned to live with the baggage tainting her new experiences and the growth she'd achieved both personally and professionally.

She lived the life she'd always wanted now. She had friends, a good job, and her own cute apartment. She'd even learned to stop looking at all men and seeing her father. She had stopped thinking that everything they said was some kind of back-handed compliment. Maybe she didn't wholly trust men, but she didn't outright dismiss them anymore. Still, she'd never felt loved, never been in love.

Did love even exist? She often wondered about that.

Rose had been sitting in her car outside the house for twenty minutes, unable to force herself to go in. She didn't want to be confronted with all those twisted memories of when her father had made his issues their problem.

It had taken her a long time to come to the conclusion that her father was a sad man, doomed to failure and loss by his own words and actions. He would never be happy or feel loved or succeed in anything. He probably would have died alone and miserable had he not fallen down the stairs drunk and broken his neck three years ago.

The twisted son of a bitch died a far better death than he deserved.

She hadn't mourned the loss of the man who brought her nothing but pain. She swore he liked it, hurting them and putting her, Mom, and Poppy down all the time.

She didn't even attend the funeral.

And now, Rose had come home at last, for her best friend Maggie's wedding. She also wanted to use this week to reconnect with her mother and sister, hoping they could finally put the past behind them and start fresh. And she hadn't seen Maggie in a while, either.

She had a week to make up for lost time with her best friend and her family.

Was that enough time to bury the past? Maybe not. But she hoped to tear down the walls she'd erected around her heart where her mom and sister were concerned.

She'd reached out to Poppy over the years and gotten nothing but scathing rejections. Poppy hated Rose for leaving her behind and blamed Rose for their father's cruelty.

The guilt weighed on Rose. The deep and heavy ache she carried never waned.

She wished she'd been stronger. She wished she'd known what to say to Poppy to make her leave and come to Rose.

She wished for a lot of things to be different.

Telling herself she'd done the best she could under the circumstances didn't help.

She didn't want to be there at all, but she'd promised Maggie a kickass bachelorette party and to be the best maid of honor any bride could want this week. She promised her best friend they'd spend as much time together as possible to close the gap that had been widening in their relationship because of work and life.

It was inevitable things would change as they got older and reached new milestones, like Maggie getting married while Rose remained single, but they'd vowed to always be best friends.

Rose would forever be family to the two people, almost strangers now, still living inside that house, but she didn't know if they'd still be in her life if they hadn't been connected by blood.

But she'd promised herself she would try one more time to overcome the past and find a way to reconnect with her mom and Poppy, because she missed them.

She took a deep breath, grabbed her purse off the seat beside her, and got out of the car. She took her suitcase from the back seat, walked the path up to the porch, and knocked on the door. It opened to her past and an onslaught of memories as the familiar sights and smells hit her. Lemon oil on the same old wood furniture along with the lavender Mom clipped from the garden, put into small vases, and placed on the dining room table and on the mantel in the living room.

The second she looked into her mother's eyes for the first time in years, she knew everything was the same but also completely different. Because Rose was not the kid who'd left, but the woman she'd become away from this place and the parents who'd tried to ruin her.

She set her shoulders and held her head high. "Hi, Mom. It's been a long time."

Her mom pressed her lips tight. "You shouldn't have come back here."

Chapter Two

*R*ose hadn't seen her mother since before her father died. She tried and failed not to be disappointed now. She'd told her mom she was coming for this visit, despite the older woman telling her it would do more harm than good for Rose to dredge up hurtful memories. "Aren't you even a little happy to see me?"

Her mom's eyes softened and her lips drew back in a rare easy smile. For a second Rose glimpsed the woman she remembered from when she was very young. "Of course I'm happy to see you. I've missed you so much. But you have a new life now."

Rose stepped into the house, set her suitcase aside, and stood a foot away from her mom. "I've missed you, too," she confessed, allowing herself to really feel it now that she was here.

Her mom's eyes turned misty right before she pulled Rose in for a hug that was nearly bone crushing.

It took Rose a second to embrace her mother and another moment for past hurts and resentments to fall away and for her to really feel the warmth and love her mom poured into her. She couldn't remember the last time her mom had hugged her like she really meant it. Though the initial greeting had been frosty, this was anything but.

Rose broke away first, stepping back to steady her nerves and get a good look at her mom. Nancy Howell had aged, of course, the years under Rose's father's domination carving deep wrinkles into her forehead and stealing the light from her eyes. She'd always seemed weary to Rose. That hadn't changed, but there was something softer about her. Less tense, more at ease, but not quite ready to fully let her guard down.

There were other small changes. She didn't have her hair pulled back into an austere chignon. It hung straight and framed her face, brushing the tops of her shoulders. Her usual makeup was missing today. While she'd been married to Rose's father she'd always worn simple sheath dresses, all in the dark colors he wanted to see her in, all of which made her mother's too pale skin look sallow against her brown hair and eyes. Today she wore a loose pair of straight-leg, light blue linen pants with a cream-colored top that complemented her warm skin tone and brought out her rosy cheeks.

She hadn't gained a lot of weight, but enough that her face wasn't all sharp angles. There was a softness to her appearance now.

Rose imagined her mother could finally eat without anxiety making everything turn sour in her gut and could sleep in peace, the worries evaporating into the past and disappearing like her father had from their lives. His presence in the house had sometimes made just breathing hard because you were always wondering what he'd say or do next.

Yes, they walked on eggshells, but it was more than that. It was like living with a faulty ticking time bomb. In the calm, you thought everything was all right. Just when you thought you could exhale and relax, all hell broke loose.

Everyone was happy to see him off to work. No one was happy to see him come home each day. But they all waited in anticipation, dread filling them up and putting everyone on edge.

But it hadn't always been that way.

She remembered a kinder, gentler man from her early childhood years. Why else would her mom have married him? If Rose tried really hard, she could even remember seeing love in his eyes and happiness in her mother's face.

Now she couldn't stand to see the contrast in the old photos on the walls. The early years when all of them were smiling and happy, arms around each other, gave way to kids with forced grins, blank stares, everyone standing close but apart. She doubted any of them wanted to be in those later photos, let alone near each other.

In contrast, Rose's friend Maggie had a great family and father. He doted on her.

He was so excited about walking his daughter down the aisle.

"Rose." Her mother looked at her, concerned. "I told you, you shouldn't have come back. This place is not for you. Not anymore."

Rose crossed her arms and brushed her hands up and down her biceps. "He's not here, but I still feel him everywhere sometimes." She changed the subject. "You look good, Mom. I love the outfit."

Her mom nervously smoothed her hands down her thighs. "Thank you. I . . ." She didn't finish whatever she wanted to say.

"He can't tell you what to wear, what a proper wife should look like anymore. What the hell did he know?" She eyed her mom up and down. "You know exactly what you like and what makes you feel pretty. And it shows."

A soft smile bloomed very slowly. "Thank you, Rose." Her mother had received so few compliments in her life, especially in the last twenty years.

It made Rose's heart ache that her mom felt so deeply about a few kind words.

"I . . . I really can't believe you're here."

"Don't get used to it." Her sister, Poppy, stood behind her mother, glaring at Rose. "We both know she's not staying and won't be back."

Her mother's appearance had improved the last few years, but Poppy's had changed dramatically for the worse. Bone-thin, dark circles marring the underside of her eyes. Her all-black outfit of leggings and a T-shirt made her skin look ashen.

Rose couldn't help the gasp. "Poppy. Are you okay?"

The glare turned even darker. "Don't pretend to care." She looked Rose up and down in one quick sweep, pressed her lips tight, and narrowed her eyes, showing her contempt, and walked up the stairs, giving Rose her back with the dismissal.

Rose could only stare at her sister with a sense of loss, grief, guilt, and deep concern, knowing she deserved her sister's cutting rebuke, but wanting so badly to help her in whatever way possible.

She jumped when her mom touched her shoulder.

"She's not the same since you left."

Understatement of the fucking century.

Rose's stomach soured at the thought of what her father must have done to turn a vibrant teenager into a sullen and withered twenty-one-year-old. Or maybe it was something else. "She's so thin . . . Is she ill?"

Her mom waved her hand out for Rose to go into the kitchen. She left her suitcase in the entry, glanced one more time up the stairs, and followed her mom back to the kitchen. She looked around the room that should have been the heart of the home but had been the scene of many of the darkest times in her life.

Not much had changed. The appliances were old and outdated. The tile counters were clean, but the gray grout had darkened over the years. The wood cabinets had been painted white. They brightened the kitchen but only made the scarred tan linoleum look even more worn.

The microwave on the counter had to be twenty years old, the toaster even more ancient.

"You've made a few changes," she commented, hoping to ease her mom.

"Your father had a decent life insurance policy, but to make it last we have to be frugal. I'd like to replace the old appliances, redo the floor . . ." She trailed off, looking around the room like she could see what it could be. "It's not important."

"The cabinets look great. I'm glad you got rid of that old valance over the window. You've got a lot more light in here. And the new furniture's nice." Rose took a seat at the simple round table with matching chairs. Her mom had added pale blue cushions on the seats, brightening the place even more.

Her mom pulled two mugs off the hooks under the cabinet and proceeded to make tea. When it was brewed, she brought the mugs to the table and set one in front of Rose.

The chamomile and spearmint scent hit her nose and took her back in time to every sad or bad thing that happened in this house that was followed by a mug of tea.

"This was probably the first new thing you bought for the house that he didn't have to approve of first," Rose guessed, rubbing her hand over the tabletop.

Her mom's gaze met hers. "You always saw things so clearly."

"Maybe," she admitted. "But that doesn't mean they ever made sense to me."

"That's why he went after you all the time. You had this way of cutting through things and stating the basic, most obvious thing that he didn't want to hear or see. Why?" she asked on a whisper.

"Because he was wrong."

"And you just had to be right." The words were bitter and angry.

As if it were Rose's fault for causing the fight. If she'd just let it go . . .

It still would have ended in a fight because that's what he wanted.

But she couldn't dismiss her mom's stinging words. "I wanted him to acknowledge and understand that he was wrong. *He* made his life hell. Not me. Not you. Not Poppy. We could have all been happy if he'd seen that what he was doing was tearing us apart and done something about it."

Her mother took a sip of tea, then pinned Rose in her gaze again. "Don't you think he knew that?"

"He used it to get you to console him. He wanted your sympathy and warmth and kindness to soothe his black heart. But it never did. Not for long. Nothing ever would because he didn't want to change. He liked hurting us."

Her mom slapped her flat hand on the table. "That's not true."

Rose rolled her eyes. "How can you defend him? You know it's true."

"He worked hard. He wanted the best for you and Poppy."

Rose scoffed. "Seriously? If he wanted the best for me, then why were straight A's not good enough? Why was getting all the scholarships and grants and getting into college not enough? Why was winning a race or a swim meet not enough? The way I looked wasn't enough. The way I spoke. The things I did. The ideas I had . . . Nothing was ever good enough. *I* wasn't smart enough, kind enough, pretty enough. I was *never* enough!" It took her a second to realize she was leaning halfway across the table. She fell back in her seat and splayed her hands on the wood and tilted her head, a disturbing thought coming to mind. "Why did you replace the table?" She watched her mother's eyes go wide at the softly spoken question that had nothing and everything to do with all she'd just said. "Mom?"

She didn't answer, just stared at her lap.

Though Rose couldn't see them, she knew her mother held her hands tightly clenched on her thighs.

She spoke without meeting Rose's eyes. "He . . . Poppy made him very angry. She stayed out late . . . She was supposed to be home on time . . . He . . ." Her mother couldn't say it, but it was written all over her face.

Rose had seen her father destroy things in a rage, but her mother's face, her inability to say the words, and the fact she put the blame on Poppy . . . "Did he hurt Poppy for coming home late? Did he blame her for making him angry? Did he tell her that if she had just done what she was told, none of whatever he did would have happened? Did he scold you for raising a disobedient daughter?" She leaned forward again. "What did he do?"

Mom's lips trembled. "He picked her up and slammed her down on the table. The top broke off from the base and she fell to the floor. He picked up a chair and . . . she broke her arm."

"*He* broke her arm," Rose snapped.

Rose saw her father in her mind slam that chair down on Poppy, who tried to defend herself with her hands up to ward off the blow.

"When did this happen?"

Her mom sighed. "She was fifteen and rebellious. He'd warned her not to be late again." Sadly, her mom really believed that if Poppy had done everything their father wanted, none of this would have happened.

So not true. Her father had pushed, shoved, slapped, and kicked Rose in the legs since she was in fifth or sixth grade. Rose had been his favorite target, and when he did go after Poppy, whom he mostly ignored, Rose had stepped in between them. She was willing to take the punishment to spare her much younger sister.

She'd even stepped between her mother and father more often than not.

But after Rose fled, Poppy had been left to fend for herself. And Rose had to live with the guilt that she'd left her sister behind, even though she knew that if she'd stayed, he'd have killed her one way or another.

Still, it pissed her off that her mother fell back on defending her father, trying to keep the peace even though he was no longer here, and blamed Poppy.

"Dad broke all of us. And let me guess, when you took her to the hospital, you didn't report him. You made up some lie to protect him and made Poppy feel guilty for being the one to set Dad off. You begged her to go along, not make things worse, just this once." There had been a lot of "onces." "You promised it would never happen again. You told her he loved her. He didn't mean to hurt her."

"Stop!" Her mom had never raised her voice. She had never showed emotion during most of Rose's young life.

But Rose heard the anger, fear, and self-loathing in that one word. And she didn't let up. "Isn't that what you should have said to him the first time he laid a hand on me? You. Poppy. How many times did you stand by and stand back and let it happen?"

Her mom leaned forward, her gaze sharp. "What did you expect me to do?"

"I wanted you to stand up for us. To tell him he was wrong. To leave. I expected you to end it!"

Her mother shook her head side to side in a slow sweep, her lips pressed tight. "You have no idea how hard it was for me."

"All you had to do was walk out the door. Call the cops. Tell someone, anyone, that could help."

Her mom frowned. "Walk out with two little girls and no means to take care of them?"

"He would have had to pay child support," she snapped. "You could have gotten a job. Grammy and Grampy would have helped."

"They were barely getting by themselves." More excuses.

"They'd have put a roof over our heads."

"He was my husband. If we'd all tried harder—"

Rose smacked her hand on the table. "That's him in your head telling you how to fix it. But guess what? Nothing we did was the cause of his abuse and nothing we did would have stopped it, aside from us leaving. That is the truth, Mom. That is the only thing you could have done. But you didn't. You still haven't. You're stuck here in this house with all the memories. You've barely changed anything because you're afraid. He's not even here and you're still worried about what he'll think about the new paint on the cabinets, or that you bought a used table, and that you changed your hair and your clothes." Rose shook her head this time, then put her hand over her mother's. "Stop."

Her mom's gaze snapped up to meet hers.

"Stop letting him rule your life."

"I'm not."

"Stop lying to me, Poppy, everyone outside these walls. Stop lying to yourself. It's obvious to me and everyone else. Just stop. Because every time you make an excuse for him, or lie, or don't do and say the things you really want, then *he* wins. Stop letting him *be* your life and *live* your life."

"You have no idea how hard it is to let it go after all that's happened."

"Don't I? I walked away, Mom. I left. And it took a long time for me to stop hearing him in my head, to make my own choices, to learn to see myself, not through his eyes, but the reality of who and what I am. It wasn't easy. And yes, sometimes I still hear him or believe something that he thought about me, but when I do, I stop. I take the time to search within myself to hear my own voice and see things through my eyes, not his. Sometimes, I still think to myself, *Would he approve? Would he finally be proud of me? Would anything I've done and accomplished have made him want to change?* And I know the answer, even if I wish it was different. The answer is always no." She let that sink in for a moment with her mom. "No matter how badly I want it to be yes because he's my dad. I want so badly for him to have turned out to be a good one, but he wasn't. He wasn't ever going to be a good father, because he wasn't a good man. You know that. You felt it.

"And now he's gone, and you don't have to ever think about him again. You can start over. You can have whatever life you used to see for yourself. You can even find someone else, who will love and respect and take care of you." She paused. "You deserve happiness like that, Mom. Be bold. Be brave. Live your life like he's not watching."

The hint of a smile and flash of brightness in her mother's eyes told Rose she'd hit the mark.

"If it helps, find joy in the rebellion. Give him a big 'F you' every time you do something you know he wouldn't like but makes you feel good."

"Is that what you did?"

"Yes. With enthusiasm. In college, I stayed up late. I went out past eight o'clock at night. I dated boys he'd have hated. I wore things that made me feel pretty but he'd have scolded me for looking like a whore. I took psychology classes." A smile tugged at her lips.

Her mom shook her head but grinned. "He'd have thought that a waste of time."

It wasn't. She learned it wasn't her. It *was* him.

She couldn't fix him by being or doing something else.

Only he could fix himself.

Once she believed that, she was free.

"Don't apologize for moving forward even if Poppy isn't ready to do the same. For what it's worth, I can see it in your eyes that the idea appeals to you, that maybe you've been looking for an excuse—"

"You mean a push."

"If that's what it takes." Rose held her mom's gaze, knowing she'd just unfairly blamed her mom for everything even though she was a victim herself, but also wanting something better for her mom. "I want you to be happy. I don't want you sitting in this house alone with nothing but your guilt and sorrow like it's some penance you have to pay. You have no idea how happy I'd be to see you out doing something that you like and being who you want to be."

"I don't have any skills."

"That's not true at all. You're a fantastic cook. You sew. You love to garden and know the names of just about every plant. You'd make a great bookkeeper or receptionist. You don't have to start a specific career. Try things out. Start simple. Just start," she gently suggested. "You don't have to know what you like, but find something you love. If the first thing doesn't fit, try something else. There's no one who is going to say anything about it. It's just you." She thought her mom needed that reminder. "Try one new thing this week while I'm here."

"Like what?"

"Anything. It's up to you. Your choice."

Her mom looked intrigued.

"Don't overthink it. Just do it." Rose heard the chime of an incoming text and pulled her phone out of her pocket.

MAGGIE: Are you here? Please say yes!!!

Rose smiled and typed back.

ROSE: YES!!!

MAGGIE: Meet me at Lucky Lou's

MAGGIE: NOW

MAGGIE: It's a bride emergency

Rose glanced over at her mom. "It's Maggie. She wants me to meet up with her. A bride emergency, or something."

"Go. Have fun. It's why you came."

"I came to see you, too, Mom. I know things haven't been good between us in a long time. I stayed away on purpose because I couldn't let the past in again."

"I know. I understand. That's why I didn't want you to come back. It makes me happy to know you're out there, living your life, being happy."

Rose smiled. "Then you know how happy it would make me if you were doing the same thing."

"Point taken. One new thing." She smiled, this time a little easier than the last, it seemed.

"Promise."

The grin turned up a notch. "Promise. Now go help Maggie. I'm sure she's missed you as much as I have."

Rose stood to leave, but hesitated. "About Poppy . . ."

"She's lost in a lot of anger and pain. I've tried to pull her out of it, but . . ."

"What happened?"

Her mom looked up at her, sadness and regret clouding her eyes. "It's . . . complicated. And too long a story to tell now. Go. It can wait."

"I'm worried about her."

"You should be. But ultimately it's up to her to change. Isn't that what you've been telling me?"

"We are only responsible for ourselves."

Her mom shook her head. "Not true. I'm responsible for you and your sister. I failed you, and I'm so sorry. Sorrier than I can ever say." Tears glistened in her mother's eyes.

The apology meant a lot. "I appreciate that, Mom. I really do." She gave her mom another hug.

"I will talk to Poppy and try to bridge the gap between us. I know she's angry I left. I just didn't think she'd hold on to it this long and hard."

"It's not just about you," her mom assured her. "It's me, your father, and her." She folded her arms around her middle. "Things got really bad at the end." Her mom shook off her glum mood and tried to appear at ease again. "We'll talk more tomorrow. Go. Have fun."

"Be daring, Mom. Watch something he'd hate on TV tonight. Eat a bag of microwave popcorn on the sofa. It'll feel good to break his rules. Trust me."

"Maybe I'll have a glass of wine with that popcorn."

Rose grinned. "That's the spirit. You'll be a rebel in no time."

She gave her mom a quick kiss on the cheek and walked to the door, but stopped and stared up the stairs, wishing she knew how to reach past all Poppy's defenses and anger. But first, she had to see to her maid of honor duties.

Whatever Maggie needed, Rose hoped she could handle it and that it was less dramatic than seeing her mom and sister for the first time since she'd left for college.

Chapter Three

*P*oppy stared out her bedroom window, watching her sister climb into the newish white Trailblazer. Poppy wanted to scream at her to leave and never come back.

When Rose left for college, their mother called her weekly, and Poppy would listen in. Rose kept the calls short, saying everything was fine, but she never pulled off making them believe everything was all right. She sounded like she couldn't wait to get off the phone.

Dad tried to get in on those calls sometimes, but when he did, Rose always hung up.

Over time, the weekly calls got answered less and less, until Rose didn't answer at all. Mom kept trying. Dad got pissed. How dare Rose upset their mom? Like her dad cared if Mom was upset. He didn't. He just needed something to be mad about. Something, anything, to start a fight.

It didn't stop Poppy from blaming Rose for being difficult. For making things worse. For leaving. For forgetting about her.

Poppy blamed her for all of it. Even *that* night. Because if Rose had been here, their father wouldn't have picked on Poppy.

Sometimes she wished he'd suffered a far worse death than he got.

Guilt ate away at her insides when her thoughts turned dark like that.

Some days it was all she could do to survive each day after what he'd done to her.

Poppy grew up jealous of her sister and angry that Rose had excelled. She resented Rose for all her accomplishments, even if their father made her believe they were nothing.

Growing up, Poppy didn't have this kind of insight. But since his death she'd spent a lot of time thinking about Rose, herself, their mother, and him.

She thought about how it all went wrong.

Rose hadn't been around when things got really bad. Mom had conveniently chosen to be in another part of the house when Dad picked Poppy as his target for the night.

She blamed her mom and Rose for abandoning her and leaving her to fend for herself against an unrelenting and callous attacker.

Her father wouldn't stop. He just kept coming at her. Day in and day out.

And then he died.

Poppy was finally free.

Except she wasn't. Not at all.

Because the past kept her locked in her memories and the anger and resentment and pain.

Depression brought on by trauma sucked her into a dark world where nothing mattered.

She didn't go to college. She didn't do much of anything. She had no ambition or goals.

It was all she could do some days to exist.

And she hated Rose for the life she'd built while Poppy's life crumbled to dust around her.

Chapter Four

*R*ose walked into the Carmel dive bar, one locals loved and the rich tourists avoided. She cringed at the sound of some drunk belting out "Copacabana" at the top of his lungs, off pitch and off key, with a smile on his face and most of the crowd singing along.

Across the bar stood the one person who always had her back, who loved her like a sister, and who was currently waving her hands in the air like a madwoman to get Rose's attention from across the crowded room.

Rose wound her way through the tables because the bar was packed just like she imagined it was every Friday night. She loved Maggie. She'd missed her a lot this past year when sixteen-hour workdays took over Rose's life and Maggie's fiancé, Marc, took all Maggie's spare time.

They both worked in Silicon Valley, Rose as a programmer and Maggie in marketing. They braved the incessant traffic to get together for lunch once a week. But over time, and as their schedules got more packed, their lunches turned into every other week, then once a month, then occasionally they'd catch up on the weekends.

It didn't matter how much time passed between visits, they were forever best friends. No matter what day or time, if one of them texted or called, the other picked up.

When Maggie fell hard for Marc about eight months ago, no one was happier than Rose. Though, admittedly, Rose was also jealous of the love Maggie had found. She didn't begrudge her friend spending time with her fiancé. She just missed her friend because Maggie had been so caught up with her guy.

For the first time in years, Rose felt disconnected from her best friend. And that probably had a lot to do with the fact they simply hadn't seen each other in person in so long, and whenever there was a chance to meet Marc, somehow the plans fell through.

Of course Rose heard all about him, even talked to him on the phone several times when Maggie had her on speaker, but it wasn't the same as seeing him face-to-face. Lately it felt like she and Maggie lived on different coasts and not just a few cities apart.

Rose flew into Maggie's open arms and fiercely hugged her friend. "Promise me we will make a point to see each other more often."

Maggie crushed her close. "Yes. Promise." Maggie leaned back and took her by the shoulders. "I'm so glad you're here. How are you?"

"I'm good." She meant it. In general, Rose had a good thing going. She loved her job, she had a few close work friends she hung out with once in a while after work, she dated when she felt like it and took a break when she got discouraged. For the most part, she had a good life. "What's the big emergency?"

Maggie waved that away and her eyes brightened with excitement. "I'm finally going to introduce you to Marc." Maggie clutched her hands at her chest. "And Gray, his best man, is coming, too."

"I can't wait to meet the man who stole your heart."

"How was seeing your mom and sister?" Maggie's eyes filled with concern.

"Mom painted the kitchen cabinets."

Maggie's eyes went wide. "Did she get permission from your father from the grave?"

Rose chuckled. "She defied the order of things and did it herself."

"Hell must have frozen over."

Rose sighed. "We talked about him. I encouraged her to continue to do what she wants now. I don't know how she stays in that house."

Maggie rubbed her hand up and down Rose's arm, comforting her the way she always did. "And Poppy? How was it seeing her after all this time?"

Rose pressed her lips tight. "She made it clear she hates me. Which is understandable. Except . . ."

Maggie motioned for her to take a stool at the high table. "Tell me," she coaxed.

"She looks terrible. Like she's a walking corpse. I don't know why she hasn't left that place, but it looks like it's killing her."

Maggie put her hand over hers. "Did you try to talk to her?"

"She wanted nothing to do with me. Mom's worried about her."

Maggie frowned. "I really thought after your father died things would get better for all of you."

"I let him go. They're still clinging to his ghost and the past and they're just . . . trapped."

"You were for a long time, too. It took you going away to school, putting distance between you, and a lot of time to get his voice out of your head."

"It's been more than three years since he passed. They need to start living their lives without worrying about what he'll think if they change something in the house or do something he wouldn't like. He's gone. He can't control them anymore."

Maggie's gaze dropped to the table, then met Rose's again. "I didn't want to say anything because I didn't want you to get sucked back into the drama here, but my mom did mention a few times before he died that it looked like your mom and Poppy weren't faring well. At first, she thought it was just them missing you, but then, well, I guess she thought it was something more."

"He didn't have me to pick on anymore, so he turned on them. Mom admitted as much. The breakfast table in the kitchen had to be replaced."

Maggie tilted her head. "He was always abusive with all of you, but I didn't think he was that kind of destructive."

"You know I left because he'd begun to escalate. I was his main target. I foolishly hoped removing myself would make him leave them alone." She'd been desperate and naïve.

Maggie squeezed her hand. "Don't feel guilty for saving your life. You and I both know if you hadn't left when you did, things would have been much worse."

Maggie knew all her secrets, even the darkest ones.

"Enough about all that. It's your special week. You're getting married!" Rose smiled brightly, because she was truly happy for her best friend.

Maggie beamed. "Can you believe it? It seems like we just met and at the same time like I've known him forever. Of course, he's great. Always trying to sweep me off my feet."

"So when do I get to meet him?"

"Marc and Gray got into town about an hour ago. They checked into their hotel and should be meeting us here any minute."

Rose raised a brow. "Marc isn't staying with you at your parents' place?"

"He's trying to be all romantic about us abstaining and building anticipation for our wedding night." Maggie rolled her eyes.

"Oh. That's . . . sweet."

Maggie burst out laughing. "I guess."

"Spill it. What's bothering you?"

"I'm . . . frustrated. In the beginning, our sex life was amazing. We did it all the time, everywhere. We couldn't keep our hands off each other. And then, things cooled down."

"As they do in relationships after you've been together for a while." Rose hoped that was all it was.

"Of course. It's expected. And when we are together, it's almost like it was in the beginning."

That "almost" made Rose raise a brow again.

Maggie waved it away. "It's really fine. Everything is fine. Just wedding jitters. Everyone gets those, right?"

"Right," Rose readily agreed.

"I mean, I've been so caught up in planning the wedding, stressing over the reception seating chart, the food, the cake, arrangements for family coming in from out of town, my dress . . ." Maggie picked up her margarita and took a big gulp. "It's been a lot. And while I love Marc, he's been no help. Lots of encouragement. 'You've got this, babe.' 'Whatever you want is fine with me, babe.'" Maggie sighed. "Is it bad that I kind of wish we'd just eloped?"

Rose shook her head. "I bet every bride feels that way at some point. But just think, in one week, you'll be married. Instead of Maggie O'Connor, you'll be Maggie—" It occurred to Rose that she'd either forgotten Marc's last name or simply didn't know it at all.

Maggie jumped off her stool and waved her hand. "There they are."

Rose followed Maggie's line of sight and caught her breath at the man walking toward her. Tall, broad-shouldered, stretching the dark blue button-down shirt across his chest, the sleeves rolled up over strong, well-defined forearms. Dark hair swept back in soft waves and greenish-blue eyes that locked on to her in a way that held her completely enthralled. She'd never felt a punch of awareness like this. One that had her awash in attraction and a need to get closer.

His sumptuous mouth tilted in the slightest grin and his

eyes brightened like he knew all the dirty thoughts playing in her mind.

"Isn't he gorgeous?"

Rose jolted, realizing she was lusting after Maggie's fiancé. Before she pulled herself together, the man was standing right in front of her. Just a little too close, considering he was marrying her best friend.

Maggie brushed past her and threw her arms around . . . someone else.

Rose couldn't look away from the man in front of her.

"I'm Gray Pearson."

"Thank god," she blurted, then gasped, realizing her blunder. "Sorry."

"No need to apologize if it means you're happy I'm not Maggie's fiancé."

The blush heated her cheeks nearly as much as Gray's rich, warm voice fired her blood. Caught and embarrassed by her reaction to him, she tried to salvage things. "I'm Rose Howell."

"Maggie's best friend. The programmer. You work for one of my competitors."

She tilted her head, confused how he knew her.

Gray smiled. "I've met Maggie a couple of times. She's always talking about you."

"You have me at a disadvantage. I haven't heard anything about you. And here I thought Maggie was my best friend, but she's been holding out. Unless you're—"

"—an idiot for not taking Maggie up on setting up a double date with you, me, and her and Marc."

Rose couldn't help the blush. "Looks like things worked out tonight."

Gray waved a waitress over.

Rose finally remembered she was here to meet Marc and turned just as the tall, blond man released Maggie from a searing kiss. He turned to face her and Gray.

The second she saw his face it felt like the air got sucked out of the room. She was suddenly lost in a memory she'd buried deep and hoped to never let resurface again, because though she'd made many dating mistakes, Marc was the worst one.

"Are you okay?" Gray asked at the same time Marc gave her a bright smile and said, "You must be Rose," like he didn't remember her.

And maybe he didn't. The asshole.

He'd taught her a valuable lesson a year ago: one-night stands are not good life choices. Fun in the moment, maybe. But when you wake up next to a stranger, you can't exactly be surprised he lied about being single. He tried to play it off, but she'd woken up the morning after and saw the text message from his girlfriend light up his phone.

ANDREA: Home tonight! Miss you! Love you!

She cursed him out for being a lying cheater and making her the other woman.

He didn't seem to have a problem with that and told her he'd had a great time. Then the asshole reminded her that she'd not only happily participated but taken seconds and thirds and ended up one orgasm up from him.

"Rose?" Maggie stared at her, concerned.

"Um. I'm fine. Sorry." She took Marc's outstretched hand because it was expected. "And you're Marc," she said lamely. She studied him for any sign of recognition, but didn't see any.

Marc pumped her hand once, then released her, hooked his arm around Maggie's waist, drew her close to his side, and smiled brightly at Rose. "I'm the lucky one who gets to marry this beautiful woman in eight days."

What happened to Andrea?

Andrea loved him.

Did Andrea find out he'd been cheating on her?

Did Marc do it habitually?

Rose didn't know. She wanted to say she didn't care, but . . . She didn't want to see Maggie hurt like that.

She wished she could figure out if he truly didn't remember her, or if he was trying to hide that he did, so she'd know what to do. Because the right thing to do was tell her best friend that she and Marc already knew each other. Intimately.

But was it the right thing? Maggie looked so happy, and Marc gazed at Maggie adoringly. Who was Rose to taint that in any way over something that happened before they met? Something that didn't amount to anything but a lesson learned and a night Rose wanted to forget as much as Marc clearly already had.

"I need a drink."

Gray glanced from the waitress, who had finally arrived, to Rose. "What'll it be?"

She had a mental list of drinks depending on her stress level and mood. Wine to unwind. Margaritas or sangria for having fun. Bellinis for brunch. Negronis for sophisticated drinks with clients. But when faced with your best friend's fiancé, who was your one-night stand . . . "Bourbon on the rocks."

Gray's eyes went wide with surprise before he smirked and gave her an approving nod. "Make that two."

Maggie held up her margarita to the waitress. "I'll have another."

"I'll take whatever IPA you have on tap." Marc wrapped his arms around Maggie from behind, snuggling her back to his front, and kissed her neck. "Sorry we're late."

Gray waited for Rose to take her stool before he sat next to her. "He's been glued to his phone for half an hour."

"Work," Marc said by way of explanation. "They can't get anything done without me."

Maggie took her seat and leaned into Marc when he took his. "You promised. This week, you and me and wedding bells."

"I can't wait." Marc's bright smile seemed genuine, but then he looked across the table at her.

Rose thought she saw recognition and regret, but it was there and gone before she was really sure.

She decided to focus on the gorgeous man beside her. "So I know you're the best man, but how do you know Marc? Best friends like me and Maggie?" Rose wished she'd paid more attention over the last eight months of Maggie and Marc's whirl-wind courtship and engagement.

Gray eyed Marc with a look that didn't convey a friendly bond. "We grew up together like brothers, but we're really cousins. Our dads are brothers. When his parents divorced when he was young, Marc spent summers and most holidays with his dad. Since his dad worked, Marc spent the day at my house so he wasn't left alone."

None of that revealed anything about their relationship, except that they were family and forced together if nothing else.

"Gray was so jealous that his mom loved me." Marc snickered.

"Only because you used to kiss her ass. The second she left us alone, you were a dick."

Marc chuckled. "Oh, come on. A few harmless pranks and I'm the bad guy."

Maggie smirked. "What did you do?"

Gray leaned forward. "He superglued my favorite lunchbox closed. I had to destroy the thing so I had something to eat because he wouldn't share his lunch with me. He put cooking oil on my bedroom doorknob so I couldn't get out."

"I locked you in the bathroom by putting a stick under the handle so it wouldn't turn." Marc didn't look the least bit repentant. Just smug.

The waitress delivered their drinks.

Gray sipped his. "Those were kid stuff compared to some of the shit you pulled when we were teens."

"Oh, no." Maggie looked from Gray to Marc. "What happened?"

Gray spoke first. "He let all the air out of my bike tires so I couldn't ride over to see my girlfriend and made me late because I had to walk, because he hid the pump from me, too."

"I did the same with your car that one time," Marc added, unapologetically chuckling.

Gray shook his head. "It was always something." The annoyance in his voice didn't convey the anger flashing in his eyes.

"You got better at seeing them coming." Marc held up his beer in salute to Gray.

Gray shook his head. "At least you've grown out of that. Mostly," he grumbled.

Marc glanced at Rose. "The truth is, I was jealous of Gray because his parents were still together and mine split up. Yes, I spent summers and holidays with my dad, but he worked so much I saw more of Gray than I did of him. And Gray's dad was always home for dinner. They played ball together, went fishing, hung out. Mine made it seem like I interrupted his life whenever I showed up."

"He loved having you around," Gray interjected.

Marc shook his head. "Sometimes. Most of the time he had work and another new girlfriend he wanted to spend time with more than me." Marc looked away and took a long pull on his beer before he turned back and held Gray's gaze. "You always had my back, even when I was about to get in trouble for something I did to you."

"Yeah, well, I know it had to suck to be bounced back and forth between your folks."

"They liked to plan my life without asking me."

"Your dad's still doing that," Gray pointed out.

Marc shook his head and gave Gray a look to stop talking.

"What's that about?" Rose asked, even though it was none of her business.

Marc obviously didn't want Maggie to know something about his dad. "Nothing. My father spoiled me to make up for not being around but he also set some high expectations."

Maggie took his hand. "Marc works for his dad's company. He'll inherit it one day. And his dad rides him hard so that he'll be ready to take the helm and lead the company when he retires."

Gray leaned in. "He wants you to be happy."

"Yeah, well, telling me what will make me happy instead of asking me what will do that are two different things."

Gray sat back and took a sip of his drink. "Are you happy?" Gray briefly looked at Maggie.

Marc raised his joined hand with Maggie's and kissed the back of hers. "When I marry her, I'll have everything I want."

The sweet sentiment made Maggie's eyes fill with unshed tears. She leaned in and kissed Marc, then turned back to Rose. "Isn't he the best?"

Rose didn't know what to say, because she was still suspicious of Marc. But she wanted to support her friend, so she held her drink up. "To the happy couple."

Gray held his drink up. "To the happy couple."

They all clinked glasses and drank.

Rose liked getting a glimpse into Gray and Marc's relationship. She understood Marc a little better after learning he was a child of divorce, that he'd been spoiled yet had expectations placed on him. She found it really interesting that he seemed resentful of his father's girlfriends. She inferred that there had been many. It surprised her that with an example like that, his father having a string of relationships, Marc had cheated on his girlfriend.

She hoped that Maggie made him want to change and be faithful to her. Rose hoped Marc loved Maggie so much that even the thought of hurting her made him feel bad.

Rose didn't know enough about his relationship with Andrea to even guess what happened between them. People broke up for all sorts of reasons.

And people changed. Marc had to be a few years older than her and Maggie. Gray a year or two older than Marc. Maybe Marc had turned thirty and really thought about his priorities and what he wanted for his future.

And he'd gone after Maggie like he had to have her now. He proposed only six months into the relationship and insisted on getting married right away. Maggie had gotten him to wait two months so she could plan a ceremony with family and friends. He'd reluctantly agreed, making it clear to Maggie that all he wanted was for her to be his wife.

In their calls, Maggie sounded so happy and lost in the romance of it all.

Rose even got caught up in it. She'd been so happy her friend found someone who loved her like that.

There had to be so much more to Marc that Rose didn't see through her anger and resentment. All the things that made Maggie fall so hard for him.

People made mistakes. They weren't the sum of just their faults and blunders.

People changed.

So Rose decided to put all that aside and focus on the intriguing man who kept staring at her. "You said I work for your competition. What do you do?"

Gray set his drink on the table. "I'm the CFO at a tech start-up. Huff Technology."

Her eyes went wide. "I applied there last year and again a month ago. You're going public soon, right?"

Gray smiled and nodded. "Yeah. We're getting close. It's a lot of work. But we expect the company to go big very soon. It's been years in the making."

"I bet you're ready for the payoff."

"It's been a lot of long days and weekends."

"And I'm sure everyone in the company can't wait to see their shares skyrocket them to millionaires."

Gray chuckled. "Well, the founders, and a few key people for sure, but everyone else who got stock options will just be very happy to see the stocks pay off."

"One of those founders is sitting next to you," Marc pointed out, making Gray look a little embarrassed.

Rose held her glass up. "To all that hard work paying off."

Gray clinked his glass to hers. "Thanks."

"You should be proud of the work you do. It's not easy to get a tech company off the ground, let alone take it public."

"True. I hope this isn't a sore point, but what happened with the job you applied for?"

"I never heard back a year ago, or since I applied again."

Gray's brow shot up. "I seriously can't believe that. You work for Lincoln Global. We actively recruit from them. I'm going to find out why you were overlooked and make sure you get an interview."

"Don't you at least want to see my résumé first?"

Gray shrugged. "Lincoln only hires the best, so I know you're better than good."

"She is." Marc sipped his beer, acting like that hadn't been some kind of innuendo, even if Maggie and Gray didn't know it. Of course, she couldn't be sure Marc hadn't intended it that way. Then he added, "Maggie is always talking about how Rose finished a project early and under budget and how she got a promotion and a raise."

"And still I feel underpaid. My company gets a huge bonus for completing the project early, but I'm the one who has to work long hours on a tight schedule."

Her salary seemed like a lot of money, but when her normal workweek exceeded sixty hours, and she added in Silicon Valley's high cost of living, and that men in her company were promoted over her, it didn't seem enough.

"Sounds like you're underappreciated and you should definitely be working at Huff Tech." Gray looked serious. "I mean it. Whoever overlooked your résumé should be fired for letting you get away. I'm not that stupid."

She wondered if he was still talking about the job, or something much more personal.

"Make him work for it, Rose." Marc snickered. "He's used to having to work hard for what he wants."

Gray held her gaze. "It's worth it when it's something I really want."

Maggie leaned in with a huge smile on her face. "And is she the one you want?"

Rose felt the blush rise from her chest up to her cheeks.

"Definitely," Gray answered without taking his eyes off her and setting her blood on fire.

"Well, uh, you haven't made me an offer yet."

One side of Gray's mouth drew back in a half smile. "I'm working on it. I don't want to slip up and offend you. I want to be sure you get everything you want." The deep timbre of his voice, the heat and sexuality humming in it, shot right through her.

She pressed her thighs together to stave off the building heat between her legs. She'd never been seduced quite like this.

"Stop flirting and do the deed," Marc teased, breaking the spell between her and Gray.

Gray took a sip of his drink and continued to hold her gaze. "There's something to be said for taking your time." Gray slowly leaned into her and whispered in her ear, "You positively glow when you're turned on and I find that sexy as hell." He leaned back just enough to look her in the eye to let her know he meant every word. And nothing but pure desire burned in the depths of his blue-green eyes.

Did she seriously ban one-night stands from her life? Because right now, she'd walk out of this bar and jump right into his bed without a single reservation. The only thing she'd probably regret was not getting to do it again.

Gray sat back, but as he moved she felt the whisper of his finger brush across her knee, sending a delicious shiver of electricity up her thigh.

Maggie clasped her hands together at her chest. "I'm so glad you two hit it off. We'll all be spending a lot of time together this week."

Wasn't it a cliché for the maid of honor and the best man to hook up?

In this case, Rose didn't really care. It had been a long time since she'd met a man like Gray. On second thought, she'd never met a man so open and forthright about wanting her. Even now, she saw the simmering desire in his eyes. She'd seen it the second he walked in and they caught each other's attention.

She liked a man who knew what he wanted and went after it. Especially when she was the object of his desire.

Gray casually looked at Maggie, then faced Rose again and spoke to Maggie while staring at Rose. "I'm all yours for the week."

She really liked the way this man flirted.

Marc tapped Gray on the shoulder. "I know you went all out for my bachelor party."

Gray eyed Marc. "You'll get exactly what *you* wanted."

Marc gave Gray a knowing look. Gray's less-than-enthusiastic response didn't faze Marc in the least.

Rose refrained from rolling her eyes at Marc's lascivious look. She wondered if these two seemingly different men would be friends if they weren't family, because Gray didn't seem quite as enthusiastic about whatever Marc had asked him to plan for the bachelor party.

Maggie touched her hand. "Please tell me you didn't get a cop stripper for the bachelorette party."

Rose scoffed. "Please. Everyone knows firemen are the hottest strippers."

Maggie's cheeks blazed pink. "I'm not getting a lap dance from some half-naked guy."

Rose deadpanned. "I'll take one for the team."

Gray burst out laughing.

Rose couldn't help but smile at him before she turned back to Maggie. "Don't worry. I've got your back. We're going to have a great time."

"You more than anyone," Marc teased about the lap dance.

Maggie wasn't as outgoing or daring as Rose. That's why she needed Rose to nudge her out of her comfort zone once in a while.

Rose had planned the perfect bachelorette party for Maggie, so that *she'd* have fun.

But Marc's comment deserved an answer. "I like to have a good time, so long as no one gets hurt." Like his ex-girlfriend if she found out about his cheating last year.

Maggie winced at the high-pitched scream the newest kara-oke singer belted out. No one should attempt Whitney Houston unless they were a trained professional. Even then, they should think twice. "No matter what, we're all going to have fun this week." She turned to Marc. "And next Saturday, we're going to be husband and wife and we'll officially move in together and be happy the rest of our lives."

"That we will," Marc assured Maggie, kissing her sweetly.

Gray eyed Marc, then took a sip of his drink, catching Rose watching him over the rim. What looked like disapproval for Marc quickly turned to something deeper when he held her gaze. Some silent acknowledgment that their initial spark of attraction ignited a flame of desire even he couldn't stop or ig-nore. She felt the pull to get closer to that flame. To him.

They'd be together most of the week.

She hoped whatever it was growing between them didn't burn her.

She was intrigued by his offer to help with an interview, but the man held a lot more appeal.

With Maggie getting married and starting a new chapter of her life, Rose had done some soul searching and discovered that even with her past she believed love and happiness and for-ever with someone was possible.

And maybe a gorgeous guy who liked numbers and flirted at a level ten and a programmer with a head full of code who needed a strong, confident, kind man who knew how to pay her a genuine compliment instead of pointing out all her faults added up to something that made sense.

Gray picked up her drink and handed it to her. "You're thinking too much. I like it better when you're smiling at me."

Those sweet words brought on the grin he wanted to see and she couldn't stop because he made her want to smile. "Tell me, Mr. CFO, what do you like to do for fun?"

"He watches cooking shows," Marc answered for him.

"Do you like to cook?" she asked, because she liked to cook and bake, but was far from a master chef.

"When I have the time. I travel some and have a lot of dinner meetings, so I eat out a lot more than I'd like."

"Really? You don't like eating out?" That surprised her.

"I do. It just gets old after a while. Deals are usually made over drinks and steaks. Sometimes I just want a big plate of spaghetti and meatballs."

"I suppose when you're that high up in the company, everyone you meet with wants to be wined and dined."

"Even some of the women I date," he added. "I like a woman who appreciates a slice of pizza as well as a good cut of steak."

Maggie rolled her eyes. "Don't get her started on how pizza is a breakfast, lunch, and dinner food."

"It is," Gray agreed, holding her gaze. "Do you eat it cold?"

"It's either gotta be cold or hot, not in between."

"Where do you stand on pineapple?"

She put her elbow on the table and planted her chin in her palm. "I'm for it, especially if it comes with crumbled bacon. Ham is good, but bacon . . ." She sighed, practically tasting it.

Gray nodded. "You and I will get along great then."

"I think so," she confirmed.

"You two are just . . ." Maggie's gaze bounced from her to Gray and back again. "There's something going on here."

Rose couldn't deny it.

Gray gave her a barely there nod, confirming it.

Marc smacked the back of his hand against Gray's shoulder. "You've got a way of reeling women in."

Gray didn't take offense; instead he smiled at Maggie. "You caught a keeper. I'm still trying to find mine." His warm gaze landed on Rose again.

She appreciated that he genuinely liked Maggie.

"I know a good thing when I see it." Marc's gaze swept over Rose before he turned to Maggie.

Her friend seemed to melt at his words and didn't even notice the ripple of an undercurrent in the conversation.

Or maybe Rose read too much into everything because she was feeling guilty. And honestly, she felt a little guilty about flirting with Gray without telling him she had a past with his cousin.

She never knew drinks could turn into something so complicated.

"What is going on inside that beautiful head of yours?" Gray was too observant.

But she liked the way he paid attention to her. "Weddings." That didn't really explain anything.

But Gray seemed to understand in part. "They do get you thinking about love, relationships, and life."

"Yes," she agreed. "Not to mention family."

"Maggie mentioned you were staying with your family while you're here."

Marc answered for her this time. "She grew up with an alcoholic father and had a shit childhood."

She didn't remember telling him that when they met a year ago, so she assumed Maggie had filled him in.

"Sorry to hear that," Gray said, eyeing Marc, then turning to her. "Are you sure you want to stay there while you're in town?"

She appreciated his concern. "My father passed away three years ago. It's just my mom and sister living there now. I haven't seen them in a long time."

Maggie took her hand. "And just like when we were kids, when family stuff gets to be too much, you can always come stay with me."

Marc brushed his hand across Maggie's shoulders. "So you're not going to come over to the hotel and sneak into my room?"

Maggie looked confused. "You're the one who wanted to wait until our wedding night."

"I didn't want to stay at your parents' place because you know I can't keep my hands off you. They barely know me. The last thing I want is them hearing us going at each other all night."

Maggie blushed. "They'll probably pretend they didn't hear anything because they're too excited about getting a grandbaby."

Rose eyed Maggie. "Are you two . . ."

"No," Maggie quickly answered. "We want kids, it's just we've . . . Everything's happened so quickly. We want to take some time before we . . ."

Marc kissed Maggie on the side of the head. "We want to enjoy being newlyweds for a little while. But soon. Because I can't wait to be a dad. And Maggie will be such a wonderful wife and mother."

Maggie blushed again and leaned into Marc.

They really did seem happy and on the same page about their future.

"You guys are going to be great together." Rose meant it. In the moment, she even felt it.

Marc held her gaze. "I'm glad you think so. Your opinion matters a lot to Maggie. I want her to be happy. And starting with our wedding day, I'm going to spend every day making sure she is."

The skeptical part of Rose wondered why he'd start on their wedding day, instead of making a point to make Maggie happy every day they were together.

The trepidation in Gray's eyes said he'd caught it, too.

Maggie shifted back into her seat, picked up her margarita, and downed the last of it. A sense of unease settled over all of them.

Marc broke the tension. "Who wants another round?"

"I've already had two." Maggie set down her empty glass.

Gray shook his head. "I'm good."

"I'm driving." Rose was always careful about how much she drank, especially when she was driving.

She remembered so many car rides as a kid wishing for the police to pull her father over and at least give him a ticket, if not arrest him, for driving while intoxicated. Some kind of consequence for putting himself, his family, other drivers, and pedestrians at risk. Even now she could feel the weight of the tension in that car, how she'd hold her breath hoping they got home okay.

Marc waved for the waitress. "You guys don't know how to have a good time. It's Friday night. No one has work tomorrow. We're supposed to be celebrating."

Maggie patted Marc's thigh. "You're right. I'll have another. Rose can drive me home tonight and I can pick up my car here tomorrow." Maggie straightened her back. "Oh. Let's order appetizers. They make the best potato skins here. And those chicken flautas you love, Rose, with the mango chili sauce to dip them in."

Rose wasn't that hungry, but she went along. "Sounds good. And I'm driving you home, so I'll have a soda."

Marc placed the order with the waitress, adding another bourbon for Gray, who just shrugged and went along, too.

The karaoke got worse as the night went on because people were drinking, lost their inhibitions, and were having a good time. The mood at the table got a little boisterous when they debated the best baking show. She and Gray agreed *The Great British Bake Off* won hands down for elevating home bakers and showing camaraderie during competition. Plus the unbelievably artistic execution for breads and desserts that were too pretty to eat.

Marc didn't watch many cooking shows, but adorably backed

up Maggie's pick for the *Kids Baking Championship*. Rose and Gray couldn't disagree that the kids were phenomenal and super-cute. But they did argue that there was something charming and calming in *The Great British Bake Off* that made the whole experience of watching relaxing. The show allowed you to wallow in laziness and binge-eat breads and sweets while wishing you were tasting the treats shown on TV.

Of course, the *Kids* show also made you crave cake.

When Marc and Maggie started arguing if they should get a cat or dog before they had a child, Rose and Gray bowed out after agreeing with Maggie that they should get a dog. Marc didn't necessarily want a cat, but argued they could leave the cat at home alone for a few days so they could take off for the weekend without having to board a dog or get someone to puppy sit.

Marc turned to Gray. "Help me out here. You travel several times a year for business alone. Wouldn't having a cat be easier?"

Gray shrugged. "Maybe. But I grew up with dogs. There's nothing like coming home to a wagging tail and a pet who's just so happy to see you. Cats aren't like that. At least all the ones I've met at exes' places."

Marc turned to Maggie. "See. Chicks like cats."

Maggie rolled her eyes and turned to Rose. "Help."

Rose slid off her stool. "I'll let you explain how sexist that is and that chicks adore guys who like dogs and cats."

"Duly noted." Gray lifted his chin at Marc. "Dogs are chick magnets."

Marc sneered. "You live alone with no pets."

"If I had a woman who wanted to get a dog together, I'd do it."

"But cats are cool. You can teach them tricks. They chill."

Rose couldn't disagree with Marc. "I'll leave you two to work this out. Back in a minute." She headed to the ladies' room, dodging appreciative patrons as a girl with pink hair belted out the lyrics to Kelly Clarkson's "Since U Been Gone" like a pro. She was probably the best singer of the night. Rose hoped they gave her another turn soon.

Maggie rushed up behind her in the hallway leading to the bathrooms and wrapped her in a hug from behind, her chin on Rose's shoulder. "Hey. Friends don't let friends pee alone."

Rose burst out laughing and kept walking even with Maggie holding on to her. "Someone's feeling good."

"Three margaritas and a week with my best friend . . . I'm so happy."

Rose pushed open the ladies' room door, stepped in, and waited by the sink because both stalls were occupied. "And are you also so happy because you're marrying your cat-loving fiancé?"

Maggie took her by the shoulders and turned Rose to face her. "Do you like him? I really, really want you to like him, so that when you and Gray end up together we'll all be friends and double-date and our kids will grow up together. Oh, they're cousins so we'll be family!"

Rose pressed her fingertip into her right ear. "That was really loud. And Gray and I just met. Don't start planning a double wedding."

Maggie released her shoulders and pointed at her. "He is so into you."

"I really like him." So much so that it made her a little giddy.

"He's so hot. That thick hair. Those eyes." Maggie sighed. "The way he looks at you."

Rose smiled at her tipsy friend, an excited flutter in her belly, because she and Gray felt so meant to be. Even if that did sound crazy since they just met. "Trust me, I felt the impact of every look." Like a caress, a pull, a longing. Something to savor and want more of all at the same time.

She'd be happy to sit and stare at him forever.

It felt so right it didn't feel real.

Maggie suddenly frowned. "You haven't said anything about Marc."

"You haven't let me get a word in," Rose teased. "He's great. Not like anyone you've dated."

"That's what I like about him. I know things moved fast." Maggie tilted her head. "Kind of like how you reacted to Gray and he did to you. The second I met Marc, something just clicked. He pursued me. He called, texted, and asked me out like he couldn't wait to see me again. I got caught up in the whirlwind of it all, and before I knew it, he was at my place all the time and we were talking about the future, kids—"

"Dogs versus cats," Rose interjected with a soft laugh. "You fell for him."

"I liked the attention and rush of it all."

"And you're happy?" Rose didn't mean to say it as a question because it seemed evident that Maggie was excited about getting married. But in the moment, looking into her friend's eyes and seeing something shadowed in the depths, she wondered if Maggie's wedding jitters were something more.

"I'm happy," she declared with a firm nod. "Absolutely. Even if he doesn't want to sleep with me until our wedding night."

"Girl, you should get some of that before you say 'I do' to be sure," someone called out from one of the stalls. "You don't want to find out he's a dud instead of a stud in the sack."

Maggie gaped at the closed stall doors. "He's not a dud." Maggie turned to her. "He's really quite good at it."

The prim answer made Rose chuckle before thoughts of her night with Marc surfaced and she almost agreed with Maggie out loud. "Good for you. Maybe one of these days you should surprise him at his hotel."

"Wearing a coat with nothing on under it," the woman in the stall called out again, then flushed the toilet.

Maggie blushed. "Trust me, I don't need to do anything but show up. He's always so eager to strip me down and have his way with me."

The woman in the stall walked out. "So long as he lets you have your way with him."

Maggie high-fived the woman. "Damn straight." But Maggie's vibrant smile dimmed. "I just wish we talked more. I mean, we do, it's just . . ."

Rose rubbed her hand up and down Maggie's arm. "What is it, Mags?"

"We talk. We do. About work, what to eat, where to go out, stuff like that. I just wish he'd open up more about himself."

"Just ask him," the woman said as she passed and opened the bathroom door. "Men don't volunteer stuff the way we do." With that bit of advice, she walked out just as the other woman in the second stall emerged saying, "She's right. Guys are always up for sex, but when it comes to their feelings . . . They bury that stuff deep. But if he loves you, he'll want to share. Maybe he just needs more time. If you're getting married soon, then you've got all the time in the world, right?"

Maggie's eyes lit with an "aha" gleam. "That's right. We have a lifetime to explore everything about each other."

Rose gave Maggie a nudge toward the open stall. "There you go. Things are moving fast right now, but you'll continue to build on your relationship. Nothing is set in stone. It doesn't always have to be a certain way. You and Marc can make it what you want it to be so you'll both be happy."

"Marriage is all about compromise," the woman said, drying her hands on a paper towel. "Good luck."

Rose nodded at Maggie. "See. You and Marc have decades of conversations ahead of you."

Maggie agreed with a firm nod, then pinched her lips. "But we're getting a dog. I'm not compromising on that." She firmly shut the stall door and any further discussion on that topic.

Rose chuckled under her breath and took the stall next to Maggie, her thoughts on years of seeing Maggie and Marc together, watching their relationship grow and flourish, and how Rose held back something that could potentially strain their friendship. Or blow it up.

Chapter Five

*R*ose stared at her reflection in the bathroom mirror. She'd told Maggie she'd meet her back at their table. She needed a minute to think about how and when to tell Maggie about her and Marc. Or if she should tell her at all. The longer she waited, the worse it could be. She didn't want her friend to think she harbored any feelings toward Marc. She also didn't want Maggie to think she didn't like him.

She didn't really know him.

Which made her think about Maggie's comment about her and Marc talking more. Maggie certainly knew Marc better than Rose did, but did Maggie really know him? Did she know what kind of man he really was deep down?

Had they ever talked about their past relationships?

Did Maggie know he'd once cheated on a girlfriend?

Was that something he'd done more than once?

Did that mean he'd do it again?

Her mind spun out.

Rose didn't want her friend to get hurt, but was it her place to bring any of this up? Especially right before their wedding?

Lost in her thoughts, she quickly dried her hands, then walked out of the bathroom and stopped short when she spotted Maggie and Marc in the hallway.

Marc's gaze connected with Rose's.

Maggie had her back to Rose. "And we're getting a dog."

Marc brushed the backs of his fingers along the side of Maggie's face and smiled down at her with amusement. "Whatever you want, sweetheart." He kissed her on the forehead. "I'll meet you back at the table in a minute."

Maggie slipped past Marc and headed out into the bar.

Rose tried to follow, but Marc slipped his hand around her arm and stopped her. Rose dipped her gaze to his hand on her, then met his eyes. "What are you doing?"

His gaze softened on her. "Remembering the last time I touched you."

She sucked in a gasp of air, wrenched her arm free, then held her breath.

Marc stuffed his hands in his pockets. "Please don't tell her about us."

"You mean about how you told me you weren't seeing anyone, then slept with me and cheated on your girlfriend?"

Marc sighed. "That's not fair."

"That's the truth," she shot back.

"But it's not the whole picture."

"Have you known the whole time you've been seeing her that she and I are best friends?"

"No."

The answer came a little too quickly.

"I don't believe you."

"Okay, when we first started dating, yeah, I thought about it. I didn't know your last name, so when Maggie mentioned her best friend, Rose, I thought maybe she could be you . . . But how crazy would that be? And then I saw pictures of the two of you at her place. That's when I knew it really was you."

It dawned on Rose that Maggie never sent pictures of Marc or posted them on her social media. Not that Maggie did that a lot in the past anyway. But still, if she had a great guy in her life, Rose thought she'd especially want to share that news with the world.

"So because you knew I was Maggie's best friend, you asked her not to post or send any photos of you." She didn't phrase it as a question, because she was starting to understand Marc a lot better.

He shrugged. "I like my privacy. She respected that."

"Or is it that you didn't want to get caught by me or someone else?"

He pulled his hands free of his pockets, held them out to his sides, and let them drop. "No. That's not it at all. I liked Maggie the second I met her. I just wanted a chance with her without our night together interfering in that." He frowned at her, frustration in his eyes. "It's not like you and me were ever a thing. And after what happened, I figured you thought I was a dick, so if I told Maggie I not only slept with her best friend but also cheated on my girlfriend at the same time, she'd call it all off. And even if I got her to understand the situation, you'd probably badmouth me to Maggie and warn her away from me anyway."

Rose couldn't deny she'd have cautioned Maggie about Marc's past behavior. "So what are you saying?"

"I'm marrying Maggie. We're making a life together. And I don't want anything to screw that up. So please, don't say anything," he implored, very sincerely.

She wanted to believe it was genuine. "You're asking me to keep a secret from my best friend. You know we tell each other everything." Rose pressed her lips tight. "I told her about that night."

"But she doesn't know it was me."

"If we tell her right now, together, she'll understand."

Marc raked his fingers through his hair. "No, she won't. You don't want to hurt her. I don't want to hurt her. And though this happened before I met her, I think she will be hurt, or at least uncomfortable with the fact that you and I slept together. She says all the time how much she misses you and that you two don't get to spend enough time together. Don't let this come between you, too." He made a really valid point.

"I need some time to think about it."

He took her arm again and leaned in close. "It was one night. And while it was a damn good and memorable night"—his gaze swept down her body, making her feel very uncomfortable— "it's not like we have feelings for each other. We both got what we wanted and—"

"Is everything all right here?" Gray asked, walking up to them in the hallway.

"Fine." Marc released her and smiled over his shoulder at his cousin. "Rose was just making sure I intend to make her best friend happy." He faced her again. "There's nothing I wouldn't do to marry Maggie and have the life I want."

The reassurance didn't satisfy her.

In fact, she wondered what he'd been about to say before Gray interrupted them. Because there'd been something in Marc's eyes that said they got what they wanted that night they were together, but Marc wanted even more now.

But she had to have misread him.

And she'd much rather think about being in Gray's strong arms. He was a guy who seemed direct and truthful about what he wanted and how he felt about her.

Marc held her gaze for one long moment, then stepped into the men's room, leaving her alone in the hallway with Gray.

"What were you two really talking about?"

She cocked her head. "Why do you think we were talking about something else?"

"You answered my question with a question, which makes me think you're avoiding answering me. And Marc tends to say things that seem real but can also mean something else entirely."

That got her attention. "Are you saying he's a liar?" She knew he was a cheat.

"Everyone lies." True. "Marc says things that are true but also not."

She met Gray's direct gaze. "Should I be worried about my friend?"

"They've been dating for months. I'd think if Maggie thought something was off, or Marc wasn't treating her well, she wouldn't have agreed to marry him."

She huffed out a frustrated breath. "That's a very diplomatic answer."

"It's the only one I've got because they are getting married and I'm not about to make waves when they've had nothing but smooth sailing as far as I know." Gray eyed the men's room door.

"Tell me about the comment you made earlier about Marc's dad still planning his life. What's the subtext?"

Gray's eyes lost all their warmth and his lips pressed into a tight line. "I knew you were smart, but your curiosity and intuition are going to get me in trouble."

She loved the sincerity, but . . . "That is not an answer, but thank you for the compliment." She really did appreciate it.

The easy smile came back. "My early morning is booked with work calls. Have brunch with me and we'll talk."

"Why can't you answer me right now?"

"Because then I'd have to come up with another reason to see you tomorrow."

"We'll be seeing a lot of each other this week."

He softly brushed his fingertips from her elbow down to her hand and linked his fingers with hers. "The more the better."

She met his earnest gaze.

"Say yes."

"Yes."

He squeezed her hand and gave a soft tug to get her to move closer, but she stopped short when the men's room door opened and Marc crowded into the hallway with them.

Marc's gaze dipped to their joined hands, then met Gray's annoyed face. "Sorry to interrupt." He turned to her. "Maggie's probably wondering what happened to all of us."

Rose slipped her hand free from Gray's and felt the loss of the warmth radiating through her, and the current of awareness between them dimmed, making her feel the need to move closer to him. "I'll join her back at the table. It's getting late. I'm going to head out soon anyway."

"Don't leave yet. I'll walk you out to your car," Gray offered. "We'll finish making plans."

She nodded and walked back into the blaring music, but still overheard Marc ask, "Plans? I thought you were here to be my best man, not get laid."

"You're an asshole."

She smiled at Gray's comeback, wound her way through the tables, and took her seat at theirs.

Maggie swayed to the slow song as she sat with her elbow on the table and her chin in her palm. "I love this song. Maybe I should add it to the playlist for the reception." Maggie turned to her. "I'm so glad you're here."

Rose side-hugged her friend. "Me, too."

"Where are the guys?"

"On their way back soon." She squeezed Maggie tighter. "Gray asked me out to brunch tomorrow morning."

Maggie sat up straight. "Really? That's fantastic. I knew you'd hit it off."

"You did? You never mentioned him on our calls."

"Every time I wanted to set up a double date and get you and Gray together, Marc was either too busy or just wanted to spend more time with me because he'd been swamped at work." She covered Rose's hand on the table and squeezed. "But I'm so glad it's happening now. It's true what they say, love is in the air at weddings."

"We haven't even gotten to the day yet." But Rose felt something happening between her and Gray, even if she wanted to play it off as no big deal for now.

As first impressions went, Gray had an impact on her.

But so had Marc. And look how that turned out.

She pushed that thought right out of her head because Gray and Marc seemed so different. Gray said what he meant. Marc tended to say what sounded good, and all too often what the other person wanted to hear, even if it wasn't wholly true.

Rose pushed her drink away. "It's been a long day. Do you want to get out of here soon?"

Marc joined them at the table. "Babe, no. Stay. Don't send me back to my lonely hotel room. It's still early."

Maggie gave Marc a tipsy grin. "You could invite me back to your place."

"Are you sure your parents won't mind that you ditched them for me?"

Maggie grinned. "While they thought our staying in town separately before the wedding was a sweet gesture on your part,

I'm pretty sure they know we can't keep our hands off each other."

Marc leaned in and kissed Maggie like no one was watching.

Rose immediately turned her head and found Gray just steps away.

He closed the distance and stood beside her. "Looks like they're thinking of starting the honeymoon early."

"Maggie's staying with Marc tonight. Walk me out?"

Gray held out his hand. "Absolutely." His warm hand clasped hers and everything felt right inside her. "I paid the tab."

Marc came up for air and glanced over at them. "Huh? What?"

"I paid the bill. Meet you at the car in five."

"Sure. Yeah." Marc dove in for another kiss.

She and Gray left them in their love bubble and headed for the door. The second they exited and the door muffled the loud music, Rose sighed. "That's better. I can actually hear myself think now."

Gray glanced over at her. "And what are you thinking?"

"That this turned out to be a better night than I thought. And I had high expectations because I got to see my best friend again."

Gray stopped with her beside her car. "I wasn't excited about spending an entire week here with Marc, but meeting you, getting to spend time with you . . . I'm feeling like a week might not be enough."

She eyed him. "Well, if someone actually calls me back about the job I applied for, who knows? You could be seeing a lot more of me."

"I'm going to find out why nobody acted on your résumé when they are constantly looking for top talent, especially with your experience."

"Thank you for the offer, but really, you don't need to go out of your way for something that's not even your job. I'll follow up again next week."

"I want to do it. If nothing else, I'd like to know why a résumé like yours is being overlooked and someone like you isn't even interviewed, let alone given an offer." He seemed as perplexed as she. "But right now I'm thinking of all sorts of offers I'd like to make."

"You've already asked me to brunch."

He moved a step closer. "And I can't wait. Would you like me to pick you up?"

"Since I assume we'll be eating at the hotel, I'll meet you there. What time?"

"Eleven."

"Until then." Rose took a step away, but came up short when Gray continued to hold her hand. She looked down at their entwined fingers, then back at his gorgeous face and read the desire in his eyes, knowing hers reflected the same heat and need his did. "Something else you wanted?"

"So many things. I want to kiss you so bad it hurts."

She went still.

"But as much as it pains me, I think I'll wait, so you'll be thinking of me tonight just as much as I'm thinking about you."

She tilted her head and gave him a flirty grin. "Don't you think kissing me will make me think of you even more?"

"I knew you were a temptation I couldn't resist when I first saw you." He released her hand so he could cup her cheek. His warm skin against hers made her burn. And then he leaned in, pressed his lips to hers, and set her body on fire with the soft caress. She sighed at the sweet contact. Then he took the kiss deeper, sliding his tongue past her lips, tasting her like he had all the time in the world. It was deep and slow, an exploration and a revelation all at once, because she didn't want him to stop. Ever.

But he did, with the brush of his lips over hers once more as he pulled away just an inch so he could look into her eyes. "A week is definitely not going to be enough."

Chapter Six

7 days to Maggie's wedding . . .

Rose woke in the morning excited about seeing Gray. The man knew how to kiss. And how to make her want him. She couldn't wait to see him again. It made her smile to think he'd asked to meet for brunch. Not lunch. Not dinner. But the first available time he had today.

The warm glow filled her to bursting through her shower and getting ready for the day, but with three hours until her date with Gray, she couldn't keep her thoughts and feelings about being home at bay.

She stood in her childhood room overwhelmed with memories. She tried to grab hold of the good ones, but they were wiped out by the dark ones. She could hear her father's demeaning words laced with threats, both spoken and unspoken. They were as real as the chill in her bones when she thought about how she'd had to tiptoe through this house and her life back then, praying she didn't catch his attention. She'd tried to be so good, but nothing she ever did was good enough.

He hurt her. He tried to destroy her.

But in this room, in the quiet where she could hear the whisper of her own voice, she'd told herself he was wrong. She was good. She did her best. She tried.

She didn't know what made her turn around. A shift in the air. A thickening of the atmosphere. The tension that washed over her. But when she faced the door and found Poppy, she wasn't surprised at all that Poppy was the cause of the disturbance.

"He haunts this place." The words held all the pain and anger in Poppy's eyes. She leaned against the door frame, arms crossed under her breasts, her black hair hanging down to her chest and partially cloaking her face. "He's ruined it like he destroyed me."

"Oh, Poppy. Don't let that be true."

"It is."

"It doesn't have to be. Don't let him continue to hold you back and rule your life. He's gone. He can't hurt you anymore."

"What the hell do you know about any of it?" The flippant remark, said with such anger, felt like a slap in the face.

A rush of adrenaline made Rose's heart pound harder. "Who stood between you and him for a decade? Who did he go after when he hit one too many red lights on the way home and needed to rail against someone? Who did he berate and demean and shove and push over and over and over again? I think I know better than anyone what you went through when I left."

Poppy pushed away from the door, her arms going straight at her sides, fists clenched. "Then why would you leave! How was

I supposed to protect myself when I never learned how because you always did it for me?"

Those fierce words smacked Rose right in the face and made her head snap back. "Are you seriously blaming me for shielding you? For real? You think I should have let him pick on you, my baby sister, and not done anything about it?"

"Maybe then I could have stood up to him."

"You're doing just fine with me. I have no doubt you tried to hold your own against him. I know how frustrated and angry you were because he always made you feel like nothing you said, nothing you did, not even being right was good enough. He dismissed you. He underestimated you. He never listened. He didn't care. He didn't see how amazing you are. He was your dad and he didn't love you." The ache in her chest saying those words and knowing they were true made it hurt to breathe.

Poppy wrapped her arms around herself again in a protective hug, her head down, dark hair shielding her face.

Rose recognized the gesture. So often she physically closed in on herself as a means of emotionally holding it all together. "I know exactly how you feel. I'm sorry you're angry and hurting and you feel stuck. But that's on you. He's gone. You can do whatever you want to do now."

"Maybe you've been able to forget the past, but I can't."

"Oh, I remember all of it. Just being here brings it all back into focus. It took a long time for me to break free of the habits that kept me scared and even longer to get his voice out of my head. But I did it. You can, too."

"You just don't get it." Poppy held tight to her petulant attitude.

Rose didn't fall for it. "I don't know exactly what happened between you and dad, but I know you're still scared. You need to break free of that fear."

Poppy's head shot up. "I'm not afraid."

"Really? You were too angry at me and afraid to leave here and come stay with me."

Poppy's gaze dropped to the floor.

"Is this the life you want? No friends. A dead-end job at a fast-food sandwich shop. Living at home with Mom. Unhappy. Unfulfilled. Angry at the world because you were dealt a crap hand. Dad ruined your childhood. Don't let him ruin the rest of your life, too."

"I did that all on my own!" Poppy rushed out of the room.

Rose stared after her, not shocked by the outburst but by what Poppy said. She had no idea what Poppy meant.

Maybe Poppy needed time to think about what Rose said and open up about what happened to her after Rose left. Perhaps Poppy needed to speak to a therapist, someone who could help her sort through her feelings and emotions and unravel the past so she could understand that none of it was her fault. She hadn't done anything to deserve their father's abusive treatment.

The walls felt like they were closing in on Rose. She took one last look at the room, decided that they all needed a change and she'd start with her room, and headed downstairs with a list of items in her head she wanted to buy.

She wanted to be the catalyst for her mom and Poppy to start really living their lives.

If nothing else, a bedroom refresh would allow her to feel more comfortable and rooted in who she was now and not feel like that scared little girl anymore when she came to visit. Because she intended to make a point of coming back and reconnecting with her mom and sister. It was time. She was strong enough now to face the past and know she'd survived it and moved on.

One day, Poppy would, too.

Rose would help her move forward. They'd been close once. They could be again.

They'd always be sisters, but Rose wanted them to be best friends again, too. She wanted Poppy to know she could count on Rose to be there for her no matter what.

She'd keep trying to break down the walls Poppy erected to keep people out, so she felt safe. Rose knew how lonely that could be.

She'd do whatever it took to heal the rift between them.

She wanted to see Poppy smile again.

She wanted them to share more memories and make new traditions together.

When she got married, she wanted Poppy and Maggie right beside her.

She wanted Poppy not only to find someone special but to know that she was worthy of love.

Rose thought of Gray and how he made her feel.

When she left for college, she'd been at her lowest, desperate for acceptance and any scrap of kindness. So needy that the first few relationships she attempted to have with guys ended in disaster because she'd clung to them. She'd tried too hard, and the guys' initial interest quickly faded. They knew she was messed up.

Not anymore.

Gray saw a strong, independent, smart woman, and he wanted her.

Rose wanted Poppy to find her inner strength and independence as well.

Because knowing Gray desired her made her feel powerful and sexy, and when you felt that way, there was no room for doubt.

And the delicious anticipation of seeing him again could quickly become addictive.

"Where are you off to?" her mom asked.

Rose stepped into the living room and smiled. Her mom was on the couch sipping a cup of tea with a chocolate cookie on a napkin sitting on her thigh.

"Eating cookies so early in the day," she pretended to scoff. "Really, Mother. You've gone too far."

Her mom laughed at her dramatic tone.

If her father had seen her mom like this, he'd have berated her not only for being lazy but for eating sweets that were meant to be a dessert.

Treats were for any time of day. Period. End of story.

Anyone who didn't agree, Rose didn't want to know.

Her mother smiled and blushed and looked caught all at the same time. "Don't tease."

"Seriously, Mom, I'm just happy to see you breaking stupid rules that aren't even really rules at all because you're an adult. If you want to have ice cream for breakfast, hey, you're the only boss of you now, so go for it."

Her mom's gaze drifted to her lap and her smile turned upside down.

Rose wondered what she'd said to upset her mom, then remembered how often she and Poppy got in trouble for stealing cookies, though they were rarely in the house. Then it dawned on Rose. "I always blamed Poppy and she blamed me for the missing cookies. Dad yelled at me. He spanked me. But it was you." It all made sense now, but Rose didn't want to believe it.

Her mother spoke to her lap. "I'm sorry, Rose."

"You're sorry. You let me take the blame for that and you never stepped in to help me. How could you do that?"

"I tried to stop him all the time in the beginning, but the more I tried, the worse things got. He'd be yelling at me, you, Poppy sometimes, and I just couldn't take it."

"But it was okay for me to take it."

Her mom's head shot up. "No. No, sweetheart. When I tried to step in, he'd be that much harder on you. You remember how he'd berate you for needing your mother, that you couldn't stand on your own. But you could. You did. Maybe I couldn't stop him from going after you, but I took such satisfaction in watching you hold your own against him. You were strong when I couldn't be."

The double-edged sword of growing up the way she did. Her childhood sucked. But it had made her who she was today. Tough. Resilient.

She'd needed every bit of that strength her mother took such pride in to survive and overcome her past.

"Please don't be upset," her mother said.

"I'm angry." Rose wanted to rage at her mom for making things harder on her.

"If it wasn't the cookies, he'd have found something else to complain about. You know that."

Rose knew all too well how her dad could take something small and turn it into the biggest, most important thing in the world. He never let anything go. He never just dropped it.

"I know that you should have—" Rose stopped right there, because she wanted to rebuild her relationship with her mom and not keep tearing it down.

Her mom stared at her. "I wanted to do a lot of things, Rose. I wanted you girls to be happy and safe. That's why I was so pleased to see you leave for college. I knew away from here, you'd thrive. And you did. And I am so proud of you."

Those words, the heartfelt sentiment, softened Rose's heart. "Thank you. That means a lot."

"I missed you every day," her mom admitted. "I know my actions didn't always show it, but never doubt how much I love you."

"I always knew *you* did. I love you, too. I've missed you and Poppy. I want us to be a family again."

"I want that, too."

"Then we need to stop letting *him* come between us." Rose walked away, needing some time to let her emotions settle, so she could really let the past be the past and they could move forward.

Chapter Seven

*M*aggie woke up with a pounding in her ears that matched her heartbeat. Thank god, the drapes were closed, the room dark, or the headache behind her eyes would make it impossible to see. Thankfully, she fondly remembered last night.

She loved spending time with her fiancé and with Rose.

Her fiancé. She said the words to herself one more time. They were getting married exactly a week from today. Soon. A wave of butterflies took flight in her stomach. Excitement mixed with nerves.

She couldn't believe she'd found the one she wanted to spend the rest of her life with. The thought made her happy and apprehensive at the same time.

What if she was wrong?

What if it didn't work out?

What if it did? Her heart overrode those doubts because she wanted to get married and have a family just like the one she grew up in.

Marc wanted that, too. He couldn't wait for them to start.

Unlike Joel, who broke things off with her when she'd made

it clear she wanted to be a mother more than anything. He'd made it clear he liked things just the way they were between them, just the two of them. He didn't want to have children at all.

She'd thought he was the one, too, and she'd been devastated when they'd broken up.

It had been a hard few months, and then she'd met Marc in the grocery store. He was there buying flowers for his aunt's birthday and asked her opinion. She'd picked out a bundle of beautiful pink roses surrounding tall stalks of white snapdragons. She'd commented that the bottle of prosecco he'd already chosen was her favorite.

She liked his smile and his charm, and she liked that picking something his aunt would really love mattered to him. He'd asked her out right then and there, saying he'd love to share a bottle of prosecco over dinner.

She'd accepted, thinking dipping her toe back into the dating pool with a family-oriented guy like Marc, who was also gorgeous, was a good start to putting herself out there again. She also liked that he made no attempt to be coy about how into her he was. He told her that if she said no, he'd be devastated.

She liked him immediately.

He'd called the next day with the details for their evening out that night.

They met at the restaurant because, though she was intrigued by him, she wasn't fool enough to give out her address without at least getting to know him better. At that point, all she knew was that he had an aunt with great taste in sparkling wine.

That night, he'd made her feel like the only woman in the room. They talked about their disastrous dating lives and how they were both looking for something more. She'd been open about the fact she wanted a family. He'd expressed how much he wanted to settle down with a wife and kids.

It all seemed so perfect and right that all thoughts that he'd be her rebound guy turned into his being her forever man.

She tried not to jump in with both feet, but found he pulled her in right along with him.

And now they were actually tying the knot in just days.

She smiled at the ceiling and turned her head toward Marc's side of the bed, but didn't find him lying next to her. He sat on the edge, staring at his phone.

He never seemed to be far from it for long these days.

She felt bad he couldn't step away from work even for a few days without them constantly contacting him.

She felt a little rough this morning, but that didn't mean she couldn't make Marc's morning a little brighter. She slid up behind him, draped her arm over one shoulder and rested her chin on the other, catching a glimpse of his phone before he startled and dropped it on the floor.

"Babe. Seriously, don't sneak up on me like that."

She giggled. "I thought you'd sense me coming up behind you."

Apparently he'd been so engrossed in the text messages, he hadn't felt the bed dip behind him.

"Who are you texting?" She tried to keep her voice light and undemanding, but she didn't like the way the text she'd seen made her feel jealous and suspicious.

We should meet.

Those words evoked a whole slew of memories of other times she'd caught him hiding his phone from her over the last month. And this wasn't the first time she'd seen something on his phone that didn't make sense.

He picked up the phone, set it facedown on his bare thigh, and turned his head toward her. "It's just work. A problem they need me to handle even though everyone knows I'm away from the office this week because my gorgeous fiancée and I are getting married." He kissed her softly. "They wish I was there in person to take care of it. But I just want to be here with you."

She fell into another kiss with him, but her initial worry about the text didn't dissipate. His reassuring words didn't make her feel better.

Several more texts made his phone vibrate.

He didn't stop kissing her.

She pulled back. "Tell them you're unavailable for the next *two* weeks and not to bother you. This is *our* time."

"I wish I could, but this is important. I've got a few hours before I'm meeting up with Gray, so it's no big deal to handle it now, so I can be all yours later when you need me."

"I always need you," she pouted, feeling like a shrew for nagging him about being responsible about his job and not giving her his undivided attention.

"I know, but you also understand that I'm trying to take

more of the burden off my father." Marc's father had suffered a stroke about two years ago. Since then, Marc had stepped up in the business that he'd eventually take over one day.

"It's Saturday. Can't it wait?"

"Better to deal with it now and get it out of the way so we can enjoy this week leading up to our wedding." He kissed her again, then stood, naked, all those gorgeously sculpted muscles on display. "Besides, don't you need to get back to your parents' place so you can shower and change and get ready to meet up with Rose later? Maybe you two can meet for breakfast."

"She's having brunch with Gray this morning downstairs in the hotel restaurant."

"What?" Marc gaped at her. "She didn't waste any time . . ."

That got her attention. "Why do you care?"

"I don't." The clipped response made it seem like he did.

"Is there some reason you don't want Rose and Gray getting together?"

Marc shrugged. "I don't think he's good for her."

"What? Why?"

"Gray likes the chase. Look how hard he went after her last night, offering her a job without even really getting to know her."

"He was right about her working for a company every programmer would kill to work at. She's brilliant at what she does. He'd be lucky to have her at his company."

"Of course you think that. He thinks she's hot and practically hands her the job of her dreams just so he can get with your best friend."

Maggie scoffed. "He offered to get her the interview she deserves."

Marc's lips drew back in a derisive half frown. "What's it going to look like when he sets his hot new girlfriend up at the company? What happens when the other employees feel like she's getting special treatment because she's with him? What happens when he gets tired of her and they break up and now she's working in the same building as him all the time?"

Something about Marc's vehemence seemed off. He never got this worked up about anything.

Marc had never been interested in meeting Rose. Now he was trying to look out for her. It didn't add up. "So let me get this straight. You think my best friend is hot." He'd said it twice. "And you don't think Gray is good enough for her."

"That's not what I said."

"Um, yeah, you did."

"I just don't want things to get complicated and messy between all of us. She's your best friend. He's family. If this doesn't go well, more than likely you'll lose your friend because no matter what, Gray will be at all the family get-togethers. And if he's not, my family will blame me."

"What happens if Gray and Rose really hit it off? That means we'll all spend a lot of time together. Is that a problem for you?"

"Why would it be?"

"Because you think she's hot. Maybe you're jealous." Maggie couldn't come up with another plausible explanation for his odd behavior.

He laughed, though it didn't sound genuine at all. "Seriously, sweetheart? Why would I be jealous when I've got the most beautiful, kind, loving woman in the world, who is way hotter than her best friend any day of the week, and especially when she's naked and thoroughly rumpled in my bed? Right where I want you." He leaned in and kissed her again, this time pushing her back onto the sheets and covering her with his body.

"I thought you had a problem that couldn't wait."

"They'll have to get by without me for now. My girl always comes first."

She rocked her hips against his. "Is that a promise?"

He chuckled, sliding his hand down her belly and between her legs. "I'll prove it to you."

He did. Twice.

But when she came out of the bathroom, dressed and ready to leave, he was right back on his phone texting, this time with his back to the window. Maybe it didn't mean anything, but if the problem was so urgent, why not get on the phone and handle it? What was so important that it had to be dealt with on a Saturday morning?

Why did it feel like making love this morning was a distraction from the texts and how he felt about Rose and Gray seeing each other?

She wanted to chalk it up to stress and nerves and wedding jitters.

But she found herself letting a lot of things go recently because he distracted her with an abundance of affection and pretty words that soothed her. In the beginning of their relationship, his attention seemed so nice and sweet and loving. But after a while, especially after he asked her to marry him, it changed in her mind to something that seemed almost calculated.

She blew that off because she knew he loved her. So much so that he couldn't wait to marry her. And her heart sometimes felt so full it might burst with how happy he made her when he was so considerate.

Like this morning.

Making love always made her feel the connection she had with him. In bed, everything felt right. Out of it, they were good friends.

Everything seemed the way it should be. The way she'd hoped it would be when she got married.

But even in her bliss she felt a sliver of disconnection growing between them that unsettled her.

He said and did everything right. Yes, he supported her in every way. He backed her up when she needed it. He offered helpful suggestions when she got into a jam. He never offered an opinion she didn't agree with.

They never argued about anything.

And then they met Gray and Rose at the bar last night and something subtle came over Marc.

She'd finally gotten them all together and it had been so much fun watching the sparks fly between Rose and Gray—the way they had when she'd first met Marc. She really hoped something wonderful came of it. Rose deserved a man like Gray, who'd be supportive and treat her the way she deserved to be treated.

Rose and Gray had found common ground on many things last night, which made Maggie realize that she and Marc had only ever veered from total agreement about getting a cat or dog.

It seemed trivial. They were lucky to have such a carefree and happy relationship.

One like her parents shared for decades.

She was making something out of nothing.

I don't think Gray is good for Rose.

None of Marc's reservations made much sense. If things didn't work out down the line, Maggie believed Rose and Gray would behave like grown-ups whenever they saw each other. Because they would eventually. Maybe even often.

At first she thought Marc was kidding, but the niggling feeling that there was more to it came back to her.

Now that the blush of lovemaking had faded, and thanks to two glasses of water her hangover had stopped pounding away in her head along with her heartbeat, she remembered the way Marc had been so focused on Rose last night.

She wished she could put her finger on what seemed off about Marc and why, because she didn't want to believe there really was something going on that she should be concerned about.

"Hey, babe, you heading out?" Marc said, distracted by another incoming text.

"Yeah. Did you fix the problem with work?"

"I think so. Though I'm starting to think this whole thing isn't worth the hassle and I should end it."

"Will that be a problem for the company?"

"No."

Odd. He seemed so sure, but usually when he talked about business he got upset that he had to run most everything through his father.

He stuffed his phone into his back pocket and came to her. He cupped her face and kissed her softly. "I'm going to miss you tonight."

"If you run off with a stripper, I'll kill you."

His grin made her smile back. "Not a chance. Besides, I have no idea what Gray has planned."

She didn't believe the white lie. "Uh-huh. Right. He'd never let you down."

Everything easy about Marc went hard. His hands dropped away from her face, he took a step back, and glared at her. "What do you mean by that?"

She held her hands out, then let them drop back to her sides. "Nothing. You're the one who brought up the strippers yesterday. So don't try to act like that's not where you'll be tonight, or that Gray didn't set up the bachelor party you wanted."

"Of course he did. Gray does *everything* right."

She stared at him, not recognizing the irritation, when he'd always been an easygoing man around her. "Why does that upset you? You're getting what you want."

Marc shook off his surly mood and smiled at her. "Sorry. It's just Gray and I have history."

"You mentioned as much last night."

"It's stupid. Kid stuff. I shouldn't let those old feelings creep up and ruin our morning."

"For what it's worth, he seems really happy for us. He set aside time this week to spend it with you and for our wedding. I know families have their squabbles and grievances, mine is no different, but don't let the past spoil what should be a very happy week for us."

"You're right. I won't. And I'll put this work issue I'm dealing with to rest, too, so I can focus all my time and attention on you."

She took a deep breath and confessed, "It's a big deal, getting married. We've got everything planned for the wedding, so hopefully we can just sit back and enjoy it. But that doesn't mean it's not stressful. It's a big change for both of us."

"Are you having second thoughts?" The concern in his eyes matched her own that he'd even ask.

"No. Are you?"

"Not at all. I know exactly what I want. And I'm looking at her."

She sighed and tried to let go of all her worries. "Then it will be you and me standing in front of all our friends and family next Saturday, starting our life together as husband and wife."

Marc didn't look as relieved as she hoped, but he did smile and give her another sweet kiss to send her on her way.

Things felt off this morning, but she looked forward to picking up her dress later with Rose. They'd talk. Rose would tell her what she already knew. Everything was okay and her wedding was going to be epic.

Chapter Eight

*R*ose arrived in the hotel lobby right on time for her brunch with Gray. She felt a million times better than she had when she left her mother's house thanks to some retail therapy. Her car was packed with her finds from the cute downtown Carmel shops.

She'd loved seeing the artist cottages built in the late 1800s and early 1900s. The Hansel and Gretel Cottages as well as the Storybook Cottage and the Obers Home were her favorites. They were straight out of a children's book come to life. They made Carmel-by-the-Sea feel magical.

After her date, she'd head home, redecorate her room to flip the bird at her dad and show her mom and sister that they didn't have to live in his world anymore. They could redecorate the house and redefine and reinvent their lives, too.

She spotted Gray the second he stepped out of the elevator into the huge lobby and smiled at him.

His gaze swept over her in one hot stroke that left her a little breathless and her mind taking a turn to sultry thoughts of his hands and mouth touching every inch of her. "You look fantastic," he said by way of hello and kissed her on the cheek.

She was so glad she'd packed an extra casual dress. The short-sleeved, dusty pink dress fit snug up top with a cinched waist that flared out into an above-the-knee-length skirt. The flirty dress was perfect for shopping in the upscale and trendy shops and for their brunch date. She was so glad he liked it.

"You're all business today, but still gorgeous." He looked good in the white button-down dress shirt, a black silk tie, and black slacks. She bet he had ditched the suit jacket upstairs in his room.

He took her hand and led her toward the restaurant to their left. "Video conference calls this morning. I don't know why people like to see me when a phone call would do."

"Were you talking to women?"

"In two cases of the three, yes."

She looked up at him, then swept her gaze down him as he'd done to her. "I can't imagine why they'd want to stare at you for an hour."

He chuckled. "I'm the lucky one who gets to stare at you for however long I can get you to stay."

"Do you always work on Saturday?"

He frowned. "No. But since I'm taking so much time off this coming week, I had my assistant set some of the more urgent calls for this morning. Usually, if I work on the weekends, it's more social or charitable kind of stuff."

"Making deals while playing golf or over drinks at a charity benefit," she guessed.

He nodded. "My golf game sucks. It's more dinner parties than the links."

"Sounds like you lead a very busy life."

"If I had something better to do with my time, I'd be happy to ditch work." He gave her a pointed look to let her know he'd happily spend time with her.

"Lucky me. I get you all to myself for a little while."

"I'm the lucky one. Unfortunately, I can't spend the rest of the day with you. Marc's meeting me here later so we can take off for the bachelor party."

"I'm meeting Maggie at two and going with her to pick up her wedding dress and mine before her bachelorette party this evening. I can't wait to see her in the gown."

Gray held up two fingers to the hostess.

"Right this way." The hostess gave Gray a seductive smile.

Rose couldn't blame her. The man was too good to be true. Tall, dark, handsome, smart, successful, nice, and he had a killer smile and body to go with all that and everything else she was uncovering about him.

The hostess sat them at a table by the windows that overlooked a fountain and pretty garden. "Your server, Jeanine, will be right with you. Enjoy your meal."

Gray held her chair out for her, then took the seat closest to her rather than across the table, even though he couldn't see outside. Instead, he stared at her.

"Why aren't you married or attached to some lucky woman?" she asked.

The half grin made him even more endearing. "I love it that you don't hold back."

She eyed him. "I hope you won't, either."

"I've never been married. Attached a few times in long-term relationships."

"How long?"

"Two that lasted nearly three years and one that lasted just under two. I'm not a serial dater, but I can figure out if I'm compatible with someone usually within the first three months if it lasts more than a few dates. As for why I'm not married or attached, I haven't met the woman I can't let go of yet."

That "yet" told her he wanted to find that person, and part of her already wanted it to be her.

"What about you?"

She gave him as honest an answer as he'd given her. "For a long time, I sucked at dating. I was in it for all the wrong reasons."

He tilted his head. "How do you mean?"

"I wanted them to validate me, to make me feel like I was worthy."

"I can't imagine you'd need anyone to do that for you. You're smart and beautiful, and from all I've heard, you've done very well professionally, especially given the competitive company you currently work at."

"Well, thank you. I wasn't fishing for compliments, but I'll take them."

"I've got more if you ever do need them."

Her smile grew even bigger. Her cheeks were going to hurt by the end of this if he kept it up. "I'll let you know."

"Happy to help. Anything to keep you smiling like that."

She shook her head. "Yeah, I just don't get how any woman let you get away."

"I guess I wasn't the one they wanted to hold on to."

"Their loss. My amazing gain."

Jeanine arrived at their table and introduced herself as their server. "Will you be having the brunch buffet?"

She glanced at Gray, who nodded with her, then answered, "Yes."

"Can I get you both something to drink? We've got an amazing peach-raspberry mimosa."

"Sounds good to me."

"Me, too," Gray answered.

"Coming right up. Whenever you're ready to eat, the plates are at the far right table." She pointed in that direction. "Then just wind your way around to all the stations. I suggest you try the crepes."

Jeanine left to get their drink order.

Rose turned to Gray. "Are you always going to get the same drink as me?"

"So far we agree. Let's see how long we can keep it up. Besides, I don't like orange juice, so the peach-raspberry sounded good."

She smirked.

"What?" he asked.

"I don't like orange juice, either." It was a small thing, but she enjoyed the discovery of all they had in common.

"Did you figure out the right reasons to date someone?"

She fell back into their previous conversation. "I learned that I had to be okay with myself, so I could be good for someone else. I did the work to understand why I acted the way I did and was such a bad date and girlfriend."

"It couldn't have been *all* your fault."

"It wasn't. I picked the wrong kind of guy for me, too. But I've had some good relationships with guys who were right for me at the right time. But I haven't dated anyone since last year because I've been busy and I made a huge mistake that kind of made me gun-shy to try again." She felt good about putting it out there, even without naming Marc as her mistake.

"Until me."

"You are too compelling to pass up. So far," she added with a flirty smile to let him know she was teasing.

"I'm glad to hear it. And even though you're best friends with the woman who is marrying my cousin, and this could get awkward down the road, I couldn't pass on a chance to get to know you better. I've been looking for someone like you who is also looking for the right one to come into their life, because that's what I want, too." He studied her. "Unless I'm wrong."

"No. I do want something real and deep and that's why I've kind of been sitting on the sidelines waiting for it to happen."

"What happened a year ago that turned you off dating?"

She didn't know if she should tell him, but she also didn't want to say nothing or to lie. "I was out at a bar, celebrating someone from work's birthday. Just a fun night out, blowing off some steam after I'd also finished a big project that took months and turned me into an all-work-no-play hermit. I wanted to have some fun. I met a guy at the bar, we danced and talked and flirted. He seemed great. One drink led to four and led to me going home with him. We had a great night." She eyed him to see if he had anything to say.

"I'm with you so far. Sounds like you two were on the same page, things got hot, clothes came off."

She let her initial worry that he'd judge her wash away. "Exactly. I woke up the next morning and thought that was fun, maybe I'll see him again. But probably not. We hadn't made any promises and that was okay with me. I'm not usually the one-night-stand kind of person, though I had done it a couple times before in college, so I was okay with walking out the door without any expectations of a phone call or a repeat."

"Sounds fair."

"And then his phone lit up with a text and I was furious."

Gray sat back. "Oh, shit. Wife?"

"Girlfriend. If I'd known, I would have gone home alone. And I asked if he was married or attached when he offered to buy me the first drink. He said no. I thought I'd made myself clear, and he made me the other woman."

Gray's eyes narrowed. "It really pissed you off."

"Big time. I've been cheated on. I know how it feels, and I'd never do that to anyone."

"I know what you mean. I'd been seeing someone going on a year when I found her with another guy."

"What did you do? Did you hit him?"

He shook his head. "I wanted to, but what you feel and what you do are two different things."

That simple yet telling statement resonated through her.

"But more than seeing him with her, it was the look in her eyes that really made me angry. She looked smug, like she'd pulled one over on me and I deserved it. We hadn't been getting along for weeks. Things were getting to the point where we either had to have a long talk about how to fix it or cut our losses and get out. She chose the third path just to hurt me."

Rose reached over and put her hand over his. "I'm really sorry that happened to you."

He turned his hand, linked his fingers with hers, and squeezed. "I'm sorry that guy lied to you, just so he could be with you. I'd do just about anything to have you, but that's not one of them."

She gasped at his bold statement.

"I don't play games, Rose. I'll always be honest with you."

"I think that's what I like most about you. You've been up front and open since the moment we met."

"Because I want this to be real."

"So do I."

"Then let's get something to eat and spend more time together."

She stood with him and they walked hand-in-hand to the buffet line. She missed his touch the second he released her hand to offer her a plate and take one for himself. They walked along the buffet, picking out many of the same items.

They both got pancakes. She put cut strawberries and a dusting of powdered sugar on hers. He drowned his in butter and syrup. They both got scrambled eggs, bacon, and fruit salad, and bypassed the pastries.

"They're too sweet," he complained.

She stared at the bucket of syrup on his pancakes, then at him, and laughed. "Really?"

He rolled his eyes and escorted her back to their table, where Jeanine had dropped off their mimosas and water.

Gray set his plate down, held her chair out for her again, helped her get seated, then sat beside her. He picked up his drink and held it out to her. "To keeping this real."

She clinked her glass to his. "Absolutely."

They ate, chitchatting about his working out of his hotel room and her redoing her childhood bedroom and why it was a cleansing of the past and embracing who she was now.

"When you have to take something away—good or bad—people have a hard time letting go. Adding something good to your life is easy. Accepting something bad is hard." Gray chewed the last piece of bacon from his plate. "I really wasn't excited about working from here for the next week. I knew it would be a huge hassle. But then I met you, and it's an annoyance I can live with because I get to spend time with you."

"You'll probably be sick of me by the end of the week."

He put his hand over hers on the table. "I seriously doubt that."

She hated that she was keeping something from him. Something that could change his mind.

She needed to tell Maggie about her night with Marc, then she could tell Gray.

But first, Gray owed her an explanation.

"I'm really enjoying our time together, too. And I hope this doesn't spoil things."

Gray read her mind. "But you want to know about Marc."

"He's marrying my best friend. And to be honest, Maggie and I have had a hard time connecting this past year. Work and life have kept us both busy. I knew about Marc, but until last night, I'd never met him. She didn't share any pictures."

"He's got this thing about his privacy."

She had a good idea why, but wanted Gray's take on it. "With social media it's not easy to keep your private life private anymore. Why is he so against pictures of him getting out?"

Gray frowned, wiped his mouth with his napkin, then set it on the table. "Marc doesn't care or apologize if others think he lives his life a bit recklessly."

"How do you mean?" She had a pretty good idea.

"Maggie is probably the longest relationship he's ever been in. When he called to tell me they'd gotten engaged, I seriously thought he was calling to tell me he'd blown up another relationship because he'd . . ." Gray paused, unsure or unwilling to say the last part.

"He cheated." It wasn't a hard guess, since she'd played a part in his cheating on his girlfriend.

"He has a pattern. When one relationship is crashing, he

starts up another one before he actually bails out of the last one. Sometimes the women figure it out and leave. Other times, they're still holding on and he strings both women along for a time until one or the other figures it out."

"What an asshole."

"Agreed. One hundred percent. But you have to understand, Marc's parents cheated on each other. That's what broke them up. Then he watched his father go through a string of women, most of them overlapping. As a teen, Marc thought his dad was a player and that was a good thing. His father's self-worth was tied to the women he had coming and going in his life. He'd tell Marc not to get tied down. The minute things weren't fun anymore, get out. There were too many women out there to get stuck with just one."

"And then Marc met Maggie, he fell in love with her, and he decided she was better than any other woman." Rose really hoped that was the case.

Gray's gaze dropped to the table. "It appears that way, yes. They seem happy together." That wasn't the resounding confirmation she wanted.

"But?" She waited for him to look at her again.

"No one was more surprised than me that they were getting married, but he seems committed and that's a good thing."

She gave him a sideways look. "Seems?"

Gray sighed. "Marc works for his dad, who is getting older and has some health issues. About two years ago, he had a mild stroke. No lasting side effects, but it scared him. Marc talked to his dad about cutting back at work and letting him take the lead. His dad agreed, so long as Marc took a good long look at his life and changed his ways, too. He told Marc that he regretted not taking his relationships seriously and focusing on family instead of . . . basically chasing women."

"I take it when he had the stroke there was no one there for him aside from Marc and your family."

"He was home alone and felt like something was off. He called the woman he'd been seeing and asked if she'd come to the house. She said she had something else going on and couldn't get away. Luckily, he decided not to wait and see if he felt better. He went to urgent care. If he'd waited even ten more minutes . . . It could have been a lot worse. They treated him and he's good. But it was a wake-up call. He changed his diet, cut back on his drinking, took some time to think about what he really wanted in a partner, and found it in Peg. She's kind and sweet and takes care of him. Because she does, he spoils her in every possible way. I've never seen him so . . . in love."

"And he wants that for his son."

"He's always been demanding of Marc when it comes to school and the business. He basically laid down the law. Stop treating his personal life like a party that never ends and get serious about his future. He told Marc, and I agree, if his personal life was going to continue to be a source of strife all the time, then work was going to suffer and eventually the business would fail."

"So in the course of reflecting on his personal relationships, he figured out that those bad affairs contributed to some of his business troubles."

Gray nodded. "He could literally see the ups and downs in his life and business and how they correlated. When things were good, they were really good. And vice versa."

"So what you're saying is that Marc's father basically told him to get his personal life in order if he ever wanted to take over the business. He hooks up with Maggie. She's fantastic. Easy to get along with. She's happy in her life. She always has been. I aspire to be her kind of blissful."

Gray nodded with a grin. "I like her a lot."

"But you're concerned, and so am I now, because he's a serial cheater who asked Maggie to marry him after only eight months after his dad basically gave him an ultimatum."

"I'm not saying what they have isn't real, or that he's not capable of a lasting relationship. I've seen his father do a complete one-eighty. Maybe that inspired Marc to do the same. I want Marc and Maggie to be happy. I hope they will be for a long time to come."

"That's very optimistic."

"I have no reason to feel otherwise, other than the fact that Marc and I have a past riddled with competition, pranks, upset, and jealousy."

"Are you jealous of Marc? Because you shouldn't be."

Gray shrugged. "It's not jealousy on my part, just that I can't believe he found someone and is getting married before me. Up until he told me he proposed to Maggie, I would have sworn he'd spend his whole life a bachelor and be happy about it. But every time I'm with someone, yeah, I see his jealousy that I've got something he can't seem to manage."

"Maggie is smart. If she thought for a second he wasn't committed, that there was any sign of something going on, she'd call him out on it."

Then again, Maggie had been devastated when her last relationship fell apart. Joel broke things off because Maggie wanted children and he didn't. The painful decision knocked Maggie off her axis, and then only a few months later she started dating Marc, who seemed all too eager to start a family. Rose worried that her friend might be on the rebound, but she seemed so happy that Rose hoped that wasn't the case.

"You're right," Gray agreed with her. "And really, it's none of my business. I know Marc's past. While we see each other for family things and call each other once in a while to catch up, we're not best friends. I was surprised he asked me to be his best man instead of one of the many other guys he hangs with. Maybe he asked me because he wants me to see that he's changed. Maybe he wants to rub it in my face that he's happy with someone and I'm alone."

That didn't speak well of Marc at all.

"Or maybe it's because I'm his cousin, and my uncle expected him to pick me because weddings are about family. I don't know."

Rose sighed out her frustration. "It's hard to wait and see if Marc has changed when he's marrying someone I care about." And Rose had seen firsthand how callous he was about his relationships. She hoped that was in the past.

Gray nodded. "I get that. All we can do is support them no matter what." Gray put his hand over hers again. "While I'm grateful they brought us together, I don't want to spend what little time I have with you talking about them."

"I know. I'm sorry. Aren't you and Marc leaving soon for the bachelor party?"

Gray sighed. "Yeah. A night of drinking and tame debauchery."

She eyed him, confused. "Is there such a thing?"

"In a strip club, yes. It's all, here's a bunch of mostly naked girls. Don't touch." He smirked. "It's an illusion. They act like they want you, but all they want are big tips. It's their job. But some guys like to get lost in the fantasy."

She cocked a brow. "You're not one of them?"

"Who do you think I'd rather spend an evening with? A stripper who means nothing to me and I have to pay to keep her attention? Or you? Someone I'd really like to get to know better. And much more intimately."

She blushed and crossed her legs under the table to stave off the building ache in her core. "I wish we could spend more time together, too." She glanced at her phone on the table and noted the time.

"You have to go, don't you?" Gray didn't hide his disappointment.

She nodded. "Maggie and I will try on our dresses while we gossip about you."

He grinned at that. "My loss."

"Mine, too. I really enjoyed brunch and being with you."

"I have a feeling I'll be surrounded by women tonight and all I'll be thinking about is you."

"When you say those kinds of things, it just makes me . . ."

"What?" He leaned in for her answer.

"It makes me want to do this." She closed the distance and kissed him. A soft brush of her lips at first, his eyes on her as she watched them spark with desire and need. She pressed her lips to his again. This time with more intent, sweeping her tongue along his bottom lip.

His fingers slid into her hair at the back of her head, and he took the kiss deeper, his tongue gliding along hers in a sure and steady slide that left her breathless.

She cupped his hard jaw in her palm and leaned into him.

Gray kissed her one last time and pressed his forehead to hers. "You are . . . so much more than I expected."

"I didn't know what to expect when Maggie said we'd all be spending a lot of time together this week. I wasn't happy about coming back home, but I'm so glad I did." Maybe she hadn't resolved her past or bridged the gap between her and her mom and Poppy, but meeting Gray and finding this kind of instant connection was definitely worth it.

Gray leaned back, giving them both some space to cool off. They were in public, and several people at nearby tables stared at them. One woman even gave her an approving grin.

"Why didn't you want to come home? Your father is gone now."

"I haven't been home since I left for college."

"Why?" he asked because she avoided a real answer.

She never talked about her dad, but with Gray, she found it so easy to open up. "All I ever wanted to do was get away.

Escape. Live my life without always feeling like everything I did was wrong or stupid. And I did. But I left my mom and sister behind. Without me, Poppy became my father's favorite target. She blames me for abandoning her. I blame myself."

"You didn't. You saved yourself. She's angry at the wrong person."

"That's what I tell myself, but it's little consolation when my sister hates me. As children we were so close, though I know it's a little naïve to think we can pick up where we left off . . . Now . . . she can't stand the sight of me. And I feel so guilty." She pressed her lips tight and tried not to let the emotions overwhelm her. "My mom didn't want me to come back at all. It somehow gave her comfort to know I was out there, living my life, happy and away from him."

"As it should. I doubt she wanted you to stay and suffer with them."

"He died three years ago. Fell down the stairs drunk. Snapped his neck and cracked his skull open. I didn't go to his funeral. I didn't come home. I didn't care that he was gone. As far as I was concerned, he didn't bring anything into my life but pain and anger. It's sad to say, but I didn't miss having him in my life at all."

"You didn't owe him anything. You don't owe them."

"I feel like I do. When Maggie told me she was having her wedding here, I couldn't let my best friend get married without me. I couldn't keep making excuses not to see my mom and sister. So here I am."

"If they've experienced what you went through with your

dad, then surely they understand why you didn't want to come back and face those terrible memories."

She appreciated that he understood how hard it was for her to be here. "My mom does. Poppy is lost in her anger. I'm her big sister. I should have protected her."

Gray brushed his fingers up and down her forearm. "Didn't you do that all those years you were under his roof?"

She couldn't deny the truth. "Yes. I simply couldn't do it anymore. If I hadn't left, I wouldn't be here right now." She'd never admitted that to anyone but Maggie.

Gray's eyes softened with understanding and compassion. He leaned in, slipped his hand along her cheek, and pulled her close so he could kiss her forehead. The tenderness of the kiss made her eyes tear up. "Aw, sweetheart, I am so glad you survived."

She leaned into his palm. "Thank you. But this conversation is getting way too serious."

He used his thumb to tilt her head back so he could look her in the eye. "It's not easy to share the deepest parts of ourselves, but it means a lot to me that you'd trust me with something so personal."

She did trust him. When she revealed why she'd stayed away and why she'd come home, she felt he'd understand and not judge her. "I like you. You're easy to be with."

"I feel the same way about you." Gray's gaze shot to the restaurant entrance. "Unfortunately, I'll be spending the rest of my day and night with him."

"My loss," she admitted, echoing his earlier disappointment.

He gave her a searing look. "You make me want to pretend I'm sick or something to get out of this."

"He's counting on you to give him the best bachelor party ever. With strippers," she added with a smirk.

He rolled his eyes. "You're the only woman I want to spend the night with."

Her ears burned with the blush that rose from her breasts all the way up to her hairline.

He caught himself. "I didn't mean it like that. Well, I do, but . . ." He shrugged because he'd been honest but knew they needed more time to get to know each other.

"Well. Um. Something to look forward to, then," she teased, but also meant it.

"Lucky me," he said, a twinkle in his eyes that didn't dim the heat still there.

Marc arrived at their table. "You two look cozy."

Gray released her and sat back, though they were still sitting very close together. She didn't know if Marc had caught them kissing earlier. She didn't care.

Gray signed the check Jeanine had dropped off while they were talking. He stood and pulled her chair back for her so they could be on their way. She hated to make a hasty good-bye, but didn't want to spend a whole lot of time with Marc if she could help it.

Except she had years of running into him and spending time with him ahead.

"Do you need to run upstairs to your room before we head out?" Marc asked Gray.

Gray shook his head. "I'm good to go."

Marc shifted his focus back to her and moved closer. He leaned in before she knew his intent and kissed her cheek, then his knuckles caressed her from her shoulder down to her elbow out of Gray's view.

She immediately stepped away and into Gray. He put his hand on the same arm Marc had touched to steady her. It did more than that. His warmth washed away the uneasy feeling Marc gave her with that too-intimate touch and anchored her to Gray.

Marc's gaze went from Gray's hand on her to her eyes. He hid whatever he felt, but Gray stiffened behind her. "It was so good to see you. Have fun with Maggie today. I can't wait to hear all about what you've got planned for her bachelorette party."

"It probably won't be as wild as your night, but Maggie will love it."

"I have a feeling you like to get a little wild sometimes," Marc teased, but she couldn't help but think he was baiting her, reminding her of their night together.

All it did was make her angry and suspicious, especially after he'd explicitly asked her not to tell Maggie about that night.

She didn't dare answer, or risk Gray sensing something more going on between her and Marc. She wanted to tell Gray the truth, but Maggie deserved to hear it from her first.

She turned to Gray. "Thank you so much for brunch. I had a wonderful time. I hope we see each other soon."

"I'll walk you out to your car."

Marc waved his hand toward the restaurant entrance. "Yes. Let's."

Gray narrowed his gaze on Marc. "You can meet me at my car." He pulled the keys from his pocket and tossed them to Marc.

"Just trying to be a gentleman for the lady."

"I've got it covered," Gray assured him, then touched her back to escort her out to the lobby.

Marc walked ahead of them out to the parking area. He briefly glanced at Gray, who nodded in the opposite direction from where she'd parked. Marc went that way in search of Gray's car.

She led Gray to hers. "You didn't have to walk me all the way here."

"I'd rather spend a few more minutes with you than with him." Gray stood in front of her beside her car. "Is something going on between you two?"

She didn't know what to say.

"He caught you in the corridor at the bar last night. Now he's cozying up to you in the restaurant." More than annoyance filled his tone. Marc had touched a nerve in Gray. "It's like we used to be. He'd see me with someone and immediately start insinuating himself into her space and trying to get her attention away from me." Gray rubbed his hand over the back of his neck. "I'm not seeing things that aren't there." He waited for her to say otherwise, but she couldn't. "He's getting married. He shouldn't be looking at you the way he does or saying the things he has." Irritation grew to anger.

"Old habits die hard," she suggested, trying to soothe him.

"I used to just blow it off, but with you . . . I really don't like it."

She saw that clearly and appreciated his honesty and that he wanted to somehow protect her from Marc's games. "Trust me, I'm more interested in you than in spending time with him."

Gray moved in and pressed her up against her car, dipping his head low so he could whisper in her ear. "Good. Because I really want you to be mine."

She slid her hands up his chest and rested them on his hard pecs. He had a lot of strength and power hidden under that dress shirt. And there really was something a little wild inside her, especially when it came to this man, because she boldly said, "What if I already think of you as mine?"

His gaze swept over her with a possessive sweep. "You'd be right."

"Then you have nothing to worry about and a lot to look forward to when you get back."

He traced his finger along the side of her face and tucked a lock of her hair behind her ear. "You make it damn hard to leave."

She gazed up at him, hoping he saw her own disappointment. "But you promised Marc an epic bachelor party and I've got a big surprise for Maggie. This is their week."

"We could make it ours, too."

She loved that he wanted that. "I love stealing these moments with you."

Gray leaned in and brushed his lips softly over her cheek, washing away any lingering memory of Marc touching her there. "Take all the moments you want," he whispered, then pressed his lips to hers in a searing kiss that promised all their moments would be as passionate as this.

She fisted her hands in his shirt, rose to her tiptoes, pulled him closer, and they lost themselves in the moment.

She was still clinging to him when he broke the kiss. She caught something over his shoulder and fell back to her flat feet, angry their private moment wasn't so private. "We've got an audience."

Gray looked over his shoulder and spotted Marc leaning against a black Tesla, arms crossed over his chest. "I'm sorry. I've got to go. We're meeting up with friends, then doing dinner and the whole stripper thing. It's going to be a long night."

She swept her hands over his shoulders and down his chest to his rapidly beating heart, feeling good that he'd gotten as worked up as he made her. "You don't have to apologize. Have fun. I'll see you tomorrow."

He pulled his phone out, tapped a few buttons, and held it out to her. "Put your number in for me."

She did and handed it back. "Thank you again for brunch."

"You're welcome." He kissed her on the forehead. "See you soon." He turned and walked away, checking something on his phone as he covered the distance to where Marc waited for him.

She didn't move until her phone beeped with an incoming text. She pulled it out and immediately smiled at the alert.

UNKNOWN: I miss you already.

She looked up and found Gray staring at her from across the lot, a wide smile on his face. He waved good-bye and got into his car.

She immediately saved his number in her contact list and sent him a text back.

ROSE: Think of me tonight because I'll be thinking of you.

She got an instant response.

GRAY: I can't stop thinking about you.

He drove toward her and stopped, rolling down the window. "Kiss me good-bye, sweetheart."

She smiled and moved to his car. "I thought I already did."

"Satisfy my greedy nature where you're concerned."

She kissed him softly, then teased, "I look forward to it."

He groaned but smiled at her.

"Can we go now?" Marc complained.

Gray gave her one last lust-filled look and drove off, leaving her thinking about all the ways she'd like to satisfy him and her growing need for him.

She'd never been this attracted to a man or so impressed with one. Gray had that amazing combination of self-assurance, sex appeal, and kindness that drew her in and made her believe good and decent men existed.

And she was keeping a secret from him that could destroy the relationship they were building.

Chapter Nine

M aggie and her mother, Brenda, were at the dress shop, waiting for the salesperson to bring the gown out from the back. Maggie was still thinking about her morning with Marc. For some reason, she couldn't get those text messages out of her mind. So far, she'd accepted his excuses that it was all work. But she couldn't ignore the growing feeling in her gut that he was hiding something.

"Maggie, are you all right? You seem preoccupied."

She didn't want to lie to her mom, but she couldn't bring herself to talk about her swirling thoughts. She couldn't wait to get Rose alone so she could dump out all her concerns. Surely Rose would tell her she had nothing to worry about, and she and Marc would live happily ever after just like her parents.

So she prevaricated. "I'm just worried that even with the alterations the dress won't fit properly. We don't have a lot of time before the wedding."

"Everything is going to be fine. I bet the dress will fit you beautifully. You're going to be a gorgeous bride."

Will I be a happy one? The thought came unbidden.

Because right now all she could think about was how Joel had left her because he didn't want children. And Marc seemed to want her because a family would make his own father happy.

That's not the only reason, she reminded herself. They were good together. Friends. Lovers. They always had fun.

"Honey, is it something else? Are you nervous about the wedding? Because I can tell you, I was before I married your father, too. It's natural. This is a big step. It's a commitment. But you and Marc love each other."

"We do."

She'd loved Joel, too. It had been there for her and Joel from the moment they met. But in the end, that love hadn't been enough to keep them together. It wasn't that she'd fallen out of love with him. It took her a long time to realize she'd always love him, but she couldn't give up having a family.

Falling in love with Marc had been different. They started with an instant attraction that grew into something more over time as they dated and saw more of each other. Probably because she'd needed to make room in her heart for him.

But had she given her relationship with Marc enough time to reveal the truth of who they both were, separately and together, and to know they truly did belong together forever?

"Love will see you through this," her mother continued.

But love hadn't been enough to keep Joel and me together.

She needed to stop thinking about her ex.

For as long as she could remember, she wanted to be a wife and mother. She wanted a happy marriage like her parents. A simple life grounded in family. She wanted the contentment she always saw in her mother and to feel the pride she always saw in her parents' eyes when they looked at her.

She thought about a sweet little boy with Marc's good looks, his charming smile, and his easygoing personality. And a little girl who looked like her, who grew up with pigtails and laughter and a best friend like she had in Rose.

She wanted that dream to be reality.

"How did you and Dad get through thirty years of marriage and make it look easy?"

"Most of the time, it was easy. We like each other as much as we love each other. That's not to say we haven't had our fair share of disagreements, angry words, and hurt feelings. We've had rough patches and tough times just like any other couple. But we stayed together and made our relationship stronger by putting in the effort to fix what was wrong, even when that meant we had to compromise and change." Her mother gave her a soft smile. "You and Marc have been happy and in love for the last eight months, right?"

"Yes." Maggie didn't even hesitate because everything had been wonderful.

"And you've got big plans for the future. Sometimes, sweetheart, it's overwhelming to think of it all, but if you just focus on one thing at a time, it won't seem like so many changes all at once."

Maggie felt centered again. "Right. I'll focus on the wedding."

The bell above the door dinged, making her turn. "Rose. You're here." Relief swept through her.

Rose smiled. "I am. And look who came with me." Rose waved a hand out toward her own mom, who walked in behind her.

Maggie hugged Rose, then released her. "I thought it might be fun for all of us to do this together."

Though Maggie had always avoided going to Rose's house, she had always been fond of Rose's mother, Nancy.

The two older women hugged, with Brenda saying, "Nancy, it's been too long since we've seen each other. Just because our girls are grown, that doesn't mean we can't still get together and talk about them."

Nancy blinked back tears. "I've missed you, too. I should have called, especially after you sent that beautiful bouquet and came to Lawrence's funeral."

"It looks like you've been getting on okay," Brenda said, eyeing Nancy's pretty outfit.

Maggie couldn't remember a time when Nancy wasn't in a dark dress. The navy slacks and lilac blouse were chic. The bright color brought out the pink in her cheeks and gold flecks in her eyes.

Nancy nervously brushed her hand over the V neckline of her blouse. "I'm doing lots of new things these days."

Rose put her hand on her mom's shoulder. "And it looks good on you."

"How is Poppy?" Brenda asked.

"I tried to get her to come, too, but she prefers to be home. She's not the same since her father died."

"It was a difficult time for both of you after Rose went away to college. I know I missed Maggie a lot. I'm sure you missed Rose just as much. And your husband . . . Well, he didn't hide how he felt about her leaving. I'm so glad that I was there to help."

Maggie exchanged a look with Rose, who appeared to be as surprised and shocked by the statement as she was.

Rose glanced at Brenda. "You helped my mother out when my father was . . ." Rose didn't seem to know how to finish the sentence.

Brenda put her hand on Rose's shoulder. "I always knew what was going on in that house with you. I promised your mom you would always be safe with us and you could come and stay whenever you wanted. I let her know that offer applied to her and Poppy, too, should the need ever arise."

Nancy took Brenda's hand. "Thank you for always giving her a place where she could be just a girl having fun with her friend. And for not judging me for staying with him."

Brenda squeezed Nancy's hand. "We all do the best we can. Let today be the first of many that we get together to share the good times in our daughters' lives and build on our own friendship as well."

The two women held each other's gazes for a moment, then released each other, both seeming to have let the past go, so they could look to the future.

Maggie hugged her mom. "You're awesome." She couldn't contain the pride and love she felt for her right now.

Her mom gave her a squeeze. "I followed your lead, sweetheart. I saw how you tried to protect Rose. I was so proud of you for caring so much about your friend."

Maggie released her mom and stared at Rose, who looked terribly uncomfortable, stunned, and so appreciative at the same time. "I couldn't have asked for a better friend than Rose. She always had my back, so I had to have hers, too."

Rose launched herself into Maggie's chest and wrapped her up in a big hug. "I love you, Mags."

"I love you, too."

They were both teary-eyed when they broke apart and Paula, the shop owner, walked in carrying two garment bags, one much bulkier than the other.

"Ladies, no crying yet. Though we are ready for it." Paula waved a hand toward a box of tissues on the table. "But we haven't even gotten you into the dresses yet."

Rose took the smaller bag and headed to the back dressing room.

Maggie followed Paula to the larger room.

Brenda and Nancy took a seat in the waiting area and started chatting like no time had passed.

"Do you need me to assist you?" Paula asked Maggie, unzipping the bag and revealing the gorgeous lace dress with a sweetheart neckline.

"Let me just slip it on, then you can help me fasten the pearl buttons up the back."

Paula backed out of the room. "Take your time." She closed the drape.

Maggie wanted a moment alone to see herself in the dress. She quickly slipped out of the simple green sundress she'd worn, took the gown off the hanger, and stepped into it, pulling it up as she slipped her arms into the long lace sleeves.

She stood looking in the mirror, amazed how well the white-on-white gown fit her despite not being fastened in the back. Lace overlaid the tight bodice to the cinched waist, then draped down to the floor in a full skirt that made her look like a princess.

"Oh, my, Rose, you look beautiful. That color with your dark hair is gorgeous," Maggie heard her mother gushing just outside her dressing room.

"You look amazing," Rose's mom praised, too.

"Maggie picked a beautiful dress." Rose would look good in anything, but Maggie had picked a one-shoulder, high-low dress with a flared skirt to make sure her maid of honor stunned. The tight bodice and drape of the skirt would make Rose look like a goddess.

She wanted her friend to feel as beautiful as she looked.

"Can I come in?" Rose called out to her.

"Yes. I guess I need more help than I thought."

Rose walked in and Maggie turned. "Oh, my god," they said in unison. "You look amazing," they said together again, and laughed.

Rose held her hand up, finger pointed, and made a circle motion. "Turn. Let me button you in so our moms can see you. Really, Mags, you're breathtaking in that dress. Marc is going to lose his mind." Rose started at the bottom and quickly worked her way up to Maggie's mid-back with the tiny little pearls.

Maggie caught her eye in the mirror after she'd finished. "Do you really think he'll like it?"

"Yes. Absolutely. But it's not about the dress, Mags. He is so lucky to have you."

"Then why can't he stop looking at you?" Maggie blurted out, feeling like a fool for bringing it up.

"What?" Rose looked stunned, but not confused.

"I thought you liked Gray."

"I do. We had a fantastic brunch together this morning. He kissed me. Again. Made my head spin, and my heart . . ."

"What?" Maggie asked, feeling so much better that Rose looked so enamored with Gray.

"It melted." Rose sighed. "I never thought that was a real thing. But oh, god, my heart just leapt and melted and felt so full." Rose pressed her palms to her rosy cheeks. "Am I crazy? We just met."

Maggie let go of whatever was making her suspicious of Marc and her friend. "It's not crazy if it feels right."

"It feels amazing. He's . . . amazing," she repeated.

"I'm so happy for you."

Rose's glow dimmed. "About Marc—"

"Forget it," she said quickly, not wanting to upset Rose. "We had a really nice night and morning together."

"Oh, really." Rose teased her friend.

"Really. He can't wait for us to get married. And neither can I. I think all the stress is getting to me. He's been trying to tie up loose ends at work before we go on our honeymoon." She shook her head. "I'm making something out of nothing. You're beautiful. Of course he'd look at you. Tonight, he'll be staring at a dozen half-naked women."

"But he doesn't want any of them. He only wants you," Rose assured her. "But there is something—"

"Are you two ever coming out of there?" Maggie's mom shouted.

Maggie rolled her eyes, but smiled. "Let's not keep them waiting any longer."

Rose looked disappointed she didn't get to finish what she wanted to say, but nodded and opened the drape, then stepped out and to the side as Maggie emerged.

Nancy gasped and covered her mouth with her fingers. "Oh, Maggie. You're stunning."

Brenda smiled like a proud mom. "Gorgeous, sweetheart. It's perfect. Just like you."

Maggie turned to hide her tears, but gasped when she spotted a familiar face staring in through the shop window. But before she could blink away the tears and focus, the person rushed away, making her think she hadn't seen him at all.

Why is Joel in town?

She shook off the notion. It had to be someone who looked like him.

Paula handed a shoebox to Rose.

"What's this?" she asked.

Maggie loved a surprise. "Something to say thank you for

spending this week with me and for you to wear with that killer dress."

Rose opened the lid and gasped. "Maggie, they're gorgeous."

Maggie had picked out the silver heels, with the straps that crisscrossed over the toes and foot and wound once around the ankle, specifically for Rose. Now the shoes would highlight Rose's gorgeous legs and feet.

"They're sexy, but you'll probably hate me by the end of the wedding because they'll be killing your feet. Though I'm sure Gray will be all too happy to give you a foot massage."

Rose sat to exchange her wedge sandals for the strappy heels.

"Who's Gray?" Nancy asked.

"He's Marc's cousin and the best man," Brenda filled her in.

Maggie grinned at Nancy. "He and Rose are totally into each other. They've already had their first date. Brunch this morning." Maggie beamed at her best friend, so happy that she and Gray were getting closer. After the wedding, they could all spend time together as couples. She'd get to see Rose more often.

Rose met her mom's inquisitive gaze. "I met him last night. We hit it off. It's new. But there's definitely something there." The blush on Rose's cheeks and excitement in her eyes said it all. Rose was smitten.

Maggie couldn't be happier to be the person who brought them together.

What a story it would be to tell their grandchildren how Maggie had fallen in love with Marc and introduced her best friend to his cousin and they fell in love and got married, too. Their children would be family by blood and she and Rose would be like sisters as they'd always been.

That little daydream made her smile.

"That's wonderful," Nancy said. "You've never really shared anything about your personal life." There was a lot of joy and regret in her words.

"There's not a lot to tell about Gray. Yet." Rose stood and showed off the heels. "These are actually really comfortable. I love them." Rose gave Maggie a huge hug. "Thank you, Mags. You didn't have to do this."

"I wanted to. Besides, I wanted to be sure you looked your best in all the wedding photos," she teased.

"Everyone will be looking at you," Rose assured her.

Paula fluffed out the skirt of Maggie's gown and stepped back, checking her out to be sure everything looked right. "It's perfection on you," she declared.

Maggie brushed her hands over the lace and her fluttering stomach. "I love it."

Paula clapped her hands together. "Then I'll help you out of it and we'll get it back into the bag for you to take home for your big day."

Maggie looked at her mom, Nancy, and Rose. "Can you believe I'll be married by this time next weekend?"

Her mom brushed away a tear. "I'm so happy for you. You're a beautiful bride. You'll be such a great wife and mother." She turned to Nancy. "Where did the time go?"

Nancy sighed, her gaze filled with fondness. "It seems like

yesterday we kissed them good-bye outside of their kinder-garten classroom, and the next thing I knew we were sending them off to college."

Maggie caught the guilty look in Rose's eyes. She'd left for college and never come back. Until now.

Nancy had to be feeling like she'd missed so much of Rose's life. She probably didn't recognize the person Rose had blos-somed into away from home. Away from her family. On her own.

It broke Maggie's heart to think about Rose's past and how different her life had been back then, while Maggie had loving, understanding, and supportive parents who'd never hurt her.

Remnants of the scared, broken little girl Rose used to be remained deep inside her.

She'd asked if it was crazy to feel the way she did about Gray. Maggie heard what Rose didn't ask but felt all the same. Did she deserve it?

Yes.

Maggie believed with her whole heart that Rose deserved every happiness.

And so did she.

She hadn't settled for half the life she wanted. She'd held out for more.

She found the right man. Soon they'd have children.

That's the life she wanted and couldn't wait to have with Marc.

Chapter Ten

*A*fter hauling in all the new things she'd bought for her bedroom at the cute Carmel boutiques, Rose spent the late afternoon redecorating her old bedroom, because she really did want to visit more often. She'd gotten caught up doing the room makeover and needed to hurry up and finish getting ready for the bachelorette party. She slipped her feet into her wedge sandals and checked herself in the full-length standing mirror in the corner of her bedroom. They looked great with her navy blue jumpsuit.

Her phone buzzed with another incoming text.

She immediately smiled and assumed it was Gray. He'd sent her three other texts today, all of them saying the same thing as the one she read now.

GRAY: I'm still thinking about you.

She'd never had a guy this sweet and charming in her life. For her, it took a little getting used to, but she really liked it.

She stood in front of the mirror, held up her phone, took a picture of herself, and sent it to Gray.

ROSE: Ready for the bachelorette party!

GRAY: All I see is a beautiful woman and a bed. Not fair.

GRAY: I wish I was going out with you tonight.

ROSE: I'll see you tomorrow. Unless you're too hungover.

GRAY: Nothing will keep me away from you.

She grinned and turned to face the room that now looked like a tranquil retreat, with the new white comforter that had an oversized sprig of long, thin leaves down the center and the matching pillow shams propped against the wood headboard. She'd exchanged old posters on the walls for silver-framed botanical prints of sprigs of leaves. She liked the fern one the best. Directly above her headboard was the only other bit of color she'd added to the room. She'd scored a large painting of pink roses in bloom on a white background.

The whole space felt simple. Elegant. And with the right touch to put her stamp on this room. What once felt like a cell now felt like a place she'd like to visit.

They were simple changes, but they made all the difference.

"What the hell is this?" Her sister stood in the doorway

holding the painting Rose had left outside Poppy's bedroom door.

Earlier she'd peeked inside Poppy's room and found it stark and devoid of comfort or personality, nothing to reflect the woman who occupied it.

No mementos from the past. Not a single photo. Nothing of the old Poppy.

She'd gotten rid of everything but her clothes and furniture, sending up a huge red flag for Rose, who tried to find a smile for her sister, but couldn't. Not when Poppy stood there, defiant and angry and broken.

"It's a gift. For you. I thought you might like it."

Being named after flowers made them tend to gravitate toward their floral equivalent. Rose loved roses. Who didn't, really? Poppy loved poppies of all colors. But her favorites were the pink ones, because they were less commonly seen.

They had once both loved pink.

"Why would you get me a gift?"

"Because I love you." It felt so good to say it, even if it made Poppy sneer at her.

"Bribing me isn't going to change the way I feel about you."

"I know. But it's not a bribe. It reminds me of when we were kids . . . It's one of my favorite memories."

"What?" Poppy's incredulous tone didn't mask the hope Rose saw in her eyes.

"You remember. When we were little, you used to draw me roses and I'd draw you poppies." Rose went to her desk and pulled out several pieces of paper in all different sizes, all with pink roses on them. "You were always a better artist than me." She held them out so Poppy could see them.

Her eyes went wide, like she couldn't believe what she was seeing. "You kept those?"

"I wish I'd kept more of them. Remember how mad Dad would get that we'd ask for more boxes of crayons because we needed a new pink one?"

Poppy seemed to get lost in the memory. "You'd beg me to ask him."

"Because he was more likely to get them for you than me."

"That didn't last long," Poppy snapped.

"It wasn't your fault he turned on you, Poppy. You didn't do or say anything to deserve the way he treated you."

"It's *your* fault," Poppy accused, but there wasn't as much punch behind the accusation as there had been yesterday.

"Is it my fault he was unhappy with his life, that he didn't love himself or us? Really? Was it Mom's fault for marrying him and having us? If I'd been nicer, quieter, more outspoken, smarter, faster, better, would it have made him stop? Would it have made him look at me and see me and love me? Would he have ever, even once, praised me for something I did? What did I have to do to make him stop? I tried as hard as I could to be what he wanted me to be. I twisted myself up and tore myself down until there was nothing left of me. I spent years wanting to escape, to get away, until one day I realized the only way out was to end it all once and for all."

Poppy's eyes went wide with shock, but deep down Rose saw the understanding.

"How close are you, Poppy, to hitting that bottom? Are you still freefalling deeper and deeper into that dark pit of despair? Or are you lying there, thinking of ways to make it all go away? Maybe you'll get lucky like me and you'll realize someone loves you even when you can't love yourself and you want everything to stop. Maybe it's your best friend standing next to you when you want to do something drastic . . . She'll pull you back from the edge, and hug you until it hurts so bad to even think of leaving the one and only good thing you have in your life."

Tears glistened in Poppy's eyes. "Rose . . . I never knew."

"You didn't want to see it. Mom didn't want to see it. Dad just kept on pushing and taunting and hurting me and I couldn't stand it anymore. But I endured it. For you. For Mom. So I could be with Maggie who always held her hand out to me and picked me up when I fell into that deep dark pit of despair." Rose pointed to the painting. "That's me, holding my hand out to *you*, offering you a hand up, telling you I'm here for you. All you have to do is reach for me and I will be there reaching back."

Poppy's lips trembled. "You don't understand. I'm not like you. It's not the same. I can't shut it off. I can't let it go."

Rose took a step toward her. "Yes, you can. Maybe not on your own. But I'm here to catch you, to hold you up, to offer you whatever support you need. You can put it behind you. All you have to do is want it and try." She took another step closer. "It won't be easy. It will take time to heal and figure out who you are now. You'll grieve for who you used to be, who you might have been without him pounding you into the ground."

Poppy studied her. "Is that what you've done? Reinvented yourself?"

"I worked with a counselor at school. I made a lot of mistakes. But then I started figuring myself out. I realized I was worth it. I deserve to be happy." She took another step. "And despite whatever happened with Dad, whatever you had to do to survive, you deserve to be happy, too."

Poppy didn't say anything, she just stood there, tears in her eyes, looking lost and desolate.

"I'm sorry it took me two years after I left for college to get to a place where I could call you and not feel like this place was sucking me back into that deep dark place. I'm sorry I left you. I'm sorry I couldn't be to you what Maggie had always been to me. You deserved that. You needed it, and I couldn't be that for you anymore."

Poppy frowned, her eyes glistening with unshed tears. "And when you tried, I pushed you away again."

"I understood why you did it. That's why I kept trying. I'm still trying, Poppy. I will never stop trying." Rose tempted her with something entertaining. "Maggie's bachelorette party is in half an hour. There's a seat at the table for you. Come with me. Have some fun. Look at someone who's found happiness and embraced it."

"You added me to the reservation?" Hope filled Poppy's voice for the first time.

"No, Poppy. I included you in it when I made it weeks ago."

She wanted Poppy to know she was part of Rose's plans. Part of her future.

"Really?" That one word held a world of anticipation and gratitude.

"Yes, really. Now go and get ready. We need to leave in ten minutes."

Poppy hesitated. "But . . . Are you sure?"

"That I want my sister to share a really special occasion with me? Yes!" She closed the last bit of distance between them and took Poppy's free hand. "I want you to come. And Maggie is really hoping you join us. She misses you, too."

* * *

Poppy set the painting on top of her headboard and leaned it against the wall. She stepped back and stared at the beautiful flower, holding back tears as she remembered how close she used to be to her sister.

She couldn't believe Rose had kept all those drawings.

Poppy had gotten rid of all reminders of the little girl she used to be. She couldn't look at the inconsequential things in her room and know she didn't deserve any of them. Not after everything that happened.

Poppy was stuck in the past and weighed down with guilt without remorse, and because of that she felt even worse. Because she should feel sorry about what happened to their father, but she didn't. Not at all.

She couldn't tell Rose that. Not when they had a chance to be friends and sisters again.

If they could be that to each other again after all this time . . . after all that had happened.

It still made her angry that Rose left, even though deep down she knew it wasn't Rose's fault. But now the anger didn't feel so visceral. It had begun to fade when Rose confessed how dire things had been for her. At the time, Poppy hadn't seen it—they'd been children, after all—and that added to her guilt. She wasn't the one Rose leaned on; instead Maggie had been there to help Rose survive.

Back then, Poppy had been trying so hard to please her father, she'd often taken his side and used her father's taunts as sage advice. "If you'd just do what he wants . . . If you'd say what he wants you to say . . . If only you'd try harder . . ." Always she'd end with "he'd stop."

The pain flared inside her for being so naïve.

Until her father turned on her and she wanted Rose there to tell her it wasn't her fault.

Poppy tried to think if she'd ever uttered those words to Rose. She hoped she had at least once, though she wished now she'd said it every time.

It was no consolation to think she'd been just a child. She'd made mistakes.

Rose had paid the price for shielding Poppy as long as she could.

And of course there was her mom, who tried in her own way to protect them but ultimately was too afraid to save them.

She understood all too well because when Rose moved into

her own place and offered to take her in, Poppy found herself too afraid to face his wrath if she left and he found her again.

They'd all lived in survival mode, just trying to get through each day without an incident.

She was trying to understand and accept what happened to all of them, but it was so hard.

"Poppy," Rose called through the door, snapping Poppy out of her dark thoughts. "Hurry up. I'll be waiting for you downstairs."

Tonight was a chance to feel and be normal.

She went to her closet and pulled out a black sleeveless dress with a ruffled skirt, and a pair of flats. She quickly discarded her oversized black sweater, jeans, socks, and combat boots. She used to love wearing colors. Until everything in her life turned dark.

She slipped on the dress, slid her feet into the shoes, and rushed into her bathroom to do something with her hair. Mostly, she wore it down, hanging limp. Not tonight. Instead, she brushed it out, then twisted it into a loose bun, leaving a few of the layered strands to frame her face.

She pulled open a drawer she hadn't gone into in years and found her old makeup. She dusted on some pink blush to give her pale face some color. She already had black eyeliner and mascara, but added two shades of purple shadow to brighten her hazel eyes, and finished the look with a sweep of pink-tinted lip gloss.

She stepped back and looked at herself in the mirror, seeing a glimpse of the girl she used to be. The black hair really didn't do anything for her, except make a statement about how she felt on the inside, and make her outside look pale and wan.

She needed to take better care of herself.

She needed to start caring again.

She wasn't sure if she knew how to do that anymore. She had to start somewhere, and tonight she was going to try to have a good time—for Maggie, for Rose, and for herself.

And, she thought a bit ruefully, black was always chic.

But a dress, fixing her hair, and some makeup didn't erase the truth. Poppy was still hiding in her anger and misery. And still holding on to her secret.

Chapter Eleven

*R*ose laughed along with Maggie, Poppy, and the four other college and high school friends making up the bachelorette party as Rachel tried to pin the penis on the naked fireman poster Rose had tacked to the wall. Luckily no one in the main part of the restaurant could see what was going on in the private room, but they could probably hear the raucous laughter.

"To the right," Jamie called out, trying to help, but they'd all had a couple of glasses of wine with dinner, making Rachel a bit uncoordinated. Luckily all of them had taken a car service to the restaurant and they'd take one home, too.

"Your other right," Jamie called out, sending Rachel's hand to the left as she pushed the pin in, giving the fireman an impressive penis in the middle of his stomach.

Rachel pulled off the blindfold and stared at her handiwork. "So close," she shouted, then burst into laughter.

Maggie picked up her phone and smiled, then turned the phone to Rose, showing off a photo. "Look at our guys."

Rose spotted Gray immediately. He sat at the back of a pack of men with Marc seated up front of the long table. All the guys held up glasses of whiskey. Gray's exuberant smile, along with all the others, said they were having a good time.

"Mom said you met someone." Poppy leaned in to get a look.

"That one." Rose pointed to Gray.

Poppy bumped shoulders with her. "Nice, sis. He's hot."

Maggie pouted. "Hey, check out my man. He's hot, too." Maggie was at least one glass of wine ahead of the rest of them.

Poppy patted Maggie's shoulder. "He's definitely good-looking."

"But does he have as big a dick as this?" Jamie called out, holding up her paper penis.

Maggie considered it. "Close," she said, deadpan, making everyone laugh again.

Jamie put the blindfold on; Rachel spun her around in two circles and nudged her toward the poster.

Maggie texted Marc back and held the phone up for Rose to see her reply.

MAGGIE: Looks like you guys are having fun.

Another picture popped up immediately and a shot of jealousy went through Rose.

Gray was sitting on a booth bench, a low table littered with whiskey glasses in front of him, and a topless girl standing between his legs. The stripper's face was cut out of the picture, but Gray had a half grin, his gaze on her ass. But when she looked closer, the amusement in his smile didn't reach his eyes.

Poppy saw the pic, too, and eyed Rose. "Are you mad?"

It took a second for the wild jealousy running through her to ease and for Rose to think clearly. "It's a strip club. Of course the girls are all over him. It doesn't mean anything. It's an illusion." She wondered if Marc had sent the picture to rile her up. She wasn't going to give him the satisfaction. They were out with six other guys. He could have sent a picture of any one of them with a stripper. "Send that to me, so I can razz Gray."

Maggie forwarded the pic to her, and Rose immediately sent it to Gray.

ROSE: I hope you gave her a really big tip.

Poppy leaned in to see Gray's response, but nothing came in. "He probably isn't looking at his phone," Poppy said.

Maggie smirked. "He's too busy looking at all the tits and ass."

Rose laughed, along with Poppy, but there was an uneasy feeling in her gut when it came to Marc and the bachelor party.

"You're really okay with this." Poppy studied her.

"Gray and I may have just met, but I trust him. He's given me no reason not to, and was completely up front about where they were going tonight and that he'd rather be with me than at that club." She shrugged. "The man has been nothing but considerate and forthcoming with me. I have zero worries."

He hadn't given her any reason to think he wasn't sincere about wanting to get to know her better.

Poppy nodded. "He'd be stupid to do something with one of them and lose you."

It touched Rose deeply that her sister felt that way.

"Marc sent more pics of the guys." Maggie held up her phone with three more pics, one of all the guys with strippers dancing in front of them. The other two were of only Gray with a stripper who had a similar look and body type to Rose.

She wondered if Marc sent the photos to taunt her or Gray.

Maybe Marc wanted her to think Gray wasn't that into her. But it had backfired because Gray made it clear before he left he'd take a night with her over a night at a strip club.

And she believed him.

Maggie bumped her shoulder. "Marc shouldn't have sent the photos. Why are nearly all of them of Gray? Why send them at all?"

Rose wondered the same thing. "They're probably drunk and having a good time. He's not doing anything wrong. I know Gray likes me."

"Of course he likes you. You're the best," Maggie said, then typed something into her phone. She turned it so Rose could see.

MAGGIE: Go Gray!!! She's smokin' hot!!!

"There. Now they know we don't care." Maggie bit her lip and looked at the pic of the group of guys again. "It's all just fun to them," Maggie said, trying to sound like it didn't upset her.

Guys going to strip clubs bothered a lot of women, Rose included. Though she wasn't going to hold it against Gray.

Especially not when she spotted Maggie's surprise waiting

on the other side of the privacy screen. She checked the time. "Let's have our own fun."

Maggie nodded. "Let's."

"It's your turn to pin the dick on the fireman."

Maggie stood. "With pleasure."

Rose took the blindfold from Jamie and helped secure it around Maggie's head. "Hold on one second. I have a surprise for you."

"What is it?" Maggie asked with a nervous laugh.

"Well, I thought you might like something a little . . . hotter." Rose waved the guy in.

He set a speaker on the table, hit play on his phone, went up to Maggie as the thumping beat filled the room, took her hands, and put them on his chest.

Maggie's smile grew even bigger. "For me?"

The fireman stripper pulled off her blindfold, smiled at her, and said, "All for you, sweetheart." Then he did a body roll against her, and Maggie laughed and blushed bright red.

Rose would be a hypocrite for judging Gray for going to a strip club when she'd hired a stripper for her best friend.

The guy knew how to dance and tease, and it only took a minute and his shirt coming off for all the other girls to get in on the action, dancing with him.

Rose pulled out a chair and set it behind Maggie. The guy put his fireman hat on her and backed her up into the chair until she sat and stared up at him. He turned his back to her, his very fine ass in her face, and shook it. It didn't take long for the dance moves to have them all going and for him to kick off those fireman boots and pants. He gave Maggie a lap dance wearing just a pair of red bikini-style undies and all his rippling muscles on display. The man was built.

All the girls took a turn getting their lap dance. Even Poppy found herself dragged into the chair by Claire, who was probably the shyest of the group, but she came out of her shell for the sexy dancer.

Poppy laughed and covered her face with her hands, spreading her fingers wide so she could see every movement of the guy shaking and rolling his body in front of her.

A couple of the tipsy ladies got a little handsy, but the guy was a professional and kept things rated R.

At some point, Maggie handed her phone to Poppy and asked her to take pictures. Most of the women had already taken several snapshots with the stripper.

When things were just about to wind down and the guy's time was almost up, Maggie grabbed Rose's arm, pulled her forward, and shoved her into the guy's bare chest.

"I got you, sweetheart," he said, spinning her around and dipping her.

Rose went with it, having fun and being in the moment as the other ladies cheered her on.

"Thank you for the dance." Breathless, Rose smiled at him. "You've been fantastic. But it's time for our bride-to-be to open her other presents."

He bowed to the clapping crowd, grabbed his stuff, and

headed for the door. Rose followed after him and caught him pulling on his costume in the narrow hallway. "Thank you so much, Kevin. You made Maggie's night."

"You're welcome. You've got some moves. Wanna go out sometime?"

"Thanks, but I'm seeing someone." It felt good to say that, even if things were new between her and Gray.

She handed him an envelope with a hefty tip and walked back into the party. The women had all taken their seats, except for Poppy, who handed Maggie the first of the many gifts they'd set on a nearby table.

"That one's from me," Jamie called out. "Marc's eyes are going to pop out when he sees you in it."

Maggie held up the sheer white baby-doll nightie that was split all the way down the front and held together by a single clasp between the breast cups.

All the ladies giggled and oohed and aahed over it.

Maggie opened the next salacious gift, but Rose got distracted when her phone vibrated on the table.

She picked it up and smiled when she saw Gray had finally texted her back.

GRAY: Tell Maggie I'm sorry, but I'm going to kill Marc for being a dick, pushing all those strippers on me, and sending you pics to try to rile you.

GRAY: I'm sorry if it upset you.

GRAY: You're all I think about!!!

She appreciated so much that he texted in the middle of his evening out to reassure her.

ROSE: While the pics did make me a little jealous, you did tell me the strip club is not your scene and it showed on your face in the pics. And then I got distracted by the fireman stripper I hired for Maggie. ☺

She wanted him to know she didn't have anything to hide, either.

GRAY: LOL. Touché.

GRAY: You're the only woman I want that close to me. All I want to do is touch you.

She wondered how drunk he was to text that. Then again, he'd never been shy about saying what was on his mind.

ROSE: I want to be the only one touching you. We're good.

ROSE: And yes, I'm still thinking about you.

She thought about her next text and whether she should send it or not and went with it.

ROSE: I can't wait to see you again.

Her phone rang immediately and she smiled when she saw Gray's name. She stood and moved to the back of the room so she didn't interrupt all the fun the women were having watching Maggie open up one sexy present after the next.

"Hello, handsome."

"I didn't want to text this." Gray's rich, deep voice warmed her whole body. "I wanted you to hear it from me. I wish you were here. Well, not here. But here. With me. I wish you were with me right now." The sincere words, even with the slightly drunk slur and how he had to shout it over the thumping music in the background, touched her deeply.

Her heart melted because he meant it and wasn't afraid to call her up and say it after only knowing each other a couple of days. "You and me—"

"I really like the sound of that."

She sighed with contentment. "And that says it all. You and me, Gray. We are something neither of us expected but we can't deny. This thing between us doesn't feel new, it feels—"

"Perfect. Inevitable. So damn right."

"Yes." She thought about her secret. "Gray—"

"I love the way you say my name."

She smiled, filled to overflowing with joy and need for this man. "There's something I need to tell you."

"If it's not that you're on your way to me right now, it can wait. Marc is heading my way and I don't want him to ruin our moment."

What she had to tell him could wait.

"Maggie is opening my gift."

"What'd you get her?"

"A black lace camisole and panty set to go with a blackberry-flavored lube."

"That makes me think all kinds of wicked thoughts."

His deep voice made her think of a few herself. Her vagina clenched and her panties felt damp with the heat and desire in his words.

"I want . . . Fuck, I have to go. Whatever you want to talk to me about, we can do that tomorrow. After I kiss you."

"Tomorrow then."

"Miss you, sweetheart."

"Get off the phone, Rose, and try this," Maggie called, holding up the blackberry lube. "It's fantastic."

Rose laughed.

"Go. Be with your friends. I'm going to see if I can get Marc and the guys out of here before we're all broke and too drunk to walk."

"Gray."

"Yeah?" His deep voice sounded wistful and wanting.

"I miss you, too."

"You're amazing."

She laughed under her breath. "Thanks. I think you're incredible, too."

"I don't want to say good-bye."

Her heart melted. "Then say you'll see me soon."

"Not soon enough," he grumbled, and hung up.

She joined the ladies at the table.

Maggie shot a deep purple thong at her and laughed when it bounced off Rose's chest and landed in her lap. "Was that Gray? Are they behaving?"

"Probably not," she teased. "But Gray was worried I was upset by the pictures Marc sent you."

"I hope Gray has some of Marc that I can use against him when he irritates me."

Rose shot the thong back at Maggie. "You better hope he doesn't see the pictures of you with our sexy fireman. And I'll remind you, you said you didn't want a stripper, but we both know you did."

Maggie blushed. "Did you see his ass?" She bit her lower lip. "Damn."

"He even asked me out," Rose confessed.

Maggie shook her head with way too much enthusiasm, then turned a bit green from all the wine she'd drunk. "He never had a chance. You are so into Gray."

"You are," Poppy chimed in. "The second you heard his voice on the phone, you smiled so big. Your whole face lit up."

Rose couldn't deny something so obvious. "People talk about meeting *the one* and say that when you do, you'll know. I've never felt that kind of spark and connection with anyone else but Gray. He's so easy to be with and talk to, and I miss him when he's not around. Is that crazy?"

Maggie shook her head. "It's the way it should be." Melancholy clouded her eyes and turned her soft smile into a frown. "Gray called you because he cared whether you were upset about the pictures Marc sent and what he was doing. He wanted you to know nothing was going on, right?"

"I never thought anything was going on," she assured Maggie and Poppy.

"He probably knew that but wanted to be sure because it matters to him." Maggie sighed. "Marc loves to have a good time. I don't mind. Mostly. Sometimes I catch him looking at other women, or even flirting with them. It's his personality. I always know he's going home with me. But sometimes I wish he was more sensitive to my feelings." She glanced at her phone, then stared at Rose. "Why send those pics of Gray to me instead of sending a picture of himself having fun? Why try to stir up trouble between you two?"

Rose's heart beat faster. "Gray told me that they've always been competitive with each other and that there's some jealousy there."

"Right. Marc is jealous of Gray. I hear it in the way he talks about his cousin. How angry he gets when his father compares him to Gray." Maggie paused, her focus turned inward. "He's jealous you and Gray hit it off. What does that say about how he feels about us? Does he think you're a better catch than me?"

"No," Rose rushed to reassure her friend. "Not at all. He loves you. You're getting married. Whatever petty jealousies they feel toward one another has nothing to do with us. Marc is lucky to have you and he knows it."

"That's what I thought, too. But the closer we get to the wedding, the more I feel like there's something he's holding back. I wanted this week to be special, but something just seems off." She frowned and looked lost. "Are my expectations too high?"

Rose shook her head. "No. We've had a lot of fun," Rose reminded her. "We laughed and sang along to bad karaoke at the bar. You were the most beautiful bride in your gown. And I think you might be pregnant after that lap dance tonight."

Maggie burst out laughing. "Most of all I loved being with all of you." She took in all the ladies at the table, most of whom were lost in their conversations, or eating the desserts that had just been brought in.

Rose had a feeling the alcohol and stress had a lot to do with Maggie's sudden sadness and quick return to joy. She took a party-store veil one of the other ladies had brought and plopped it atop Maggie's head. "You are getting married, my friend, to a man who will never deserve you, but you'll be happy knowing he's going to try every day to make you smile."

"Damn right!" Maggie tossed back the rest of her wine.

Poppy slid a piece of cake in front of her. "And if not, there's always chocolate."

Maggie held up a forkful of chocolate cake in a show of solidarity, but paused before eating it. "At least he wants kids." She stuffed the bite into her mouth.

Rose knew her friend would be such a great mom. She'd be a mom like Brenda had been to Rose when her own mom couldn't be what she needed.

"Can you believe our moms coordinated my staying at your house when we were young?"

Maggie sighed again. "I overheard a few conversations back then when your mom would tell my mom it might be better if you stayed the night with us." Maggie's sad eyes met Rose's. "I think it mostly happened after a particularly bad night you had at home and you were . . . a little worse for wear."

"It makes me feel better to know in some way she tried to protect me. I mean, I wanted her to take us away, but . . . She did something." Rose needed to accept that her mom, like many abused women, had been afraid to leave, but she'd done the best she could to survive. Her actions and decisions all stemmed from paralyzing fear.

Her mom's rebellions had been small but aimed at keeping Rose safer than she was at home. It only staved off the inevitable, but Rose had always enjoyed those reprieves at Maggie's house where she could just be, without the constant fear of the next attack on her, whether it was verbal or more.

Maggie had always been her safe harbor.

Rose held up her glass and clinked the side with a butter knife to get everyone's attention. "Thank you all for coming tonight to celebrate our amazing friend Maggie, who is not only beautiful inside and out, but strong, talented, and smart. May you have a lifetime of happiness and love. To Maggie!"

"Maggie!" the women all shouted and drank.

Maggie reached over and squeezed Rose's hand. "I have the best of all best friends."

Rose stared at her with watery eyes. "No. I do."

They shared smiles, and Rose felt better knowing she'd ended Maggie's night on a high note.

Now all she had to do was make sure Maggie had the best wedding ever.

Maybe the best thing to do was tell her the truth about Marc. Maggie already suspected Marc was hiding something from her, but he had refused Rose's offer that they tell Maggie together.

Rose simply couldn't keep this secret from her best friend.

Tomorrow, no matter what came up, she'd tell her.

Chapter Twelve

6 days to Maggie's wedding . . .

Rose wiped the back of her hand over her sweaty brow, pulled her ball cap back on, and stared over at Gray, who looked almost the same color as his name. He'd called early that morning and asked her to meet him at Del Valle Regional Park. The foothills and lake were pretty, but with little tree cover, the six-mile hike in the sun was hotter than hell in early June.

What were they thinking?

"Are you okay?" She handed him the spare bottle of water she'd stuffed into her backpack.

"I think I might have actually sweated out all the alcohol."

"I still can't believe you wanted to go for a hike after you partied so much last night."

"One, I wanted to see you. Two, unlike Marc, even when occasionally hungover, I get up early. And three, I find a workout kicks the hangover faster than just trying to sleep it off." Gray downed the entire bottle of water.

"Are you sure he's okay?"

"I called and checked on him. I got a barely audible answer that he was fine and we'd catch up with each other later." Gray shrugged. "I'm guessing much later. So thank you for driving all the way back here to meet me."

"I didn't mind. At all." The two-hour drive had been filled with anticipation to see him again.

Gray smiled. "I would have come to you, but Marc's car is back in Carmel at the hotel, so I'll be driving him back there later tonight after I pick him up at his place in San Jose. Though I'm thinking it may not be until tomorrow if he's as bad off as I think."

"Maybe you should have gone over to be sure he's okay. Alcohol poisoning is no joke."

"Like I said, I wanted to see you. I called his dad and told him to go over and check on Marc. He lives closer. And his dad has a key. I don't. And if Marc is passed out, his dad can get into the condo and make sure he drinks some water and eats so his system can recover."

"Maggie's going to be concerned if he doesn't go back down to Carmel today."

"I'm sure she'll understand. You said you guys had a few last night, too."

"Maggie was drunk, but I've seen her worse off."

"You seem fine today."

"As party coordinator, I had to maintain some semblance of decorum to be sure everyone had a good time and got home safe."

Gray chuckled. "I'm sure you were the picture of dignity getting a lap dance from the fireman stripper," he teased.

"How many strippers ended up in your lap last night?" she shot back.

"Too many," he grumbled.

She was teasing but it didn't really matter to her, because he'd called her first thing this morning and said, "I miss you, come see me."

Gray's eyes clouded with regret. "That's the last time I go out with Marc. His idea of a good time and mine are not the same."

"You didn't have fun?"

"Not really. Marc racked up a huge bar tab on my dime and drank himself into oblivion. And he's a dick when he's drunk. He kept saying stuff about me and you and us getting together."

She cocked her head, her full attention on him. "What did he say?"

Gray shrugged like it didn't matter, but the angry look in his eyes said it did. "At first it was nothing really. He told all the guys that I fell hard for Maggie's BFF."

"Oh, really?"

He eyed her. "Definitely." But the spark of amusement and heat in his eyes quickly dimmed. "He gave them a description of you. How gorgeous you are and stuff."

She raised a brow. "Stuff?"

"Let's just say he was detailed about your"—he looked her

up and down—"many fine assets. The guys were impressed and I was happy to be the guy who had such a beautiful woman interested in me."

"Definitely interested," she confirmed, mimicking him, even though he knew it.

But her stomach went tight at the thought of Marc describing her *in detail* like that to Gray and their friends, indicating he'd paid particular attention to her. Or knew her well. Which he did, but Gray didn't know that. And Marc could tell him at any time that they had slept together.

Of course that meant that Maggie would find out, too, and Marc didn't want her to know, so he'd probably keep his mouth shut, giving her time to tell Gray herself after she spoke to Maggie.

She wanted Gray to hear it from her.

Gray's grin didn't reach his eyes and fell away all too quickly. "But as the night wore on, he kept coming back to you and me and things got . . ."

"What?" she asked when he didn't finish the sentence.

"I know we were in a strip club and sex is on the brain, but him talking about you, me, us, asking if and when and how good it was . . ." Gray shook his head, disgust and anger in his eyes and the locked set of his jaw.

"Sounds like he gets a little immature when he drinks. I'm sure you blew him off and he got the hint that it's none of his business."

"You'd think, but he kept going until I finally told him to shut the fuck up."

"And did he?"

"Yeah. After he and the guys had a good laugh at my expense for defending you so vehemently that Marc teased I was completely whipped." Gray rubbed his hand over the back of his neck. "I'm sorry. I didn't want to tell you, but . . . I don't know. I'm so tired of this thing Marc and I do whenever we're together too long. We become those two teenage boys fighting for attention and trying to one up each other."

"Except you aren't trying to do that with Marc. You're secure in who you are and where you are in your life. You don't need to flaunt your girlfriend to feel like you're a man."

"My girlfriend?" He eyed her with amusement tilting his lips into a slight grin.

She blew that off, because she didn't presume anything. "You know what I'm saying. Marc uses the things in his life to make people think more highly of him. People think highly of you because of who you are, not what you do or have."

Everything about him went still. "Do you feel that way?"

"I think you're probably the best man I've ever known."

He fell back a step, his eyes going wide, then he closed the distance between them, cupped her face, tilted his head, and kissed her, knocking her ball cap off in the process.

The kiss was deep and all-consuming. A claiming.

She went up on tiptoe, wrapped her arms around his neck, and pressed her body along his, not caring one bit that they were both sweaty. All she cared about was being close to him.

He broke the kiss and stared hard at her. "I . . . I don't know what to say to that."

"Okay." It surprised her that she came up with a single word. He'd scrambled her brain so completely with that kiss.

"I know we just started this thing, but I really want to say that you're my girlfriend."

"Okay." This time she let her smile say all the things she couldn't find the words for because she was too busy being so happy her cheeks hurt from smiling.

He dove in for another searing kiss and they lost themselves in the moment and each other.

"You guys are going to start a wildfire," a hiker said, passing them.

They ended the kiss, smiling and laughing together.

She fell back on her feet and he hooked his arm around her shoulders. "I know this great little taqueria down the road. Do you like tacos?"

"Does anyone *not* like tacos?"

He chuckled and led her back to where they had parked.

"I'll follow you."

He frowned but nodded, then gave her a quick kiss and went to his car where he pulled off his sweat-soaked T-shirt, wiped it over his chiseled chest and abs, then grabbed a clean one from the back seat of his Tesla and pulled it on.

She stood there drooling over the gorgeous display of muscles. "Smart, honest, and built like a god." She sighed, astounded he was real, even as she stared at him.

He lifted his shirt a couple of inches, teasing her with another glimpse of his taut abs. "We could skip tacos and go to my place."

"So tempting." She wanted to, but felt like everything was moving so fast that she wanted to savor the building anticipation between them. And she didn't have much time before she had to head back and meet up with Maggie again. She didn't want their first time to be something rushed before she dashed off for more maid of honor duties.

And if they were racing to being boyfriend and girlfriend and going to sleep together, he deserved to know the truth about her and Marc. That was not a conversation she wanted to have in a public parking lot while they were flirting with each other. So she stalled. "After that hike, I need sustenance. And so do you if you're going to fully recover from that hangover."

He let her off easy. "I'm dying for some tacos. And you. But one of those things will have to wait. Probably better this way, because I'm not likely to let you go once I have you in my bed."

"Thanks for understanding."

Gray held her gaze, his sincere. "There's no rush, Rose. We've got all the time in the world to be together."

"I don't need all the time, just enough that it doesn't actually feel rushed."

He gave her a sexy grin. "I will definitely enjoy taking my time with you."

With that promise and two dozen steamy thoughts filling her head, she followed Gray down the main road into town and to the little hole-in-the-wall taqueria. Gray took her hand the second she exited her car and they walked into the place, ordered, and took a seat at one of the small café tables outside on the sidewalk in the shade.

The girl behind the counter brought over their iced teas, a basket of chips, and a bowl of salsa.

Gray drank half his drink and sat back in his seat. "We forgot to pick up your hat."

She touched her hair, feeling the loose strands Gray had pulled from her ponytail. "I totally forgot about it."

"We can go back after we eat. It will probably still be there. Sorry about that."

She shook her head. "It's no big deal and kind of a long way back." She pulled her hair loose, gathered it all together at the back of her head again, then redid the ponytail holder. "Is that better?"

Gray nodded. "You're always beautiful."

"You're sweet, but I'm a sweaty mess." She took a long sip of her tea.

Gray dug into the chips and salsa. "Did you enjoy the hike?"

"I love hiking." It was another of those things they'd discovered they both liked when he called and asked her if she'd like to go with him this morning. "I haven't been to Del Valle in a long time. But I really love going to the redwoods near the coast. It's hot out here in the valley."

"I love those hikes, too. But today I really needed to sweat."

She laughed. "I guess you won't be drinking again anytime soon."

"Not like that."

The waitress came out with their food and set the steak street tacos and chicken enchilada in front of Gray and the chicken flautas in front of her.

Gray held up a taco, she picked up a flauta, they toasted with their food. "To another good day together," Gray said, then stuffed half the taco in his mouth.

She giggled. "Hungry?"

"Starving," he said around the too-big bite.

They enjoyed the shade and the good food.

She was leaning back in her seat, relaxing, enjoying the company and the quiet, when Gray tapped his foot against the side of hers.

"I knew hanging out with you this morning would make my day."

She smiled, because it didn't matter what they did, she just enjoyed his company. "I knew you'd say half a dozen sweet things to me to make my day."

"You're easy to please. A hike. Cheap food."

"Good food. Great company."

Gray leaned in. "I wish you didn't have to go back right away."

"Do you think Marc will be ready to go back tonight?"

"Unfortunately, I'm thinking tomorrow." Gray's phone rang in his pocket. He pulled it out and held it up. "Speak of the devil." He tapped the screen a couple of times and set the phone on the table. "Hey, man, you're on speaker with me and Rose."

"Hey, gorgeous, sorry to interrupt and you don't want to hear this, but . . . What the fuck, Gray! You sent my dad to my house!" Marc bellowed.

Gray went still, staring at the phone, then his confused gaze met hers. "You drank half the top shelf of the bar last night.

You were in bad shape when you stumbled into your Uber." Concern filled Gray's voice. "I'm surprised you made it into your house, let alone your bed. So yeah, I asked your dad to check on you in case you needed anything."

"You really know how to fuck things up for me."

The line went dead.

Gray sat back and rubbed both hands over his face, then let them drop to his thighs. "Sorry."

She shrugged it off. "No worries. I just don't get why he's so angry. His dad had to know what he was walking into after last night."

"My uncle seemed fine about us going out, he even teased me about being hungover. He said that's what a bachelor party was all about. He was concerned about Marc, but not upset."

"I guess you'll find out what really happened when his dad showed up when you drive Marc back."

Gray rolled his eyes. "That's going to be a fun drive down the coast."

"I hate to say this, but I've got to get on the road if I'm going to make it home to clean up and change clothes before I head over to Maggie's for dinner with her aunt."

"Is she going to be upset if we don't make it back to town until tomorrow?"

"Probably. Marc said some things to her about me that upset her. She didn't like that he sent the pictures of you to her last night just to try to rile me."

"I didn't like it, either. What did Marc say to her about you?"

"Nothing really, and it's not about that. It's a stressful situation with everything going on leading up to the wedding. Tension is running high. She wants everything to be perfect. Which is why I can't be late. I don't want to add any more stress."

"Are you going to tell her about that call?"

"No. If Marc wants to tell her why he's mad about his dad checking on him, I'll let him tell her. That's between them." She sighed, feeling her mounting worry amp her anxiety. "Do you remember I told you last night I wanted to tell you something?"

He settled his hand over hers. "Yeah. What is it?"

Part of her wished she could keep the secret and that no one would ever find out. But with Marc stirring things up, despite him begging her not to say anything, she felt like she needed to tell Maggie and Gray before it came out in a way that hurt them. She hoped being honest, and them both knowing how much she cared about them, would ease any ill feelings they might have about something that happened before Rose met Gray and Maggie met Marc.

"It's something I need to tell Maggie first, because it has to do with Marc."

Gray cocked his head. "Did he say or do something to you?"

"No. I . . . It's not a big deal. At least, it shouldn't be, but I want her to hear it from me first, then I'll tell you. Is that okay?"

"If that's how you want it, sure. I guess I'll have to wait."

She smiled, hoping to ease his mind and erase the concern in his eyes. "Just know that I'm really happy to be with you. I'm looking forward to less Marc and Maggie and more me and you."

That brought his smile back. "I really like the sound of that."

She stood with him and gave him a quick kiss. "Then I'll see you soon." She stepped back, but he pulled her close and kissed her again, showing her how much he wanted her. She didn't need the reminder. She felt it between them, even when they weren't together. Since she'd met him, she'd felt the pull deep inside her.

Gray set her away and stared down at her, his hands on her shoulders. "Have fun tonight."

"Get some rest. You look tired." She brushed her hand over his scruffy jaw, liking the feel and look of his beard stubble.

"I've got nothing better to do without you around." He opened her car door for her. "Drive safe."

"I will. And whatever happens with Marc when you see him, just know you did the right thing sending his dad to check on him."

"You're probably right about the stress of the wedding getting to him and Maggie."

"I can't wait to see them say their I dos."

"After Saturday, I can have you all to myself."

"I look forward to it." She slipped into her car and waved good-bye to him. She drove out of the lot and headed back to her hometown, where she still had a lot of unfinished business. Including telling her best friend that she'd slept with her fiancé.

Gray would understand. She'd basically already told him about her night with Marc.

The news would probably shock Maggie at first, but then she'd understand it happened long before Maggie met Marc.

There was nothing between Rose and Marc now.

Marc and Maggie loved each other and belonged together.

Maggie had nothing to worry about, especially since Rose had fallen hard and fast for Gray.

Still, Rose worried this could all blow up in her face.

Chapter Thirteen

4 days to Maggie's wedding . . .

Maggie spotted Rose the second she walked into the café Tuesday morning. Maggie had arrived early and bought herself a double chocolate muffin and two of Rose's favorite honey almond shortbread squares. Rose loved those thick, gooey, crumbly cookies.

"You are a goddess." Rose picked up her caramel latte and tapped it to Maggie's vanilla latte cup. "Cheers."

Maggie smiled at her best friend even though she wasn't in a great mood today. Worried. Frustrated. Cranky. Yes to all of those things.

And it was all Marc's fault with a heaping side of help from that stupid bachelor party.

Marc was supposed to return to town Sunday, but here it was Tuesday and he still hadn't come back. He'd skipped out on dinner with her family on Sunday night after her aunt had flown in early to meet him. He left her and Rose to take care of calling all the vendors yesterday to be sure they were ready to deliver for the Saturday wedding and reception. And now he'd texted her to tell her he wasn't coming back until tomorrow.

Not that he really needed to be here for anything, but she thought spending the week before the wedding with him was important. Plus, he left her doing all the work.

She was so happy for Rose and Gray. She wanted Marc to be happy about it, too. Her fantasy—that they'd hang out together as couples—could be coming true, except her groom-to-be was missing. And, when he did talk to her, he was perpetually irritated.

"I wish my ornery fiancé thought I was a goddess, too." Maggie sipped her latte and frowned.

"Uh-oh. That came out of nowhere. What's wrong?"

"He and Gray were supposed to come back Sunday. Now they're not coming back until tomorrow."

Rose's eyes went wide. "What? Gray didn't say anything about that to me."

Maggie tapped her nail on her phone on the table. "I just got a text from Marc. A text. I haven't spoken to him since Sunday when I called to check on him after the bachelor party. And he texts me, even though I've left him several messages asking him to call me back." She shrugged, but on the inside she was really mad and a little scared because the closer they got to their wedding day, the more distance she felt growing between them.

"Truthfully, I have no idea what's really going on with him. Ever since we came here for the wedding, something has been off. I don't know if he's having second thoughts, or what." She held up her hands and let them fall back onto the table. "On Sunday, I teased him about partying too hard and being too hungover to come back to me. I said one little comment about him running off with a stripper and he got really mad. He said if I didn't trust him and I was so insecure about him going to a strip club and about one comment he made about you, then maybe I didn't really love him and was looking for excuses to get out of marrying him."

Rose gasped. "What? That makes no sense. He had to know you were kidding about the strippers."

"I thought he would, but . . . And maybe it has more to do with me telling him I didn't think it was cool that he sent those pictures of Gray." The annoyance rang clear in Maggie's voice. "He said Gray got on his case, too, and he didn't need us ganging up on him and maybe we should be more like you and just blow it off because it didn't mean anything."

That unsettled Rose. "Um . . . I don't know what to say to that. You and I both agreed that them going to a strip club was no big deal, but the pictures seemed like Marc was trying to get Gray in trouble with me. I didn't like him trying to mess things up with me and Gray, especially since it's so new."

"Exactly what I said to Marc, which only made him angrier." She shook her head again. "He's never talked to me that way."

"Are you sure this doesn't have something to do with his dad?"

Maggie sat up straighter. "What do you mean?"

"From what Gray told me, he and his dad have a strained

relationship right now. Marc was really mad on Sunday when Gray asked Marc's dad to stop by and check on Marc."

"I don't see what the big deal is about that."

"Gray didn't get it, either. Maybe you should call Marc and just ask him."

"I've left him three messages."

Rose reached over and covered her hand. "It's worth trying again, right?"

Maggie picked up her phone and swiped the screen for Marc's number. To her surprise, he answered right away.

"Hey, sweetheart, I was just about to call you and tell you how sorry I am for acting like a jerk. I had no reason to be upset with you when I was really mad at Gray and my dad for making a big deal out of nothing when I drank too much. I paid for it with a raging hangover and pushing you away when all I want is to be with you."

Maggie's heart melted. "Then come and be with me," she said, forgiving him.

"I wish I could, but my car is still there at the hotel and since I told Gray I wasn't going back until tomorrow, he's at work taking care of some stuff that needed his attention. I'm sorry, baby, I miss you like crazy."

"It's okay. There's nothing you really have to be here for until Thursday night for the ceremony rehearsal and rehearsal dinner. Your dad and his girlfriend will be there, right?"

"Why wouldn't they be?" The tight, clipped tone sounded defensive.

"Rose said you were upset about your dad coming to check on you on Sunday. Is there something more you're not telling me?"

"Not at all. Like I said, I was hungover and not expecting my dad to barge into my place unannounced and scold me like I'm a teenager."

"He was worried about you."

"Yeah, well, that's what Gray said, too, but it was unnecessary and overbearing. We all drank too much that night. No one went to Gray's place to check on him."

"He was up bright and early to meet with Rose."

"Told you. He's hot for our Rose."

Our?

Maggie pressed her lips tight to stave off a jealous retort and the anger that came with his possessive tone when it came to her best friend.

"So did you work things out with your dad?"

"Nothing to work out. I told him exactly how I felt about him butting into my business and interfering in my life. He's getting what he wants, so he should be happy."

That jarred her. "What does that mean?"

"What?"

"What do you mean he's getting what he wants?"

"Oh, nothing. Sorry. I got distracted by this news report on TV. Dad and I are fine. He's excited about the wedding and thrilled at the idea of me becoming a husband and father. Are you sure we can't skip the wedding and move right to the honeymoon?" The suggestive tone was all too familiar and made her relax.

"I thought that's what we'd been doing for the past eight months."

"You are so right, sweetheart. Every day with you is like a honeymoon. I hope we keep it that way."

"Why should anything change now?"

"You and I are really just made for each other."

When they talked like this, it really seemed so, because they were only talking about them. When other people were involved—his father, Gray, and even Rose—it got confusing and complicated.

"Let's plan to meet up with Rose and Gray tomorrow evening," he suggested. "We'll go out and have some fun, just like you wanted us to do."

"Are you sure? It didn't seem like you really wanted to do that." Maggie hoped Rose didn't infer they were talking about her and Gray.

"You know I love Rose."

You do? Since when? They barely knew each other.

"Gray is family. I know how much you want us all to get along and hang out. All I want is for you to be happy."

Maggie got the sense he was placating her again by saying all the right things but meaning something else entirely, because it sounded like he was fine with going out with them, but he hadn't actually said so.

"I'm with Rose now. I'll see if they can join us."

"Great. In fact, I've got an idea that I'd love to enlist Rose to help me with. A little wedding surprise for my fiancée."

Maggie thought it sweet that he wanted to do something for

her and to ask Rose to help him. It would be a great way for them to get to know each other better.

"Okay. When will I see you tomorrow?"

"I'll let you know as soon as Gray and I connect and set a time."

"Great. And Marc . . . I'm so glad we talked and got everything out in the open."

"Me, too, sweetheart. Now let me talk to Rose." The soft demand in his voice spiked her curiosity again.

Maggie held her phone out to Rose. "Marc has some kind of surprise in mind for me and he'd like your help."

Rose eyed the phone like Maggie was handing her a snake. "Um. Okay."

* * *

Rose took the phone and put it to her ear, her gaze steady on Maggie's. "Hi, Marc. What's up?"

"Move away from Maggie so she can't overhear us."

Rose didn't like the demanding tone, but if it was to keep a surprise for Maggie, she'd comply. She stood and told Maggie, "I'll just be a sec. We don't want you to hear about the surprise."

Maggie nodded, though her brows drew together as she watched Rose step away toward the front window.

"Okay. She can't hear us. What's the big surprise?"

"Did Gray tell you what happened on Sunday?"

"I heard how angry you were when you called him about your dad coming over."

"That's not what I'm talking about." He paused. "You don't know. Good. He kept his mouth shut."

"What is this about?" She didn't like it that Gray was keeping something from her.

"Nothing. I told him to keep his mouth shut and he did. I'm surprised but grateful. Now all you have to do is promise the same. Do not tell Maggie about us."

She sighed. "Marc, you know I can't do that. Eventually she'll find out. If we tell her now, it's no big deal. If we don't tell her and she finds out later, she'll think it's more than it is and be upset we hid it from her. I don't want her to think we hid it because it needed to be a secret for some reason. She's already wondering why you're acting weird about me."

"She doesn't have a clue."

"She's smarter than you think," Rose snapped.

"I need this wedding to happen, Rose. Don't screw this up for me. We had a great night together."

And it was done and over and should never be spoken of again, especially since he was getting married.

"I remember every bit of that night and you. Do you really think Gray wants to know that you and I slept together? There's no way he won't picture that every time he sees me with you. I picture it every time I think about you and see you."

What the hell? "Stop."

"I wish I could, because it's really complicating things for me. You seem to care about Gray. I care about Maggie. We have plans that will give us both what we want. I can't let anything screw that up."

"She already suspects something. That's why we need to tell her the truth."

"I can't take the risk that she won't get over it and leave me. Gray won't let it go, either," he warned.

The knot in her stomach tightened painfully. But Rose stuck to her guns and tried to hold on to her belief that Maggie and Gray would see the truth. "We had sex before we met them. Over a year ago. One night. Nothing more. They'll understand that."

"We had fucking great sex. And you may have thought I was an asshole the next morning, but that night, you were all over me."

The reminder made her cringe, because it was true, they'd had a great night together. And if it had ended there, she'd have gone on thinking that, but it didn't negate the fact that he wasn't a good guy. And her friend should know that.

She needed to be the friend who told Maggie the truth, damn the consequences.

"Don't do this, Rose. If you do, we'll both lose the people we're with. You want to keep Gray, fine, but you won't if you tell him you slept with me."

She didn't want to believe that. "Look, we don't have to go into detail, just tell them we spent a single night together. That's all. Gray and I have a really great thing together. He cares about me. He's been burned in the past and I'm not going to do anything to mess up this amazing thing I have with him. And not being honest with him *will* screw this up."

"You're wrong. You better keep your mouth shut if you want

to keep him because he's not going to want you if he knows you were with me. Trust me on this, Rose. I know him. And I think you know it, too." He hung up on her.

She swore and saw Maggie headed toward her, but at the last second, Maggie rushed past her and ran out the café door, up to a man, and spun him around to face her.

Rose gasped. "Oh, my god. Joel."

Chapter Fourteen

M aggie stopped Joel before he could get away again, because she knew she'd seen him outside the dress shop. She had also caught glimpses of him around town the last couple of days.

"Joel." God, he looked good in black jeans, a red polo stretched across his broad chest and shoulders, his light brown hair tousled by the breeze, and his warm brown eyes glued to her. "What are you doing here?" A strange flutter of anticipation washed through her.

"Oh, uh, hi, Maggie. How are you?" He seemed nervous. Jumpy even, though his gaze took all of her in and his eyes filled with a need she recognized from the past, because he'd always looked at her that way.

"I'm fine. But you didn't answer my question."

"Um." He looked down the street, at the ground, then finally at her again. "I'm visiting my family. I had no idea you were in town, too."

She'd known him long enough to know when he was lying.

"Really? I saw you at the bridal shop. Your mom didn't tell you I was getting married here this weekend?"

He looked down at the diamond engagement ring on her finger. "I did hear about that."

She thought she detected some remorse in those words, but couldn't be sure.

He met her gaze again. "Congratulations, Maggie. You deserve to be happy." He took a tiny step closer. "Are you happy?"

"Yes," she said automatically. "But I don't understand why you're here."

He stared at her for a long moment, time spinning out, memories surfacing that made Maggie want to reach out and hug him. She longed to feel the love they'd once shared though they'd long ago said their good-bye.

"I—" Joel stopped, searching for something in her gaze.

She wished she knew what he was looking for, what he wanted to say.

"I . . . I hope you'll be very happy." Joel turned and rushed away, just like he'd done when she spotted him staring at her through the window.

She watched him disappear around the corner and stood there for another minute wishing he'd come back and say something entirely different. Something that would make her feel the way she felt every time she saw him. The way she felt when they were together.

"Oh, no." She still loved him.

But loving him had never been the problem. Wanting different things had torn them apart.

And now she was about to marry a man who was willing to give her everything she wanted. So why didn't it feel right to think that and believe it and see Joel? Couldn't she have the love she had with him and the family she wanted with someone else?

She loved Marc.

But it wasn't the same.

She'd had the once-in-a-lifetime kind of love and lost it.

Not everyone ends up with the one they want.

It didn't mean you didn't love again.

Her heart was big enough to love two men in different ways.

She and Marc would be happy together. They'd build a family, careers, and make memories together watching their kids grow and have children of their own. They'd be doting grandparents one day and look back on their life and know they'd had something good.

She couldn't ask for more.

* * *

Rose's heart broke for her best friend when Joel walked away. Maggie looked despondent and resigned. It was easy to see they both still loved each other. But sometimes that wasn't enough. Maggie wanted more. If she and Joel stayed together and Maggie didn't feel completely fulfilled, it would eventually tear them apart.

It had to be agony to love like that and not be together.

Would Maggie and Marc eventually be torn apart if Rose

told Maggie about her one-night stand with Marc? Would it forever be a thing between them, especially when they were all together?

She didn't even want to think right now about how Gray would feel.

Bottom line, Maggie needed to know. Today. Even if the timing sucked.

Maggie's phone rang.

Since Rose still had Maggie's phone, she answered for her. "Maggie's phone. This is Rose."

"Hi, this is Jill from Divine Dessert Diva. Is Maggie available?"

Rose waved Maggie forward. "She's right here. Please hold on for a moment."

Maggie took the phone.

"It's Jill from the cake shop," Rose said, then followed Maggie back to their table.

"Hello. This is Maggie."

Rose listened to Maggie's side of the conversation, all the while watching her friend's face turn from resignation to despair.

"Uh-huh."

"I see."

"That's terrible."

"Yes, I'd love the names and numbers for the other shops."

"Please, email them to me."

Maggie ended the call and stared at nothing, her whole body still.

Concerned, Rose put her hand over Maggie's. "What's happened?"

"The bakery had an early morning kitchen fire. They can't deliver on the cake."

Rose fell back in her seat. "Oh, no."

"They're sending me a list of other shops in the area. Maybe one of them can do it." Maggie didn't sound optimistic about it at all.

"Okay. We'll call right away. Maybe it won't be the exact cake you ordered, but I'm sure we can get something delicious and beautiful."

Maggie nodded, picked up her latte, then set it back down when she realized it was empty. She sat across from Rose, but she wasn't really there.

Rose put her hand over her friend's. "Mags, what happened with Joel?"

Her gaze finally settled on Rose. "Nothing. He's in town seeing his family."

"The same week you're getting married?" Rose didn't hide how suspicious that sounded. Because really, what were the odds?

"Yeah. I've seen him before—at the bridal shop. And maybe a couple other places. I thought maybe . . ." She turned and stared out the windows, looking for him, then shook her head and turned back. "He said he wants me to be happy." She picked up her cup again, then immediately set it down, frowned, and sighed out her frustration. "That's how we left things when it ended and now. Does he think I need to hear it again? Doesn't he know that it doesn't help to say that to me and then walk away?" There was a plea in Maggie's eyes for Rose to understand and feel the pain so clearly written all over her face.

Rose squeezed her hand. "You still love him."

"It doesn't matter." The bitter words made her lips press tight. "I'm marrying Marc," she said without much enthusiasm or joy.

Marc's recent behavior and the cake cancellation probably didn't help.

"Is that what you really want?" Rose asked the bold question, giving Maggie a chance to voice whatever reservations or feelings she had about it.

Maggie seemed to snap back to herself. "Of course. Sorry. I was thrown by seeing Joel and now the cake thing. They say something always goes wrong at a wedding. If the cake is the worst of it, I guess I'm lucky." That sounded more like Maggie.

"Well, let's start calling the other shops and see if we can get a replacement cake." Rose pulled out her phone, ready to help, and smiled at the text.

GRAY: Miss you still. Work sucks. I'd rather be with you.

GRAY: I'm coming to see you tonight even if Marc isn't ready to go back.

He texted her several times a day. They talked on the phone last night for two hours about everything and nothing. She learned that he'd loved doing tricks on his BMX bike when he was a kid. He'd been on the swim and tennis teams in high school. And he wished he'd had a sister growing up. She teased him that Marc had spoiled the idea of having a brother. He agreed, but also acknowledged that having Marc around in the summers and on holidays showed him how good he had it at home with his parents.

"You're smiling. Let me guess . . . Gray," Maggie said.

Rose held up her phone. "He texted me."

Maggie smirked. "Something scandalous, I hope."

Rose sighed. "More like sweet."

"Of course it is. Marc apologized to me. I think we're both on edge. I can't wait for the honeymoon where we can be alone and just be happy like we've been all this time."

"You really love him."

"I do. Everything's been great up until a few weeks ago when he started spending more time looking at his phone than at me. I know he's working hard to impress his dad and prove he can take over the company so his dad can retire. Add that stress in with the wedding and it's no wonder we're both tired and cranky and wanting things to just be like they were before all this."

"Once you're back from the honeymoon, everything will fall back into routine. And you two will be living together, so that will make things easier."

"I hope so. In my mind, it all seemed so easy. Find a guy who loved me and wanted a family. Get married. Move in together. Start a family. Live a happy life."

"Sounds like a plan," Rose agreed. "And I want you to have all the happiness in the world."

"But?" Maggie asked, sensing something in Rose.

"No 'but.' Just something I should have told you the night we all got together at the bar. I wanted to, but—"

Maggie leaned in. "You were awestruck by Gray."

Rose couldn't deny it. "Yes. The second I saw him . . . I don't know what happened to me. I just wanted him. I felt this connection."

Maggie's grin grew wider. "Exactly."

Rose wondered if Maggie was talking about her connection to Joel or to Marc, but didn't ask.

Maggie sat forward. "Does this have something to do with Marc's surprise? Please don't tell me the surprise he's come up with sucks."

"We actually didn't talk about a surprise. He wanted to tell me not to tell you what I'm about to tell you."

Maggie fell back in her seat and eyed her. "What? Why?"

"Because he doesn't want you to know. Because he thinks you'll be upset or angry."

"Now you really need to tell me what it is."

Rose sucked in a breath and revealed the truth she'd been holding on to for too long. "Marc and I know each other. We met a little over a year ago. Though I didn't know your Marc was the same Marc until I saw him with you."

Maggie shrugged. "So. What's the big deal?"

"We had a one-night stand." Rose held her breath, hoping this didn't ruin their relationship.

Maggie's mouth dropped open, then she closed it with a snap and narrowed her gaze. "The one-night stand where the guy was cheating on his girlfriend and you were pissed about it." Of course Maggie remembered.

"Yes. It was Marc."

Maggie brushed her hand over her hair, her eyes wide, her gaze unfocused. "What?" She folded her arms and unfolded them. "What?"

"I'm sorry I didn't say anything sooner. At first when I saw him at the bar I thought he didn't remember me."

"Did he?"

"Well, yes. But he didn't want you to know he and I knew each other. I told him we should tell you that we met way before you and he got together. It was one night, Maggie. We barely knew more than each other's names. It didn't mean anything. I never wanted to see him again."

Maggie gaped at her. "Because he's a cheater!"

Rose softened her voice, trying to soothe Maggie. "But that doesn't mean he'll cheat on you. He's committed to you. He asked you to marry him. He wants you and a family and the life you two talked about. Nothing has changed. He and I are nothing to each other. You're with Marc. I'm with Gray."

Maggie sat up straighter. "Does Gray know?"

"About the one-night stand, yes. But I didn't tell him it was Marc. I wanted to tell you first. Gray texted that he's coming to see me tonight. I'll tell him then."

Maggie sat for a long moment, quiet and contemplative. Rose gave her all the time she needed to absorb the news and work it out in her mind on her own. "That's why he seemed so taken with you."

Rose drew her lips back in a half frown. "I suppose there's a familiarity between us because of that night."

Maggie eyed her. "But you don't really like him."

It had to be hard for Maggie to realize her best friend and fiancé weren't friendly.

"I don't know Marc the way you know him, Maggie."

"But you know what he's like in bed," she shot back.

Rose didn't know what to say.

Maggie sighed. "I'm sorry. That was out of line. You met him before I met him and never saw him again. You had no idea I was seeing him."

Rose caught Maggie's gaze. "But he knew I was your best friend while he was seeing you because he saw my pictures in your apartment."

"That's why he didn't want me to post or send photos. He knew you'd see them—him." Maggie's eyes went wide. "You don't think I should marry him."

Rose didn't want to influence or upset her best friend by confessing that she thought there was something definitely off about Marc's behavior. "You're the only one who knows what's right for you."

Maggie pressed her lips tight, annoyed by Rose's non-answer. "The two of you—"

"There is no two of us. Even without finding out about the girlfriend, I was prepared to leave him that morning and not look back. I wasn't infatuated with him. We were both just looking for some company at the end of a night out at a bar. And while that wasn't my usual thing, that night, I thought why not. That's all."

"Is that how you explained it to Gray?"

"We were talking about past relationships. I told him about my dating disasters in college, relationships where I learned to be a better me and girlfriend, and yes, that I had a one-night stand a year ago that made me stop dating because I'd made a mistake in trusting someone I didn't even know."

"What do you think he'll say when you tell him it was with Marc?"

"I hope he'll understand that Marc didn't mean anything to me then or now, except that he's someone I'd like to get to know as the Marc my best friend loves. I hope I've shown Gray how much I want to continue to get to know him better. I want to build on this budding relationship because he means so much to me already and I'd never do anything to hurt him." Rose slid her hand across the table toward Maggie. "I hope you know that I'd never do anything to hurt you. I wanted to tell you right away, but when the initial moment passed and I missed it, it seemed harder to bring up. Not because there's something between me and Marc, but because I didn't want you to think there ever could be. I'm telling you, I am so deep in this thing with Gray, there's no one else I see. And my love for you is so great that all I want is for you to be happy.

"I mean it, Mags, I'd like to get to know Marc as the man you love, because you see all the great things about him. I know through your eyes I will, too."

Maggie brushed away a tear. "That really means a lot to me. And I know you'd never go after a guy I'm seeing."

"Mags, you're marrying that man. And he's lucky to have you."

"So this is all that's been going on? He's just been weird because he thought you'd tell me and I'd be upset?"

"I think so. I mean, he doesn't come off very well in the story. But that doesn't mean he hasn't changed because of his love for you," she reminded Maggie.

"I've had no reason to believe he's ever been unfaithful. Except with his phone," she teased, returning to her old self.

Rose held Maggie's gaze. "Are we okay?"

Maggie nodded. "Yes. We're good. But don't tell Marc you told me about the two of you. I'm going to give him a chance to tell me himself."

"I'm not sure that's a good idea." What if Marc lied to spare her feelings? "It feels like a test when all he wanted to do was keep you from getting hurt and upset."

"He didn't want me to know he'd cheated in the past."

Rose gave her a diplomatic answer. "We don't know the circumstances and why he did what he did."

"There's no justification for cheating."

"No. But testing him or tricking him into lying isn't a great way to treat your fiancé, either."

Maggie sighed. "I'm sorry. You're right. I'll just ask him about it. Get his side. Make sure it's out in the open so we don't have any secrets or misconstrued feelings about it. You two slept together before I met him. I don't like that he asked you not to tell me and that he manipulated things so that you wouldn't know he was dating me."

"If it helps, I think he liked you so much he didn't want to jeopardize things over something that happened in his past. We've all done things we'd like to forget."

"And if that's how he feels about it, too, then we'll never mention it again."

"I'm all for focusing on Maggie and Marc's big day and you two as a couple from now on. As far as I'm concerned, it never happened."

"Agreed." Maggie picked up her cell. "Now, let's start calling about the cake. If we can't find someone to do it in time, then we'll have . . ." Maggie turned thoughtful for a moment. "Hot fudge sundaes."

"Now that's an idea. Or pie."

"Exactly. We have options."

Rose read Maggie's face. "But you want the cake."

Maggie sighed. "I really do. It's tradition."

"Then we'll find you a beautiful cake."

They spent the next hour calling all the bakeries from the list in the email and then some. No one in a thirty-mile radius had the time and availability to make a wedding cake on such short notice.

"Where do you think we can get a billion gallons of ice cream and hot fudge?"

"Maybe the caterer will know?" Rose suggested, picking up her phone the second it rang, hoping it was one of the bakeries calling back to say they had a last-minute cancellation and could do the cake. She sighed, dejected. "Sorry. It's Gray."

Maggie grinned. "I won't tell him how disappointed you look right now."

"I wanted it to be your fairy god-baker." She slid her finger across the screen and answered the call. "Hey."

"What's wrong?" The concern in Gray's deep voice soothed her.

"I need a cake and I can't get a cake."

"What kind do you want?" He sounded all too ready to fulfill her wish.

"The wedding kind."

"What?"

Rose filled him in on the bakery fire and the denials they'd gotten from all the bakeries they'd called.

"Hold on a minute, okay?"

"Sure. I'll console myself with the last bite of my cookie."

Gray laughed. "You do that, and I'll try to find a way to make you happy again."

"I'll be happy when I see you tonight."

He made a deep growling sound in his throat. "You say things like that and make it damn hard for me to do anything but come and find you." The promise of what he'd do when he did filled her with desire.

"You're blushing," Maggie pointed out.

"Hold on," Gray ordered.

"I'm trying, but you've been gone awhile and all I do is think about you."

"Rose."

"Yeah?"

"You're killing me."

"Whatever gets you here faster." She felt like begging.

"Damn, it's hot in here." Maggie waved her hand in front of her face, knowing full well Gray heard everything she said, and grinned about it.

"I'm going to set the world on fire when I get my hands on you."

"You'll have to be here to do it."

"Oh, my god, you two should not be let out in public," Maggie continued to tease.

"Hold on," Gray said again.

"I'm trying to be patient, but where you're concerned, I want it all right now."

Maggie gaped at her.

She felt damn good about being up front with Gray about what she wanted and letting her friend see how happy she was with Gray and how much she wanted him. Not Marc.

"Then I hope you're ready when I get there."

She didn't get a chance to say anything else before he put her on hold, which only made her laugh.

"What's so funny?"

"I don't think he could take any more of that."

Maggie tapped the back of her hand on Rose's shoulder. "You are so bad."

"It's so fun and sexy as hell to flirt with him like this. He's just . . . everything good," she finished, not realizing Gray had come back on the line.

"Sweetheart." His voice was deep and thick, and when he called her that it made her heart beat faster and everything in her melt.

"Yeah?"

"You're not just killing me, you own me."

"Gray." She couldn't say anything more than his name and she hoped he heard everything in her heart to go with it.

"Yeah. Damn. This is getting good."

"So good," she agreed.

"Maybe you two should be getting married instead of Marc and me."

Rose went still and stared at Maggie, wondering if she was having second thoughts.

"*With* Marc and me," she corrected, rolling her eyes at her blunder. "Sorry. I'm stressed."

"I can help," Gray said, and even though Maggie could hear him because they were sitting so close, Rose put the phone on speaker. "Hey Maggie. I called our events coordinator and asked her if she could reach out to a few of our vendors to see if they could do a last-minute wedding cake." Gray paused. "She just emailed me with the name of a bakery here in the city. They're happy to help and all they need are the details. I'll forward this to you. Give them a call with the details of what you want and they'll make it happen. The only hiccup is they can't deliver it. But I'm sure we can figure out how to pick it up and get it to the reception."

"Are you serious?" Maggie asked, hope and wonder in her words.

"Yes. All I need is your email address."

Maggie rattled it off for him. Ten seconds later, her phone lit up with the incoming email alert.

"I know you're totally into my best friend," Maggie said, "but when I see you, I'm going to kiss you for this."

"Rose is only happy if you're happy, so it's really in my best interest to help you out, because I'm happy when Rose is happy," Gray said.

"That's it, Rose, you win. Marc apologized and turned around and lied about why he wanted to talk to you. You and Gray spend five minutes on the phone and it's filled with sexual innuendos, flirting, and romance."

"Why did Marc want to talk to you, Rose?"

She eyed Maggie, who whispered, "Sorry," for bringing up Marc and hinting at what Rose hadn't told Gray yet.

"I would really like to tell you about that when we're together. It's an in-person kind of thing." She didn't want to tell him over the phone without being able to see his face and how he took the news. She wanted him to see in her that it didn't mean anything to her.

"You've got my attention."

"She's had your attention from the second you met," Maggie interjected. "If what she says changes that, then you haven't been paying attention to what she's been telling you and you don't feel for her what you say you feel for her. This happened before you met, so it shouldn't affect you and her and what you have right now." Maggie always had her back.

"This is about that asshole you had a one-night stand with, right?"

Rose rolled her eyes. "Yes." She sighed. "Gray, really we can talk about it when I see you."

"And you told Maggie whatever it is you want to tell me?"

"Yes." She knew it was coming but it still didn't prepare her for Gray's clipped, controlled tone.

"It was Marc."

"Yes," she confirmed.

"That cheating asshole never said a word, just secretly got off on knowing how much I liked you and wanted you and he'd already had you."

"Gray." She spoke softly, understanding he needed to work it out in his mind, but also so very aware that Maggie could hear him.

"All the flirting, catching you two talking in the hall at the bar, him calling you gorgeous on the phone, kissing you in the restaurant, saying little things about you to get under my skin."

"He kissed you?" Maggie looked furious.

"On the cheek in greeting." Rose wanted that to be clear.

"Yeah. And you backed up into me because I thought you didn't like it."

"I didn't." She wanted that to be clear, too. "I told you everything about that night and how things ended between us the next morning."

"Well, you didn't tell me everything," he pointed out.

She wasn't about to give him a blow-by-blow. "The only thing

I held back that mattered was his name. Because of Maggie, he didn't want me to say anything at all, but I thought you both should know that Marc and I met long before Maggie met him and I met you. Marc was a mistake I made." She sent Maggie an apologetic look. "You are exactly what I said you were five minutes ago. Everything, Gray. My every thought. The man I can't wait to see. The one I want." She felt the tears threaten to spill from her eyes. "If I'm not that for you, even in some small way right now, because of a guy I slept with before you were the dream I never thought could be my reality, then . . . I guess this isn't as real for you as I thought. If we were talking about one of your ex-girlfriends, I'd tell you nothing from the past matters if you want me now. And I know it's complicated because he is your cousin and there's history there and he's Maggie's fiancé, but he is not and never was mine. I was never his. We were two strangers who spent the night together. I thought you understood that. I hope it hasn't changed just because you know his name."

She held her breath and waited.

"Rose."

"Yeah."

"Are you crying?"

"A little bit. Yes."

"Why?"

"Because losing you hurts."

"Why?"

The tears cascaded down her cheeks unchecked. "Because I'm yours, Gray. And I thought you were mine."

"I am, sweetheart." Relief came out in a whoosh of air over the line. "I meant it. You own me. You're the one I want."

Maggie laid her forehead on her arm on the table and sighed. "Thank god." She glanced up at her. "Because you two were made for each other."

Rose thought so, too, but she still felt the intensity coming across the line from Gray.

"Take me off the speaker, Rose."

Maggie's eyes filled with concern.

Rose nodded toward Maggie's phone. "Call the number Gray sent you and order the cake."

Maggie grabbed her phone and walked over to the windows.

Rose tapped the speaker button and put the phone to her ear. "It's just you and me now."

"Exactly the way I like it." The teasing tone didn't conceal the possessiveness of his words or the residual anger.

"Gray. I'm really sorry I didn't say something sooner."

"I didn't name every one of my exes."

"I doubt any of them were my cousin or friends."

"Did you know Marc was dating Maggie before you saw him in the bar?"

"No. Marc is a common name. It never even occurred to me."

"You never saw a picture of them together?"

"He knew about me, so he made sure I never saw a picture so I couldn't tell Maggie."

"So he knew walking into that bar that you were in there waiting with his fiancée."

"Yes."

"And that first night when you saw me . . ."

"You were right. I thought you were Maggie's fiancé and I was immediately disappointed that I didn't have a shot with you."

"You saw Marc after that and you were about to say something but he introduced himself to you and pretended he didn't know you."

"Yes. And then I didn't know what to do. I wish I'd called him out on it. But how weird would that have been to announce that Marc and I knew each other but he didn't remember me or that night?"

"Yeah, Maggie probably wouldn't have taken that well, and I'd have probably steered clear because of Marc and we'd have missed discovering this thing we have between us."

"Then let's just put it out there. How do you feel about the fact that Marc and I have a past history?"

"I don't like how Marc has handled this, keeping secrets, making comments, trying to upset you with those strip club pictures, and asking you to lie for him. I don't like that he called you gorgeous on the phone, or said *our* Rose like he and I are sharing you in some way."

"If he wasn't marrying Maggie, I wouldn't see him again," she assured Gray. "As far as I'm concerned, he's not the same guy I met a year ago, but Maggie's Marc. And your cousin. I don't know that we'll ever be friends, but I can try to like him for you and Maggie."

"Don't try too hard on my account."

"I was really just saying that for your benefit. I have no intention of going out of my way to be nice to him. Except for Maggie, because I don't want to lose my best friend over him. I don't want to lose you because of him, either."

"You didn't do anything wrong. I'm not upset or mad at you, I was just surprised, and yes, angry that you'd been with Marc. Mostly because I just want it not to be true so that you're all mine. I don't want him to know things about you that I don't."

"He doesn't know me at all."

Gray remained silent for a long moment and she knew he was thinking of her having sex with Marc.

"It was just sex, Gray. Nothing more. I'm sure you've had sex with women and it meant little to nothing."

"Intellectually, I know that. But knowing he had his hands on you, kissed you, saw your beautiful body naked and explored it . . ."

"You make it sound like we made love, took our time, and savored it. That is so very far from the truth. We were drunk and sloppy and eager for release." That was all the detail she'd give him. "It was what I wanted in the moment. And when I woke up, I was done and ready to leave without a backward glance. I don't want to think about it now, let alone relive it with you.

"If you think that you and I will have the same thing, you're wrong. But if you're not willing or able to put it out of your mind and just be with me, then you'll never know and we'll both lose out on something I think could be amazing. Because I've spent every night and so many of my waking moments these last few days thinking about us. Together. You are the one I want in my bed, naked, touching me, filling me, taking me into the fire even you said would burn the world.

"We can have that, Gray, but only if you let this go."

"As far as I'm concerned, he's not even an ex. Just some dickhead who never had a chance of more with you," Gray said.

"And I promise if I ever meet one of your exes, I'll try really hard not to scratch their eyes out for ever looking at you, but feel really lucky that they were stupid for letting you go and you're mine. And I will hate them for sleeping with you, but then I'll take you to bed and remind you why you want me and only me."

"Damn, sweetheart, you really know how to make me wish I was with you right now."

"Then why aren't you here?" She hoped he heard the plea in her voice, because until she saw him and felt the way he looked at her, touched her, and kissed her, she wouldn't be convinced this wouldn't be a problem for them.

And then he said the only thing she wanted to hear. "I'm on my way."

ose opened the door and found Gray standing there in black jeans and a green Henley. He'd buried his hands in his pockets and his eyes were a mix of weariness and relief.

"Hey, I—" He grunted when she launched herself into his chest, wrapped her arms around his neck, and hugged him tight. He immediately crushed her to him. He dipped his head and nuzzled his cheek to hers, then whispered in her ear, "I missed you."

"Not as much as I missed you. I'm sorry."

"For what? Having a life before you met me?" He leaned back so he could look at her, but he didn't let her go. "I could have handled the news better. The drive here gave me time to put it in perspective and realize that all the things you've said and done and made me feel are real and ours. It has nothing to do with him. And maybe I ought to thank him for asking your best friend to marry him because it brought me here to you."

"I don't think you need to go that far."

"Trust me, I won't." He loosened his hold and smiled for the first time. "I'm glad you told me. It happened. It's over. Let's just move on."

She sighed out her relief. "Thank god. I had a whole speech prepared that included a lot of begging."

"Why don't you just show me how you feel and kiss me?"

"You have the best ideas." She went up on tiptoe for the kiss. He met her halfway, his lips eager to find hers as they sank into the kiss and lost themselves in each other's arms.

"So this is the boyfriend," Poppy said from behind her.

Rose reluctantly pulled away and turned to face her sister, glaring at her for interrupting.

"Yes," Gray answered her sister, even though she hadn't asked a question. "I'm Gray. Rose's boyfriend."

She glanced up at him, so happy he made the declaration, not just to Poppy, but to her, to let her know everything was okay between them.

"Gray, this is my sister, Poppy."

He gave her a nod. "Your sister is really happy to reconnect with you. You should stay at her place sometime. We'll take you out and show you around the Bay Area."

"Yes! Definitely." Rose wanted Poppy to know she really wanted her to come.

"I'd like that." Poppy turned her focus to Rose. "You going out?"

Rose stepped back and looked up at Gray.

"Did you eat yet?" he asked, his hand still on her back.

"No. I couldn't eat after I talked to you earlier today. I was so anxious to see you. I wasn't sure you'd really come."

He used the hand at her back to pull her close again and brushed a kiss against her forehead. "I'd be the stupidest man alive to leave things the way we did and walk away."

"Is everything okay?" Poppy asked.

"Everything is great now that he's back." Rose hugged him again, just to feel him and know that he was solid and real and hers.

"Okay, then." Poppy watched her.

"Hand me my purse from the hall table and tell Mom I went out."

"She left a little while ago. She joined a book club."

Rose gaped at Poppy. "Really?"

Poppy smiled. "Yeah. She said because of you and seeing Maggie's mom again, she wanted to make some new friends. Brenda belongs to the group and invited Mom to join. I think it's more about wine and gossip than books, but hey, she's not closed up in this house."

"Like you," Rose pointed out.

Poppy handed her the purse. "Have a good night." She closed the door on any more conversation.

"So that's Poppy," Gray said with a grin.

"Yep. Isn't she fun?"

"She comes across a bit dark."

Rose walked with Gray to his car, thinking about Poppy's all-black look and the black hair. "Some of us bury our pain inside. She wears hers on the outside. I worry she won't ever get beyond it and what our father did to her."

Gray held the door open for her. "She will when she's ready. It's up to her."

"About what I told you—"

"You were open and honest about it. I couldn't ask for more."

She placed her hand on his chest. "I can't stand the thought of ever hurting you."

"I feel the same way about you. And I think we're off to a good start. We got the first big hurdle out of the way. We had a difficult situation come up and we handled it by talking about it. That's how it should be."

"That's how it will be," she promised him, and slipped into the front seat.

Gray closed her door and walked around the car and got in on his side. He started the engine and pulled out of the driveway. "What do you feel like?"

"Doesn't matter. I just want to spend time with you."

He reached over, took her hand, and linked his fingers with hers. "Sounds good to me."

While Gray drove them to town, Rose pulled out her cell and texted Maggie with her free hand.

ROSE: Gray's back. We're good. Going out to dinner.

"Who are you texting?"

"Maggie. I promised her I'd let her know as soon as you got back whether or not we worked things out."

He glanced at her, surprise in his eyes. "You really thought we might not?"

"I sensed that any other guy I'd slept with you'd brush off, but because it was . . . him, I knew it wouldn't be that easy for you. He doesn't matter to me at all. But you . . . I can't even explain it." She lifted his hand and pressed it to her cheek.

He pulled his hand free and slid his fingers into the back of her hair, leaned over, and gave her a quick kiss before returning his attention to the road.

She looked down at the incoming text.

MAGGIE: Marc is back, too. Meeting him at his hotel room to talk. Wish me luck.

Rose responded immediately.

ROSE: Good luck!

Rose wished she really meant it. She increasingly believed Maggie could do so much better than Marc. Joel always seemed more present for Maggie than Marc had this week. She'd had better with Joel. Their relationship seemed so easy and carefree. They enjoyed each other's company, laughed and played together as well as supporting each other in everything they did. There were no jealousies or arguments about inconsequential things. In fact, the only thing that ever dimmed their happiness was their disagreement about having children.

Losing Joel had really hurt Maggie.

Marc was her chance to have everything she wanted.

Rose hoped Marc was capable of loving her the way she deserved to be loved.

"Did Marc come back with you?"

"No. I didn't even bother to tell him I was coming back tonight."

"Maybe Maggie did. He's in town, too. He and Maggie are meeting up at the hotel to talk."

"I hope he comes clean about everything the way you did."

"He's probably mad that I told her."

"It would have come out eventually. And he'd have been the one to blow it. He can't keep his mouth shut about you. He liked having a secret with you. I wouldn't have been surprised if he used it against you."

"What do you mean?"

"That's just how Marc is. If he wants something, he'll use whatever means necessary to get it. Somewhere down the road, he'd have used your relationship with him to get you to do something for him."

"First, we did not have a relationship."

"I know. Sorry. Bad choice of words."

"And there's no way I'd let him blackmail me."

"Now he can't. I know. Maggie knows. So unless there's something else you're holding back, you're clear."

"You know everything."

"Then all he has to do is convince Maggie he lied to spare her feelings and not because of something else so she can accept it happened and it's over and move on."

"You do believe me, right? I'm not holding anything more back from you."

Gray stopped at a red light and looked at her. "Yes. Of course I believe you. As far as I'm concerned, you and I are together and Marc isn't a part of that at all."

"Okay." She let all her tense muscles loose and sank back into the seat. "My hope is that now that it's out in the open, Marc will stop all the nonsense and focus on his relationship with Maggie and be sensitive to her feelings."

And if Marc couldn't do that, then maybe Maggie was making a mistake.

Gray scoffed under his breath. "When it comes to being sensitive, Marc is sorely lacking. You might be hoping for too much from him. Look how he's been subtly taunting me about you."

Rose wished the wedding wasn't just days away. Then she could tell Maggie to take some time to let this whole matter settle. "I have a bad feeling this isn't going to go well." Her stomach knotted.

"If Marc really wants to hold on to Maggie, he'll do the right thing." Gray pulled into the parking lot at the nicest steakhouse in town. "Let's give them some space and not eat at the hotel."

"Fine by me. This place is really good. And it has a bar."

"I don't need a drink. You make me feel a little drunk sometimes."

She smiled. "Yeah? That's sweet. But I could use a glass of wine."

Gray leaned over and kissed her again, sliding his tongue

along hers, letting the heat build and the moment stretch before he broke the kiss and stared at her. "See what I mean."

"Yep." She popped the P on her kiss-swollen lips. "I feel it."

He chuckled and slid out of the car, walking around the front to get her door for her.

"Thank you."

He put his hand to her back and nudged her toward the entrance. "My pleasure, sweetheart."

"No. The pleasure is definitely mutual."

"And it always will be, sweetheart."

$\mathcal{M}$aggie knocked on Marc's hotel room door and jumped when he answered so quickly. He smiled at her like he was relieved to see her.

He hooked his hand at the back of her neck, drew her close, and kissed her like a man who hadn't seen his love in years.

At first, she kept her hand planted on his chest, but feeling the galloping pace of his heart and the passion he poured into the kiss, she sank into him and gave in to the way he always made her feel.

Or was it the way he wanted her to feel so they could skip over the part where he'd lied to her and go right back to the way things usually were between them?

She pushed him back into the room, breaking the kiss in the process. It allowed her some time and space to think about why she was really here.

Marc picked up a huge bouquet of red roses from the entry table and held them up to her. "I'm sorry. I should have told you I knew Rose from before we met. I should have said something the second I spotted her in the pictures in your apartment."

"Why didn't you? We could have avoided all of this."

Marc held out his hands and let them drop back and slap his thighs. "This what?"

"The lies for one," she snapped.

"It's one lie," he grumbled. "And I did it for you." He sighed out his frustration, then held her gaze, his eyes earnest. "I didn't want you to get all weird every time you saw me and Rose together. I didn't want it to come between us. Not when things were going so well, and definitely not now when we're about to get married." He took her hand and squeezed it. "Because I love you, Maggie."

"And?"

He cocked his head. "And what?"

Unsure exactly what she was waiting for, she didn't say anything.

"Damnit, Maggie." He let go of her hand and held his out to his sides. "I'm a guy. If I can avoid an argument with a woman, I'm going to avoid it, because I can't win." He dropped his hands and his shoulders sagged.

"It's not about winning. It's about being honest."

"You want honest. Okay. Here it is. I slept with Rose. I had a good time. She had multiple good times. She woke up the next morning and left. I never saw her again until I walked into the bar to meet you, my fiancée, the woman I want to marry and have a life with. Do I feel anything when I see her? No. Because I'm in love with you. I want you to be my wife and the mother of our kids. I want us to have everything we dream of having together. And I'm not going to let one night with a woman I barely knew, who happened to turn out to be the love of my life's best friend, spoil it for us. Are you?"

She took in his frustration and determination mixed with the plea underscoring his words and answered, "No. I want to be a wife and a mom. I want the life we planned."

"Then why are we arguing about Rose? She's with Gray. For now. And I plan on being very happy with you." He cupped her face and kissed her softly. "Tell me you love me. I need to hear you say it."

"I'm upset you lied. And I also know you cheated on your girlfriend with Rose."

"I was an asshole. And then I met you and I realized that loving you meant more than anything to me. There is no one else for me. All I want is you."

She'd heard Gray talk to Rose just like this and wanted it for herself, and here was Marc, his heart open, telling her everything she wanted to hear. "I do love you."

"Good. Because I am so in love with you, and all I want to do now is show you how much." He kissed her as he turned her into the small sitting area and backed her toward the big king-sized bed.

"Maybe we should wait until our wedding night," she suggested, just to taunt him.

He eyed her with a smirk tilting his lips. "Stop talking, baby."

"Make me."

He dipped low, hooked his hands around the backs of her

thighs below her ass, lifted her, and tossed her on her butt on the bed, then followed her down until she was flat on her back and under him.

She laughed, but he stopped it with a deep kiss that stole her breath. He lifted his head long enough to say, "I can't wait to call you my wife." He dove back in for another searing kiss.

She felt his words rush through her on the wave of passion he poured over her. There was no room for doubts or anger or anything else but this amazing feeling rushing through her. This was how things had always been between them. Overwhelming in the best way. Filled with heat and passion. And a desire to share all of it with each other.

Time got away from them as clothes came off, one orgasm rolled into another until they were lying in each other's arms, a fine sheen of sweat covering their skin, their breaths coming in short, fast pants, and everything felt like it was right again.

The bright room had turned to shadows.

"See," Marc said, breaking the silence. "We're perfect together."

Almost. Because in that moment, Joel popped into her head.

But they hadn't been perfect together, either.

Perfect was unattainable and unrealistic.

She'd take almost perfect and the life she planned with Marc and their future kids, and be happy knowing she'd have his love and support for the rest of her life.

Marc rolled out of bed, tugged on his jeans without any underwear, and walked over to the sofa at the end of the bed. He pulled the bottle of wine out of the ice bucket and held it up. "Can I pour you a glass?"

"Please." She sat up and stared at him, standing there with the jeans slung low on his hips, chiseled abs, his wide chest and shoulders on full display. She'd messed up his dark blond hair with her fingers but he still looked temptingly rumpled. "You ordered all this for us?"

The coffee table had a very pretty and appetizing charcuterie board with cheese, meats, crackers, and breadsticks. Beside it was a bowl of fruit salad. The swanky Carmel hotel knew how to play up the California vibe for its guests.

"I hoped we could spend the night together. Reset things between us. Remind ourselves that this week and the wedding are about us, not our friends and family, or not having a cake."

"Gray helped me get a cake."

Marc went still. "You asked him to help you?"

"No. Rose happened to be on the phone with him and mentioned that we couldn't find anyone to do the cake. He asked his company's events coordinator to help us."

"I see." He took a sip of the wine, acting casual, but he was anything but.

"Are you upset he helped with the cake?"

"I'm sure he was just trying to impress Rose." He took another sip of wine. "And you. He is CFO of a big company, makes a shit ton of money, has a big house, and has women tripping over each other to have him. He gets things done with the snap of his fingers."

"I'm sure he's worked very hard to get where he is and have the things he has, but I don't think he goes out of his way to impress anyone."

"No. He just does it with his mere presence."

"It sounds like you're jealous, and you shouldn't be. You'll be taking over your father's business soon. You make good money, enough that we'll be comfortable and can even buy a house when we're ready to expand our family. There isn't anything Gray has that you can't have, too."

He scoffed and took a big gulp of wine.

She studied him. "Unless we're talking about Rose. Is that it? You're jealous that she's with Gray now?"

"No." He shook his head. "Not at all." He shrugged like it didn't matter. "Besides, that'll end when Gray finds out I slept with her."

Maggie frowned. "You think so? Should I break up with you because of it?"

Marc stopped the wine glass in front of his mouth and stared at her over it. "What? No. It didn't mean anything. You're the one I love."

"If that's true, then why should Rose and Gray break up?"

"It's different for men and women. Women have feelings for the guys they sleep with."

"Wow. That's an absurd and old-fashioned way of thinking. Even women can have sex just for the pleasure of it without it turning into something more. Rose barely knew more than your name. I'm sorry to break the news to you, but she didn't, and doesn't, have feelings for you. She's head-over-heels for Gray. And he knows that."

Marc shrugged. "Yeah, well, don't you think it's awkward for him knowing I've seen her naked?"

"Well, I'm okay with it," Maggie retorted, though she didn't like it, but she'd come to terms with it. "But I think it's strange that we just had sex and are getting married and you're talking like this. It even sounds like you hope Gray will break up with her."

Marc eyed her. "Maybe it would be better for all of us if he did. Then there's no weirdness in the future."

"So whenever we have a holiday celebration or dinner party or whatever, we only invite one of them at a time?"

"They've barely even started seeing each other. So if they break up, it won't be a problem for them to be friendly in the future."

She chuckled. "You have not been paying attention. You didn't hear them on the phone together. They are . . . not just into each other, but deeply connected to each other already."

"Come on. They just met."

"And the sparks flew and somehow melded them together. Rose texted me earlier. They are very much still together."

Marc rolled his eyes. "Of course they are." Marc sat on the sofa and fell into the back of it. "Gray gets everything he wants."

Her stomach knotted. Everything between them felt off again. "Does it really bother you that he's with Rose?"

"What?" His brow furrowed. "No," he scoffed.

She didn't believe him. "Are you sure? Because you went out of your way to make sure she didn't know you and I were dating."

"And this is the reason why. Because all we're talking about is her."

"You're the one who keeps bringing them up after you said this was our night. You thought *I* wouldn't get over what happened between you and Rose, but it seems like *you're* the one who can't let it go."

Marc stared at her, then sighed. "You're right. It's me."

Her heart pounded in her chest. "What do you mean?" Was he really not over Rose?

"I've worked really hard since we met to be a different and better man for you. I wanted so badly to be the man you wanted and needed, not the guy I used to be who cheated on his girlfriend." He rolled his eyes. "I know I made it worse by ending things by cheating. I was stupid. But I didn't want to be that way with you. For the first time, I opened myself up to really being with you, exploring all we could be together, and building a solid friendship, so that when we disagreed or things got complicated we could fall back on that and talk to each other about how we feel."

"Then tell me, how do you really feel about Rose and Gray being together?"

"I don't want to care, but I do, because I don't want it to come between *us*."

"It won't."

One side of his mouth drew back in a half frown. "Right. Look at us."

She slipped off the bed and went to him, straddling his lap and tracing her finger down the side of his face. "Look at you with your naked fiancée wrapped around you, wanting your attention, loving you for being the guy who worked so hard to be everything she wanted, and so ready to be your wife."

He checked her out, his lips twitching as he tried to hide his smile, but she saw the heat in his eyes oh so clearly. "I'm so damn lucky."

"Yes *we* are. Now what are you going to do with your naked soon-to-be wife?"

"I'm going to start with this." He slid his hand into her hair, drew her close, then kissed her softly. "And move on to this." He kissed his way down her neck to the top of her breast. "And I definitely need a taste of this." He flicked his tongue over her nipple, then took it into his mouth and sucked hard and deep, sending a wave of heat through her system, dampening her soft folds as his fingers glided over her, one, then two, diving deep inside her.

She sighed and gripped her hand in his hair to hold him to her. "You always make me feel so good."

He released her breast and nuzzled his cheek and chin against it. "These are good, but I want more." He slipped his hands under her legs and stood with her straddling his waist, setting her ass on the end of the bed as he fell to his knees. He draped her legs over his shoulders and buried his face between her thighs, pressing her legs wide, so he could lick and lave and plunge his tongue inside her.

He kept her right on the edge, bringing her up to the brink, lulling her back into enjoying the feel of his mouth on her, then building things back up until he slid two fingers inside her, sucked her clit, and sent her right over the edge.

As the first of the aftershocks rocked her, he stood, undid his jeans, and thrust his cock into her, hard and deep, pulling her to him by her thighs. He held her hips above the bed and kept control, slamming into her again and again until she climaxed a second time and he tossed his head back and spilled himself inside her with a deep, satisfied groan before he fell forward and collapsed on top of her, his face in her neck, his breath sawing in and out.

It took a moment for him to raise his head and stare down at her. "You okay?"

"Perfect. I can't feel my legs."

"Good. Then I can keep you happy in this bed all night." He kissed her, long and deep, his tongue sliding along hers. "I can never get enough of you."

She tamped down all thoughts that something still wasn't emotionally right between them and focused on the physical and sexual connection that always worked for them. "You can have all you want for the rest of our lives."

"Promise?"

"I do," she vowed, thinking that in just a few days she'd make that vow again. But tonight, they'd worship each other's bodies and reconnect, and tomorrow they'd focus on *their* relationship and the wedding and the rest of their lives together.

Chapter Seventeen

3 days to Maggie's wedding . . .

Rose sat with her mom at the kitchen table, sipping tea and enjoying a moment of peace and quiet. For the first time in a long time in this house, it felt companionable between them. A sense of comfort came over her that she'd never felt in her mother's company.

"Did you decide on a paint color for the living and dining room?" Rose asked.

Her mom had painted a dozen different paint samples on the walls. Different shades of white, pale blue, and green. "I'm not sure yet."

"Well, if you pick one and it doesn't feel right after it's up on the walls, you can always change it again. It's just paint."

Her mom pressed her lips together and nodded.

"It doesn't have to be perfect, Mom."

All of them had spent countless hours worrying about doing everything right. Mistakes were not dismissed or overlooked.

And every time there was a rip, a tear, a slash mark in the fabric of their family.

She gave her mom a soft smile of encouragement. "Sometimes in order to make a change, you have to make a mess first."

Her mom returned her smile. It came much more easily now.

Rose kept going. "Like going through the rooms and deciding what to keep and what should go."

Her mom had filled half a dozen boxes with things from the house and two large garbage bags of clothes to donate, and Poppy had helped her haul out several pieces of furniture for the donation truck to pick up this morning. The house looked a bit bare in some areas because she hadn't had time to rearrange things and buy anything new to make the place feel like hers—not his.

"If you don't really love it, it should go, so you can make room for what makes you happy."

Her mom held her gaze. Rose wondered if she understood that statement didn't just mean the things in the house, but the people in her life, too. Without her father here, dominating the conversation, the room, the house, their lives, they could breathe and be themselves.

If her mom had put him out of the house years ago, things could have been so different for her, for all of them.

"I loved what you did with your room. It suits the new you," her mom said.

Rose's room felt like a cozy, welcoming space to come home to now. "And this place will suit the new you you're just discovering. It's a transition. It will take time. It doesn't have to happen all at once."

Her mom tilted her head to the side and stared at her tea. "Don't you think I've had enough time to figure out who I am?"

"Not when you've allowed him to live in your head. How does it feel to put paint on the walls and toss out all that stuff he wanted but you didn't like?"

"Like I'm being defiant," her mom admitted.

"Because you still feel him judging you. You still think in some way you'll be punished for wanting what you want and liking what you like. He's not here to say or do anything about it. It's time for you to live your life the way you want and stop living the one he forced you to live."

"You make it sound so easy."

"It was, wasn't it? You take out the old and bring in the new. Keep the good. Get rid of the bad." She reached across the table. "And repair the things you've damaged and broken that you want to hold on to."

Her mom squeezed her hand. "I wish I knew how to make up for all I didn't do for you and Poppy. I wish you knew how much I love you both."

"We know. And I love you, too. I've been angry for a long time about the past. I blamed you for not stopping him, for not taking us away. I was a kid who needed to be protected and I felt like you didn't do that for me."

"I didn't. Not in the way you really needed me to."

Rose took in that acknowledgment of the pain her mom had caused by her inaction. "But I also learned from my counselor to see things from others' perspectives. I don't know what I would have done in your shoes. I'd like to say I'd have walked right out the door the first time he hit one of my kids. But that's easy to say and harder to do. As a grown working adult who has bills to pay and likes to eat, I get what you were up against."

"I sometimes wonder now that he's gone and I don't feel so . . ."

"Incompetent," Rose suggested. "Someone tells you that enough times in a lot of different ways, you start to believe it. I know, Mom."

"I wonder if I'd left, gone to my family or a shelter for help, if I might have surprised myself and been able to care for you both. I was so afraid he'd take you from me like he threatened, and I'd never see you again."

Rose's chest went tight. She hadn't thought about those threats he'd made to her mom in a long time. It had taken a great deal of tears and hard work to let that go so she could find a way to feel safe, even in her own skin. "I remember, too, how scared I was that he'd make you leave and we'd be stuck in this house all alone with him." Even now, the thought of it brought on a wave of fear.

"And now we are all, each of us in our own way, alone with him in our heads."

"Coming home has brought it all back for me, but when I'm back at my place and at my job and just living my life, he's not there with me much anymore." But sometimes that kind of trauma snuck up on you when you least expected it.

Her mom squeezed her hand again. "I'm so happy for you.

And proud that you finished college and built a life of your own. And now you're here, standing strong on your own two feet with a new man in your life and the possibility of a wonderful future with him, just like Maggie has found with Marc."

Rose blushed. "I just met Gray, Mom. Don't go planning a wedding yet. But he is really great. Kind. Understanding. He compliments me all the time. He's nothing like Dad. And we enjoy each other's company. Gray and I are . . . good. It's so good. Everything I ever wanted." She paused. "I just hope I don't screw it up." The fear and pain of almost losing him because of her thing with Marc had nearly broken her heart. But she'd taken the chance and had been honest with him. It wasn't easy to give him the time he needed to sort out his feelings about it. He seemed to quickly let it go, but she expected they'd really move forward when they spent more time together and put distance between them and what happened with Marc, and focused on what they were building together.

The foundation of their relationship, though they'd just begun to build it, wasn't as fragile as she thought. It was even more solid now that they'd worked through the issue.

"You won't mess it up," her mom assured her. "Sure, you'll make mistakes, but you'll do the right thing because you have a good heart."

"I try, but sometimes I don't get it right."

"What are you talking about?"

"I kept something from Maggie and Gray. I should have told them both right away that I . . . knew Marc, but I didn't. And when I did tell them, it was almost too late for them not to think I held it back because there was something more between Marc and me."

Her mom eyed her. "Is there something between you two?"

"No. Not anymore." Rose sucked in a breath and confessed, "I slept with Marc, but—"

* * *

"But nothing," Poppy yelled at Rose. She stood in the kitchen entry, stunned and furious at her sister. "You incredibly selfish bitch. How could you do that to your best friend?"

Rose pleaded with her eyes. "Poppy—"

"What is wrong with you? You abandon your family, you cheat on your new boyfriend, and you betray Maggie. You hurt everyone and don't even think twice about it. I thought you came home to make amends. You've convinced Mom and me that we can let go of the past and move on. But she started before you got here with the kitchen, then it was her clothes, and now it's everything. But it takes more than new paint and furniture and garbage runs to change what went on here. You've pushed us to change, but you haven't, not really, if you came here to stand up with Maggie at her wedding, then you stab her in the back." Poppy glared at her. "You're just as bad as Dad."

Rose gaped at her, pain in her eyes that Poppy didn't want to acknowledge. "That's not true."

"Isn't it?"

"No. If you'd let me explain . . ."

"I don't want to hear it. You've changed. Mom's changed. And I'm stuck in the muck."

Rose shook her head. "That's not true, either, Poppy. Look at you." Rose's gaze swept over her. "You're beautiful."

Poppy had forgotten why she'd come into the kitchen. She'd been so excited to show off her new pixie cut, the dark black hair softened to a deep brown with vibrant red highlights. She'd also bought a pretty red dress to wear to Maggie's wedding. The new look made her feel confident, but still edgy.

Rose's smile faded. "But Poppy, about Marc . . ."

"Fuck you, Rose. Fuck you for making us believe you cared."

Anger flashed in Rose's eyes. She stood and planted her hands on the table, leaning over it toward Poppy. "I do care. About you, Mom, Maggie, and Gray. I'd never do anything to hurt any of you."

"You slept with Marc! You encouraged Mom and acted like you and I could be friends again. You want us to just forget what Dad did to us, but I can't forget. He hurt us. He came after me because you were gone. And I didn't know how to stop it. I blamed myself because he always twisted it around and made me think it was my fault . . . But you know, it wasn't me." All her wild emotions started bubbling up inside her, making it hard to think clearly through the rage she always felt for being so helpless when it came to her dad and the abuse he inflicted on her.

"It was him," Rose assured her, sympathy in her steady gaze.

Poppy shook her head and tried to catch her breath. "Yeah. Well. Now he's dead and I'm happy he's gone. He deserved it. And I'm glad I did it! I hated him!" she screamed, clutching her hands together at her aching chest.

Rose stepped forward, nodding her agreement, understanding in her eyes. Then her gaze sharpened with curiosity. "What do you mean, you did it? What did you do, Poppy?"

When Poppy realized what she'd revealed with her wild outburst, she gasped.

"Don't say anything more, Poppy," her mom warned. "It's okay. Everything is okay. Go up to your room. Take a few minutes to calm down," she coaxed, only making things worse.

"Calm down? Are you serious? She thinks she's so much better than us, but she left us and stabbed her best friend in the back."

"I didn't," Rose swore.

But Poppy didn't want to hear it. "Oh, but you said you did."

"What did *you* do, Poppy? What happened with Dad?" Rose's eyes filled with suspicion.

Maybe it was Poppy's guilt making her see things that weren't there. She did that a lot these days because the guilt that she was happy her father was gone was always there, lurking, making her think everyone around her was judging her. She couldn't escape it, because she couldn't escape herself.

So she lashed out. "Why do you even care? You left us to fend for ourselves. Mom cowered. She stood back and let it happen like always. You ran. You left me here all alone with him."

Rose came around the table and approached her slowly. "What happened that night, Poppy? Did he hurt you?"

"Pick a night. Any night. He always hurt me. He liked it. You know. You knew and you left anyway." The pain and tightness in her chest grew.

"Yes. I left to save myself. It was selfish, but I had to go, Poppy. I wouldn't have survived another day. You know how that feels. I know you do. So how did you save yourself? What did you do?" The coaxing tone didn't sound judgmental. More inquisitive. Like a plea for Poppy to finally release what she'd been holding in for so long.

"I did what had to be done."

"No," Mom shouted. "That's not true."

"What happened?" Rose demanded, coming another step closer.

Poppy backed into the wall, needing the support, because she felt as if she was about to shatter.

She hated feeling the weakness come over her. The same feeling her father evoked when he tore her down. This time, like that last time with him, she came out fighting. "Same thing, different day. Repeat. Repeat. Repeat! Again and again and again! But I had enough. I wasn't going to take it anymore. And I told him so. I told him I was leaving. And he came after me, racing up the stairs as I headed for my room to pack my shit and go." She could barely breathe, thinking of that night, feeling the panic of it take hold of her again. "He shoved me from behind, but I didn't go down. I turned on him."

"Poppy, that's enough." Her mom sat at the table shaking her head, her face drawn tight in denial and the desire to erase it from her mind.

Not going to happen. None of them could forget what her father had done to each of them and to their family.

It made Poppy so angry that her mom didn't want to face the

truth. Again. "What? You don't want her to know? You don't want anyone to know what he did to us. You want to just hide it from the world, so no one will know you stood by while he beat your daughters and treated them like shit. She knows! Everybody knew! No one did anything about it." She glared at Rose. "*I* did something about it. I wasn't going to let him tell me I was stupid and weak and nothing one more time. I wasn't going to take one more slap across the face, one more punch in the back, one more kick while I'm down, because no matter how many times I stood back up, he always left me flat inside and out."

"What happened?" This time Rose's voice was soft and filled with sadness, because Poppy could just as well have been describing what had happened to Rose.

"I went after him. This time *I* pushed back. *I* told him exactly what I thought of him. Just like him, I didn't let up. I went right for him and said all those things no one ever said to him but he loved to say to us. That he was mean and worthless and an ugly drunk who beat on his kids and didn't deserve anything or anyone to love him. I told him what he already knew, that Mom was afraid of him and didn't love him, that you left because you hated him and you were never coming back, and that I hated him, too, and I was leaving, and if Mom was smart and wanted to save herself she'd leave, too, and he'd die a miserable bastard all alone."

Tears blurred her vision and trailed unchecked down her cheeks.

"I told him to go to hell. Stupid drunk as he was, he tried to take a swing at me. I ducked. He stumbled over his own feet, momentum carrying him sideways, and I pushed him back, but he lurched forward again, and then . . ." She saw it all so clearly in her mind. "We were at the top of the stairs, and then *he* wasn't." He'd reached both hands out to her as he fell, but she hadn't reached out for him at all.

"He was drunk and fell down the stairs." Rose looked at her like that's all that happened.

"I *let* him fall down the stairs."

"Poppy, no," her mom pleaded. "That's not how it happened."

"You were there, standing in the background like you always did. Witness to his cruelty and Rose's and my destruction. You saw what happened. You know it's true. I could have tried to pull him back. I didn't. I didn't want to help him. I didn't care if he fell. I wanted him to die." It felt so good and so terrible to say those words out loud.

Her mom wiped at her tears.

Rose stood still, tears sliding down her face, but she never looked away.

Poppy turned to her mom. "Tell her what you saw. For once, say it out loud."

Mom didn't say anything. She shook her head and wiped at her tears.

Rose cupped her face. "Poppy, honey, you didn't do anything wrong. He did . . . He went after you. He hit you. You defended yourself. You let him know exactly how you felt about him. I wish it had been me," she confessed. "I was never brave enough to stand up to him like that. But you were. You did."

Mom stood and faced them. "Both of you were stronger than

I ever was. I'm sorry that you had to face him alone because I was too scared to do it for you. There's no excuse. And I have to live with it every day. But none of this was your fault. It was mine. I should have protected both of you. I should have left him. I didn't. And you both paid the price." She came to Poppy and put her hand on her shoulder. "You did what you had to do to survive. It wasn't for you to save him. He was the only one who could save himself, and each and every time he had a choice of whether to do that or hurt you, he chose wrong. He created his own fate. You can't reach for help from someone you've harmed over and over again and expect to get it."

"I could have been the better person."

"You had a split second to react," Rose pointed out.

Her mom rubbed her hand over Poppy's back. "What if you had tried to grab him? With his size and weight and the momentum carrying him down, he would have taken you with him. You could have been seriously injured or killed, too. I can live with losing him. I wouldn't want to live if I lost you."

In that moment Poppy understood why her mother always looked so sad and had spent the last three years barely living her life. She didn't want to truly live while her children were still suffering.

It had taken Rose coming home, looking and sounding like she'd moved on with her life, encouraging them to do the same, for the healing to begin.

Even though Poppy felt wrecked right now, she knew this was the first step toward reclaiming her life.

And that meant forgiving her mom for being weak, because

Poppy understood all too well what it felt like to be trapped with her father and helpless to do anything about it. Or so it seemed.

She pulled her mom in for a hug. Rose embraced both of them with a ferocity that seemed to repair all the fractured pieces of their bond. It felt like for the first time they were a real family again, helping each other, loving each other.

They stood in the center of the kitchen like that for a long moment before they drew apart.

Her mom brushed her hand over Poppy's hair. "I wondered why you were late coming home today from the sandwich shop. I love it. You're so beautiful."

She ran her fingers through the short strands. "Thank you."

"Both of my girls are," Mom said. "You're both so strong. And I hope now we can all heal together and be a family again, but this time a kind, loving family who supports each other."

Poppy eyed Rose. "I can't believe you betrayed your boyfriend and best friend."

"I didn't," Rose quickly assured her. "You didn't let me finish explaining what happened."

"Is there any good explanation for sleeping with your best friend's fiancé?"

"How about, it happened a year ago before Maggie ever met Marc?"

Poppy felt foolish for jumping to conclusions. "Oh."

"Yeah. Oh. It's not like we had a relationship." Rose glanced at their mom, then focused on Poppy again. "It was a very rare-for-me one-night stand. And it's one of those crazy coincidences that really do sometimes happen. I never saw him again until he walked into the bar and Maggie introduced him as her fiancé." She recounted the whole story. "It's all been a whirlwind. But Maggie and Gray both know now. It's all out in the open. We're all going to move on with our lives. In fact, Gray will be here shortly to pick me up for our double date."

Poppy couldn't believe it. "You're dating Marc's cousin and Maggie is marrying Marc and you slept with Marc and everyone is okay with this?"

"Yes." Rose sighed. "I know it's weird. Crazier things have happened and worked out."

"Maybe." Poppy sounded unconvinced. "Something like that doesn't just fade away, but if you're all going to try to make it work . . . okay."

"Great." Rose looked relieved. "I really don't want to talk about it anymore. What's important is how you're feeling right now."

Poppy sucked in a breath and really thought about it. "I think I'm okay. I've been holding all that in for a long time. My head is kind of spinning."

Rose touched her arm. "Maybe you should think about seeing someone you can talk to, who can help you work through your feelings. It helped me."

"Maybe. Right now, I'm just trying to find the me I used to be, so that I can be the me I want to be. Does that make sense?"

"Totally. I felt so lost when I left here. It took a long time to unearth who I was before things got bad, then find my way to who I really wanted to be."

"You haven't done so bad." Poppy wanted so much of what Rose had now. A career. A great guy. Her own place. Inner peace.

Rose was lucky she'd gotten away when she did and worked to overcome what their father had done to them. Poppy had been stuck these last three years. Not anymore. Her new, brighter future started now.

Rose brushed her hand up Poppy's arm. "It took a lot of introspection, making mistakes and fixing them, not listening to his voice in my head anymore, and discovering who I am and what I like and want in order to move forward. But I feel like I'm the best version of me right now, even if I am a work in progress and always will be."

What a great way to look at things.

Poppy didn't feel like the best version of herself at the moment, but she'd made some small changes. They felt right. They were a step in the right direction. Her new look would help her get a better job. She'd taken a page out of her sister's book and fixed up her room, allowing herself to feel like she deserved to have nice things and feel good about herself.

She'd even looked up college courses at a few of the schools nearby. She'd taken a few here and there, but never found her focus or drive to finish. Now, she wanted to get her degree.

The doorbell rang.

Rose smiled. "Mom, would you get that? It's probably Gray. I just need a minute with Poppy before I go."

"Sure." Her mom brushed her hand over Rose's shoulder before she left the kitchen.

"What is it?" Poppy asked, concerned her sister really did blame her for their father's death.

"I know it's hard to put the past behind you. I understand that what he did to you was terrible. I want you to know that I'm here for you anytime you want to talk, or even if you just need me to be there so you're not alone in it. There were so many times I wanted to call you, or come and see you and just be with you because you got it. You were the only one who knew what I was going through."

"I'm sorry I pushed you away every time you tried."

"I understand." Rose was the only one who truly did understand Poppy. "I wish I'd been braver back then, and strong enough those first couple of years to help you before it got so bad you felt like no one could help you."

"Don't." Poppy stopped her there. "You did what you had to do. I understand that now."

"And you did what you had to do. No matter what you might think, it's not your fault. You need to believe that, because I do. It was an accident that could have been a worse tragedy. Let it go. Let him go. And let's be sisters again."

Poppy threw herself into Rose's open arms. "I want that so much."

"Me, too." Rose squeezed her tight, then let her loose and wiped away the tears rolling down Poppy's cheeks. "I love you."

"I love you, too." They needed to say it more to each other.

They both heard their mom greeting Gray in the other room.

Poppy caught Rose's eye. "Mom protected me that night.

She told the cops he was drunk and slipped at the top of the stairs and that she was the one who'd been arguing with him. She could have gotten into a lot of trouble if they didn't believe her story."

"I'm so glad she came through for you when it really mattered. But I want you to always remember, you did not cause the fall. And saving yourself isn't the same as being responsible for his death."

Rose hugged her again with the same ferocity as before.

Poppy held on for a minute, then stepped back and waved Rose away. "Go. Gray's waiting for you."

Rose smiled and headed out of the kitchen.

Poppy followed and felt a rush of happiness for her sister when Gray smiled at her like he hadn't seen her in a year. Rose's eyes went wide when Gray handed her the gorgeous bouquet of pink roses.

Rose buried her face in the blooms, inhaling the heady scent.

Poppy smiled at Gray. "Those are her favorite." She thought of the pictures Rose had kept all these years.

"She told me you used to draw them for her when you were kids."

"Rose has a big heart. She's sentimental. Sweet, like those roses. Be sure to treat her like you would the delicate blooms."

"I will. But roses are also strong and resilient."

"Just like her," they said in unison.

"You guys." Rose blinked back tears.

Gray hooked his arm around Rose's waist, drew her close, and kissed her forehead.

The gesture was sweet and protective. Everything Rose needed and deserved.

Their mom sighed and watched with a soft smile on her face.

Poppy took the flowers from Rose. "I'll put these in water and take them upstairs to your room."

"Thank you."

Gray took Rose's hand. "It was nice to see both of you. I wish we could stay longer, but if we don't head out, we'll be late meeting Maggie and Marc." He didn't look the least bit enthusiastic about it.

"Have a good night," their mom said.

Poppy nodded her good-bye, waited for them to leave, then headed into the kitchen with the flowers.

Mom followed her. "They look so good together."

"He makes her happy. She glows when she's with him."

"Do you think this thing with Marc will get in the way of them being together?" The worry in Mom's question matched the concern in her eyes.

Poppy arranged Gray's thoughtful gift in the vase she found under the sink. She wasn't worried about the couple at all. "Those two are already in love with each other, they just don't know it yet."

Chapter Eighteen

*R*ose took Gray's hand the second the valet helped her out of the car. The wind kicked up and caught the ends of her black and white scarf skirt, blowing it back against her legs. She pressed her free hand between her thighs to keep it from blowing up and giving everyone a show.

Gray chuckled. "I love the skirt."

"It seems to have a mind of its own." Thankfully they walked under the portico outside the seaside restaurant and it blocked the wind.

Gray held the door open for her to step into the restaurant and her nerves kicked up. He stopped a few feet from the hostess and held up her hand in his. "What's wrong?"

She loosened her death grip and frowned. "Sorry. I'm nervous."

"Why?"

She met his earnest gaze. "You know why."

He pressed the back of her hand to his chest. "It's going to be fine."

"Are you sure? Because you hardly said anything to me in

the car, except that you liked my mom, and Poppy looked stunning."

"I almost didn't recognize her from yesterday to today. It's like I met two different people."

"You did. Lost Poppy and coming-out-of-her-cocoon Poppy."

Gray glanced into the dining area, then back at her, with an uneasy look.

She grimaced. "I really don't want you or Maggie to feel uncomfortable tonight, or ever, when we're all together."

He shrugged but didn't pull off casual. "I'm fine. It's just dinner."

"Gray." She wanted to believe him, but ever since she told him, it felt like he was holding back in a way. He spoiled her with the flowers, said all the right things, held her hand, kissed her, but it still worried her that after dinner last night, he drove her straight home, gave her a chaste and sweet kiss at the door, and left.

"It's just . . ." He looked away.

Her heart sank. "You can't do this, can you?"

His head whipped back to her. "What? It's just dinner."

"No." She shook her head, tears threatening to spill from her eyes. "You can't do us."

He drew her close and kissed her like his life depended on it. She sank into the kiss and him, letting everything he put into it fill her up and make her believe he had no intention of letting her go.

He ended the kiss with a sweet press of his lips to hers,

then stared down into her eyes. "You and me is easy. I see you, I think about you, everything feels good. But you're right, I stalled out last night after dinner. I wanted to take you to my hotel and make love to you all night and instead I backed off because of something you did that had nothing to do with us. I spent all morning trying to distract myself with business calls. But I barely paid attention to them because I was talking myself out of tracking you down to rectify my mistake. We didn't know each other when you met Marc. You had no idea we'd meet later. But you're right, this is weird, so I'm just going to acknowledge that and get through this night with us all knowing, and let it be odd and strained or whatever so we can move on."

"Okay. Let's go be weird together." She laughed with him when he smiled down at her.

"Sounds like a plan." He took her hand, led her over to the hostess, and said, "Gray Pearson."

"The other Mr. Pearson and his guest are already seated. Follow me."

It occurred to Rose that if she married Gray, she and Maggie would both be Mrs. Pearson.

"What?" Gray asked, side-eyeing her as they followed the hostess toward the wall of glass windows overlooking the Pacific Ocean. "You're smiling about something."

"It just occurred to me that you and Marc are both Mr. Pearson and Maggie will be Mrs. Pearson."

He stopped a few feet from the table where Maggie and

Marc stared at them, and turned to her like he'd read her mind about his wife being Mrs. Pearson, too, and smiled. "It has a nice ring to it, doesn't it?"

She stared at him, falling into the depths of his blue-green eyes and the assurance there that he liked it a lot. "Yes. It does."

Gray tugged on her hand. "Let's wish them a happy life."

Marc stood as they approached the table. "Gray," he said by way of hello to his cousin, with barely any warmth. For Rose, he smiled. "It's so good to see you again, Rose. Especially now that everything is out in the open."

"Marc," she said, and nodded, keeping her response neutral and giving Maggie a warm smile. "I love your dress."

Maggie's smile brightened. "Thank you." She brushed her hand down the pretty purple and white floral sun dress.

Gray didn't say anything to Marc; instead he held his hand out to Maggie. "You look amazing in it."

Maggie shook Gray's hand, then Gray held Rose's chair out for her. They ended up seated with Rose and Maggie opposite each other by the window, and Gray and Marc opposite each other on the end.

"Your server, Rochelle, will be here in just a moment to take your drink orders. Until then, look over the menu, including the chef specials, and have a wonderful evening."

"I could use a drink," Marc said to the table at large. "Come on, guys, let's just have a good evening and a nice meal and forget the rest."

Maggie tried to do just that. "Can you believe this place? It's amazing. And the view . . ."

Rose stared out the window with her friend. "We lived here most of our lives and never dined like this."

"Thank you, Gray, for picking the restaurant. It's beautiful."

"My pleasure, Maggie. I've wined and dined business associates here a few times when they came to town to golf at Pebble Beach."

"Do you play?" Maggie asked.

"Not as well as I'd like, but it helps to lose sometimes to the people you're trying to win business from."

"There are some amazing tennis courts here, too. Have you played down here?" Rose asked, trying to keep the conversation going.

"A few times. I prefer playing in Silicon Valley. It tends to be cold and foggy here in the morning. As you know."

"True."

The waitress arrived. "I'm Rochelle. Welcome. Can I get you something to drink?"

"Thank god, yes," Marc said. "I'll have a double scotch on the rocks."

Rochelle nodded and looked to Maggie, who stared at the smaller drink menu. "I'd love to try the peach sangria."

"You'll love it. It's sweet and fresh and so summery tasting." Rochelle looked at Rose. "And you?"

Rose shrugged one shoulder. "You sold me. I'll have the same."

"And you, sir?" Rochelle asked Gray.

"Is Jack behind the bar?"

Rochelle beamed. "Yes. He is."

"Please tell him Gray Pearson is here and would love one of his whiskey cocktails."

"Absolutely. He'll be so happy you asked." She turned to the table at large. "Would any of you like to start with an appetizer? The lobster fondue is my favorite."

"Oh, let's," Maggie said.

Gray leaned in to Rose. "You'll probably like the crab artichoke poppers."

Rose smiled at him for remembering her love of spinach artichoke dip. "That sounds amazing."

"I'll add it to the order. Anything else?"

Gray and Marc shook their heads no and Rochelle left to put in their order.

"Maggie told me that you helped fix the cake situation," Marc said to Gray. "Thanks. I want her to have the wedding of her dreams, and the cake is a big part of that."

"It was no big deal. All I did was use a contact to make another for her. But I'm glad it worked out." Gray turned to Maggie. "Were you able to get something close to what you wanted?"

"Actually, the baker had an amazing idea for the cake that she could do in time. It's going to be gorgeous."

Rose was happy to hear it. "So maybe it worked out for the best."

Maggie nodded. "Tomorrow is the wedding rehearsal and rehearsal dinner. Both our immediate families will meet for the first time. And of course you guys will be there."

Rose put her hand over Maggie's on the table. "It's going to be great."

"Is your dad coming?" Gray asked Marc.

"What do you mean?" Maggie turned to Marc. "Why wouldn't your dad come?" Maggie breathed hard and stared at Marc, who glared at Gray.

Marc turned to Maggie. "He's being difficult—"

Gray scoffed.

Marc glared at him again. "Something to say?"

Gray shook his head. "No."

"I didn't think so." Marc gave Gray a shut-up look and faced Maggie again. "My dad and I argued. We do it a lot. We said some things we didn't mean. He made some demands and I refused to give in because I'm an adult, not a child he gets to order around."

The conversation should be private, but Rose and Gray were their reluctant audience. Rose watched Gray as she listened to Marc and saw the exact opposite expressions on Gray's face than the calm, it's-not-a-big-deal look Marc wore.

"What did you argue about?" Maggie asked.

"The same thing we always clash on. How I live my life." Marc rolled his eyes to add to the exasperated tone.

"I thought he was happy for us?" Maggie sounded nervous and unsure.

"He is. He wants to see me settled down and married. He'll be there tomorrow," Marc assured her. "I'm his only child. There's no way he's going to miss my wedding. Trust me, this will blow over. It always does."

The almost imperceptible shake of Gray's head didn't make Rose believe Marc's words.

"You're sure?" Maggie asked. "Because we can't get married without your dad and his girlfriend there."

"They'll be there. Just like my mom, they're driving down tomorrow afternoon."

A man arrived with their drinks and Gray stood and shook the guy's hand while he balanced the tray in his other hand.

"Jack. You didn't have to bring them yourself."

"I've only got a minute. The bar is busy as usual, but I wanted to say hi and thank you again for the help. You're a lifesaver."

"Just doing a friend a favor, that's all." Gray turned to them. "Jack, this is my cousin Marc and his fiancée, Maggie. They're getting married this Saturday."

Marc and Maggie said hello.

Gray smiled at Rose. "And this is my girlfriend, Rose."

Jack's eyes went wide. "It's really nice to meet you. And to see him having a good time with someone."

"It's nice to meet you, too. How do you two know each other?"

Jack glanced at Gray, then back at her. "Um . . ." He started handing out their drinks.

Gray filled her in. "I dated his sister a few years back."

"Things didn't work out for them, but Gray and I are still friends," Jack added. "Personally, I think my sister screwed up. And she probably knows that, but it's a pattern with her." Jack shrugged. "You guys have a good night. I've got to get back behind the bar." He turned to Gray. "Bring her back soon."

"I will." Gray slid his arm along the back of her chair and brushed his fingers against her arm. He picked up his drink and held it aloft to her.

She tapped her wine glass to his tumbler, gave him a smile, then sipped her drink as he did the same.

"Why did you and his sister break up?" Marc asked. "Were you too busy working to pay attention to her?"

"Yes," Gray readily admitted. "But that didn't excuse her cheating on me."

She put her hand on his thigh and squeezed to let him know she sympathized.

He glanced down at her hand on him and acknowledged the intimate gesture with a desire-filled look that was also warm and affectionate.

"I'm really sorry, Gray." Maggie sat back in her chair. "That sucks. I'm sure at the time, it hurt deeply."

Gray turned away from Rose and smiled at Maggie. "It did. That experience makes me appreciate the open and honest relationship I have with Rose even more."

Marc narrowed his gaze on Gray, but Gray didn't see it because he was looking at Rose.

She understood the undercurrents between Gray and Marc because of their past, but there was something more going on tonight, and it wasn't just about her and Marc's past encounter.

Rose had hoped they'd find a friendly balance because they were each with the one they wanted to be with now, but it didn't seem like Marc wanted to do that.

"No one is ever completely honest in a relationship," Marc said, taking a sip of his drink. "You can't seriously mean you tell Rose everything."

Gray left that hanging while Rochelle arrived with their

appetizers. Rose wondered if Gray was keeping something from her, but quickly dismissed it as just another way Marc was trying to instigate something between them.

Maggie saved the conversation by changing the subject to something much more neutral. "It's a beautiful night. Have you two had time to go to the beach and walk on the sand? Marc and I spent an hour down there before dinner. It's so lovely."

Rose moaned over one of the crab artichoke poppers before she could answer. "Gray had to work all day and I was at home, spending time with my mom and sister. But maybe tonight we'll take a walk before he drives me home."

"You're not staying with him?" Marc asked, and casually dipped a piece of bread in the lobster fondue.

"That's none of your business," Maggie scolded him.

"What? Why? Is there trouble in paradise for you two?"

Maggie frowned. "Marc, stop. How they spend their time together is their business."

Marc shrugged. "He introduced her as his girlfriend. I just thought they were . . . you know . . . But maybe I'm wrong."

Maggie shook her head and rolled her eyes. "Excuse him. I thought we could sit down to a meal and not poke at the elephant in the room, but I guess we can't." She glared at Marc. "So what is it? You're happy they aren't sleeping together yet? You hope they don't? You want to stick it to Gray for some reason? Or maybe you're just mad at Rose for telling the truth when you wanted to hide it?"

"Babe, no. Come on. Poking at Gray is what I do," he teased with a grin. "He knows that. I didn't mean anything by it."

"Well, now it's a little more personal, don't you think, because Rose is my best friend, Gray and Rose are together, and I'm marrying you? Though I'm thinking twice about it if you're still hung up on her," she snapped with irritation.

"Wait. Whoa. No." Marc sat up straighter. "This has gotten way out of hand. There is nothing going on between me and Rose."

Maggie glared at Marc. "Funny. That's not what I suggested, but that's where your head went."

Gray put his hand over Rose's tangled ones in her lap. She grasped his in both of hers and kept her head down.

"Gray, tell her," Marc pleaded. "I'm just messing with you."

He squeezed Rose's hand, but addressed Maggie. "He's just trying to get under my skin for reasons that have nothing to do with Rose or you." Gray held Marc's gaze. "Stop before you say something you can't take back. If Maggie and I can accept it happened and move on, then you should, too."

"I did a long time ago. I met Maggie and fell in love with her. This whole thing is just weird."

Maggie took a sip of her drink. "It wouldn't have been if you'd told the truth months ago when you saw pictures of her in my apartment. Instead you lied and then you asked her to lie, too."

Marc sighed. "Babe, come on. We went over all this yesterday. I'm the asshole. I know. I'm sorry. But now everyone knows everything and it's no big deal."

"Then stop acting like it is and butting into Gray's relationship with Rose," Maggie snapped.

Rose flinched.

Gray linked his fingers through hers and squeezed. "It's okay, Maggie. Marc is right. This is an odd thing to have happen between all of us. Now that we've all acknowledged it, let's just have a nice dinner and talk about something else."

"It's a beautiful night out," Maggie said, talking about the same nothing again to get them all to change the subject.

"Did you know the first full moon of summer is called a strawberry moon?" Rose went along with the new topic.

Maggie leaned in and stared at her like she was fascinated. "You don't say. That is interesting. And one of my favorite fruits."

"I love them in daiquiris." Rose smirked at Maggie.

"One of the better ways to consume them. Remember the time we got wasted on strawberry margaritas on spring break?"

"What year of college was that?" Gray asked.

"Sophomore year of high school," Rose informed him. "The year my father let me finally stay out past seven o'clock."

"Seriously," Marc scoffed.

Gray bumped his shoulder to hers. "You rebel."

"Not so much. I threw up all over—"

"Tony Rupert's shoes," she and Maggie said in unison, and burst into giggles.

Rose blushed. "He'd just asked me to homecoming."

"Did he still take you?" Marc asked.

She shook her head. "My dad wouldn't let me go."

"Why?" Gray asked.

She and Maggie exchanged a look. "Because I was two minutes late getting home that night."

"Man, your dad was really strict." Marc dipped another piece of bread in the fondue.

"Yes, he was," Maggie said softly, probably remembering, like Rose, that her dad had shoved Rose into a wall so hard it left a baseball-sized bruise on her shoulder.

Gray rubbed his hand up her back and under her hair and kept it there, a soft and steady pressure that grounded her. "So no more margaritas after that, I guess."

"Oh, no," Maggie said. "Margaritas are forever."

Rose tilted her head toward Gray. "I just learned not to drink so many at a time."

Gray laughed with her.

"Remember that time we snuck out and went to that pool party at some girl's house and you got wasted doing keg stands?" Marc asked Gray.

Gray dove into the fondue, too, but before he took a bite he eyed Marc. "You mean every time I took you with me to a party and you ended up wasted and I was always your designated driver?"

Marc smirked. "I do remember that. Kinda. It's all a bit fuzzy."

"Do you even remember summers as a teen?" Gray teased.

"Not really," Marc admitted.

The guys clinked glasses across the table and she and Maggie exchanged relieved smiles that all was as it should be and everyone was getting along again.

Rochelle arrived again. They ordered dinner and got another round of drinks. The conversation flowed and everyone silently agreed to talk about things that happened in their past. She and Maggie dominated most of the conversation because they had a lot of shared memories.

By the end of dinner, all of them were back to being just two couples out for an evening together, making new memories.

Rochelle asked, "Who wants dessert?"

"I'm stuffed." Rose sat back in her chair completely satisfied after her delicious steak and lobster tail all drenched in garlic butter.

Maggie snatched up the menu. "I probably won't fit in my wedding dress after this decadent meal, but I am so not passing up dessert."

"Whatever you want, babe. I'll help you burn off those calories later."

Maggie gave him a seductive smile. "I look forward to it." Maggie turned to Rochelle. "I'll have the cheesecake."

Marc nodded. "Make that two."

Gray handed Rochelle his credit card. "Put it all on this." He turned to Maggie and Marc. "You two enjoy dessert. I'm taking Rose for a walk on the beach."

"It's cold out," Maggie warned.

"I'll keep her warm," Gray assured her.

Gray stood and helped Rose out of her seat.

Rose smiled at the couple, sitting close, smiling up at her. "Have a nice night."

"Oh, you know we will," Marc assured her.

From the looks on Maggie's and Gray's faces, she guessed they caught the double meaning in Marc's words. Maybe he didn't mean anything by it, but he sure didn't choose his words carefully.

"Good night," she said, walking past Gray toward the entrance. She walked right out the door without realizing Gray wasn't right behind her and stopped.

He came out the door a minute later. "I had to sign the check."

"I'm sorry. I just wanted to get out of there."

"He didn't mean anything by it." Gray didn't sound convinced. That was just his go-to excuse for Marc.

"Let's just go."

He took her hand before she walked away. "Hold up. No. We aren't ending the night like this. The moon is out. Granted it's not strawberry-colored, but I bet you look beautiful in its glow. And I really want to walk with you on the beach."

She sighed and sucked in a breath, resetting her attitude. "Thank you for dinner. It was delicious."

"The company could have been better mannered, but I got to sit next to you and touch you and I learned a lot of things about you through Maggie's stories. You two really have been best friends forever."

"Kindergarten until now. I don't ever want to lose her."

"You won't."

"What about you? That last comment he made . . ." Her stomach tightened with dread.

"He said it best. He's an asshole. I'm used to it."

"You should have made him pay for dinner after that innuendo."

"Believe me, that's the last check I'm picking up for him. But it won't be the last time we're all together. And he's probably going to say something insensitive again. I'm going to leave it to Maggie to shut him up. Instead, I'm going to remember that I get to do this any time I want." Gray slipped his hand along her cheek and drew her in for a soft kiss.

"Yes. You can do that any time you want."

His devilish grin said there was a lot more to come. But instead of kissing her again, he took her hand and drew her around the building to a path and stairs that led down to the beach. The wind had died down to a soft breeze, but it was the California coast at night, so it was cold. She slipped off her strappy heels and held them in her hand. Gray pulled off his shoes and socks and rolled up his slacks.

"You have really big feet."

He wiggled his toes in the sand. "Compared to your dainty ones, yeah." He stood and took her hand. They walked along the beach away from the restaurant, past an outcropping of rocks that hid them from the other diners. Beyond that, another stretch of secluded beach bordered the coastal road above them.

The crashing waves lulled them as they walked closer to the water. There were a few others out enjoying the evening but they were far enough away that it felt like she and Gray had the beach to themselves.

"I'm sorry." She didn't say why, because he'd sat through that awkward dinner, quiet and also trying his best to make it all seem normal.

Gray stopped and she turned to him. "You don't have to apologize. It was Marc. And I hate that he made you feel like you'd done something wrong."

"I did. I went home with a stranger and because I didn't know the kind of man he is, these are the consequences."

"You thought you'd never see him again."

"That did not work out so well for me. Or for you and Maggie," she sulked. "It feels like this is ruining the happiness they should be feeling leading up to their wedding. It feels like it's coming between us, especially when Marc uses it to taunt you."

"He's an asshole."

"I'm going to get that needlepointed on a pillow and give it to you for Christmas."

Gray grinned. "There's the spirit. We'll be together at Christmas. Something for both of us to look forward to."

She laughed under her breath. "Any time I get to spend with you is something to look forward to and enjoy."

"Then let's stop talking about him." Gray sat and pulled her in front of him and tugged her hand for her to sit between his legs.

She did and leaned back into him.

He wrapped his arms around her and kissed the side of her head as they watched the waves roll in and the stars sparkle overhead.

"This is really nice." She snuggled into him and felt his cock thicken against her back.

He brushed his hands up and down her forearms and kissed

her head again, dipping his head low to her ear. "I desperately want to touch you."

Out here, in the dark, the waves crashing so loud no one could hear them, it felt as if they were completely alone in an intimate bubble all their own.

"I really want you to touch me." She shifted, rubbing her back against his thick dick.

His hands slipped under her arms and brushed across her belly, then came up and cupped her breasts. She was wearing a thin black cashmere sweater with a lace-trimmed bra beneath. She arched into his hands as he caressed and molded her breasts in his big hands. He squeezed her tight nipples between his thumbs and fingers, plucking at the aching buds.

She moaned and pressed her thighs tight to ease the ache building between them.

One hand left her aching breast so he could pull her hair away from her neck. He kissed her softly and slipped his other hand up under her sweater, rubbed it over both breasts, then freed one from the bra cup and palmed her breast, with her hard nipple trapped between two of his fingers. "God, you feel so good. I want more."

She turned her head into the deep, penetrating kiss as he tugged her nipple, sending a wave of heat racing through her system.

He broke the kiss, wrapped his arm around her middle, pulled her up on his lap and back against him. One hand went back up under her sweater to her bare breast, the other hand gently slid up the outside of her leg, bringing her skirt up to her hip. He took his time, fondling her breast, kissing her neck, and sweeping that hand up and down her thigh until finally his fingers dipped between her legs and up and over her mound. He rubbed the heel of his hand against her clit and brushed his fingers over her damp panties.

"I wake up to dreams of you riding me hard," he confessed. "I have to wrap my hand around myself. But the relief I get is nothing compared to how it will feel to be deep inside you." He pressed against her clit again, and her inner muscles quaked from his touch and his words.

His cock pulsed at her backside. "Damn, sweetheart, you are so beautiful." He plucked at her nipple with his fingers and pulled her panties aside so he could touch her wet folds, his fingers barely grazing her heated skin.

"Gray, please."

"Greedy. I like it." He shifted her so he could kiss her at the same time he plunged one finger, then two deep inside her. She gasped and he took the kiss deeper, sliding his tongue along hers as his fingers caressed in and out of her slick vagina, her inner muscles clenching to pull him back in.

"That's it sweetheart, let go."

Her skirt brushed her sensitive thighs and his fingers went deep, stroking her as he kissed her again and pressed the heel of his hand to her swollen clit. She rocked against his hand, forgetting where they were and that anyone could come up on them. She lost herself in his kiss and the wonderful way he made her feel. In a passion-fueled haze, she came with a groan he swallowed with one last deep kiss before he gathered her close and held her in his arms.

"So damn beautiful." He kissed her on the head.

His thick erection was still cuddled up against her backside. She rolled her hips back into him.

"Don't. I'm so damn close. Just give me a sec."

"Do you have a condom?"

"Baby, I'll only be able to manage getting inside you before I lose it."

"I'll take it."

He squeezed her tight to his body. "That's not how I imagined our first time."

"I mean it, Gray. I want to feel you inside me. Right now."

He glanced around, then leaned to one side and pulled out his wallet. With one hand he found the condom and shifted so she was sitting on his thighs. Behind her he undid his slacks. She shifted just enough to slide her hand up and down his length while he opened the condom.

"Hurry," she said, wanting to feel him fill her.

"You're distracting me." He put his hand around hers on his dick. "You have no idea how much I like having your hands on me."

"I bet you'll like being inside me better."

He groaned, pulled her hand away, rolled the condom on, and took her by the hips. "You're sure?"

She shifted up on her knees. "Please."

His hands went under her skirt and pulled it back and over

him. The thick head of his penis rubbed against her soft folds. There was a sharp tug on her panties to get them out of the way, and then all she had to do was sink back on him. She groaned at the heady sensation of him seated deep inside her.

"Don't move." He breathed deep and his dick pulsed, sending out waves of heat through her system. All she wanted to do was move and intensify the glorious feelings. He was very close. But he slid his hand around her hip and found her clit with the pad of his finger and softly stroked it in circles. She rocked against him, unable to move up and down too much in their position, but, god, the rippling pleasure that shot through her.

"You feel so good, sweetheart. I should have taken you back to my hotel, laid you out on the bed, and fucked you all night."

"Later," she said, pushing down hard on him, taking him deep as his finger swept over that sweet spot and her muscles clenched with another orgasm. Gray gripped her hips and brought her up and down on his hard shaft and held her there as he spilled himself inside her.

His forehead rested on the back of her neck, his breath heaving in and out as his body relaxed under hers, but his grip on her hips didn't loosen. He held her close.

"I know that didn't last very long."

It didn't matter to her, because knowing that he wanted her that bad, that touching her and getting her off made him that combustible . . . It made it all the better. And he'd made sure she got off again before him when he had every right to just take what she offered.

She watched the water rush up the shore and smiled because

her happiness needed a way to express itself. She glanced over her shoulder and met his steady gaze.

He smiled back. "That was so damn good."

"That was amazing."

He hugged her to him. "You're amazing."

"I'm pretty sure you get the title, since I had far more fun than you did."

"Not true. I think making you come is my new favorite thing to do." He kissed her softly, pouring in all the passion they'd shared but in a much more sensual and slow way that strengthened the bond being forged between them. Nothing had felt as raw and intimate and satisfying as the two of them kissing after making love for the first time, knowing it was the beginning of something much more profound and beautiful than they'd ever experienced.

"I didn't plan this," he said, nuzzling his nose at her ear. "But whenever you're near, I just want to touch you and be close to you."

"I feel the same way." She was still sitting on his lap, straddling him backward.

He brushed his hands up and down her arms. "You're getting cold."

"There is quite a breeze blowing up under my skirt."

Gray laughed with her. "Sorry if you've got sand in places you don't want it."

"Luckily the long skirt and being on top helped with most of that, but you're going to have to help me up."

"Anything for you, sweetheart." He took her by the hips

again and lifted her as she stood. Her panties fell down one leg and landed at her ankle in the sand. "Oops. How did that happen?" The innocent look on his face made her laugh.

She eyed him. "Someone tore them because they were in the way."

"They were. I'll buy you new ones."

She grinned. "Sacrifices sometimes have to be made for the greater good."

He chuckled and grabbed her panties off the sand, wadded them around the condom trash, and stuffed them in his pocket. Zipped and buttoned, he stood next to her and shook his legs. "I think I have sand on my ass."

They both laughed at that. But he looked her up and down, his gaze filled with wonder and appreciation. "You really do glow when you're turned on and totally satisfied."

"Then I bet I look that way every time we're together."

He picked up their shoes, handed hers over, hooked his arm around her shoulders, and they walked back toward the restaurant.

"Do you want to come back to my hotel?"

She leaned into him. "Actually, if you don't mind, I'd like to go home and check on my sister. She and I had a fight earlier that turned into a big revelation about my father's death and I want to be sure she's okay. She went to a dark place during our conversation and though I think we ended things in a good place, I need to be sure."

"Absolutely. But what did you find out about your dad's death?"

"Poppy and he were arguing upstairs. My dad hit her. This time, Poppy didn't just take it. She fought back. She said some very true but terrible things to him. He went after her again. She pushed him. He was stumbling drunk, went after Poppy again, lost his balance, and fell down the stairs."

Gray sat beside her on the stairs leading back up to the parking lot so they could put on their shoes. "Oh, my god. That had to have been traumatic."

"Our whole lives with my dad was traumatic. Anyway, she's been carrying around the guilt of thinking that if she'd reached out for him, tried to help in some way, he wouldn't have died."

"Sounds like he could have very well taken her down those stairs with him."

"Exactly."

"Then yes, you definitely should go home and check on her and make sure she knows it wasn't her fault."

"I think she feels guiltier about the fact that she didn't want to help him and she's glad he's dead."

"Sounds like he deserved that for treating you and her the way he did."

She put her hand on his face, leaned in, and kissed him. "You're a good man, Gray. I appreciate it so much that you're kind and understanding and sexy as hell and too tempting for one man to be."

He grinned, then teased, "So you really do like me."

"I more than like you," she admitted, feeling a warmth in her heart she'd never felt for anyone but him.

He kissed her again, his lips soft and warm against hers, then looked her in the eye. "I have some really big feelings for you, too." He brushed his nose against hers and smiled. "Come on. Let me take you home."

She took his hand and stood with him. "It really is starting to feel like that now."

He hooked his arm around her waist as they ascended the steep stairs. "That's good, sweetheart. Next time, you won't stay away so long, and you'll have your mom and sister whenever you need them."

"I've missed them, but at the same time I didn't because I couldn't go back to that toxic environment. But now, it's getting to be what I always hoped it would be between us."

They made it up to the parking lot outside the restaurant.

"They aren't the only ones who are different. You've changed, too, since you left. This is a whole new chapter for all of you."

"And this time I have you in my life."

He squeezed her to his side and glanced down at her as they walked to the valet. "Yes. You do. Though I kind of want to keep you all to myself." He handed the ticket to the valet.

"So you're not done with me yet?"

"We haven't even gotten started."

"Oh, I think we're off to a very good start."

He slid his hand down her hip and back up to the small of her back. "Yes, we are. And it's driving me crazy to know you have nothing on under this skirt."

"Good. Then you'll be thinking of me tonight and through

your meetings tomorrow until you see me again. I'm wearing a dress to the rehearsal, so you'll be wondering if I'm wearing panties or not."

"You're just going to tease me like that?"

"Tempt is more like it. And after the dinner, I'll be all yours."

He plastered his hand over her ass and pulled her close. "You're already all mine, but I like your plan. Just don't expect me to wait until *after* the dinner to find out what, if anything, you have on under the dress." He didn't give her a chance to respond. His mouth crushed hers in a possessive and passion-fueled kiss that set her whole body on fire. She pressed close to him, feeling his desire, thick and hard against her belly.

"Hey you two, we can't afford another wildfire in this state," Maggie teased.

Gray broke the kiss with a disgruntled growl, but came up smiling for Maggie. "I can't seem to help myself."

Maggie held Marc's hand as he handed over his valet ticket to a young man. "We're going to go start our own fire. See you two tomorrow."

Rose waved to them and caught the look in Marc's eyes as he stared back at her. It was one of pure lust.

Gray must have caught the look, too, because he was all of a sudden standing between her and Marc. "Come on, sweetheart, it's time to go." He held the car door open for her, took his keys, and tipped the valet for bringing the car around.

She waved to Maggie as they drove away, noting that Marc hadn't taken his eyes off her. She didn't like it.

Why won't he just let it go?

She did and focused on the man who made her feel like she was the most desirable woman in the world, but also like a friend, because it was so easy to talk to him.

"Thank you for another wonderful night."

Gray glanced over at her long enough for her to see the anger in his eyes. "You're welcome, sweetheart. I had a really good time with you, too."

Yes, with her. Not with Marc at their table.

She put her hand on his thigh and rubbed it back and forth. "Don't let him spoil our night."

He put his hand over hers. "I'll be glad when the wedding is over and you and I can see each other without him around."

She turned her hand and linked her fingers with his. "We know where each other works, but I have no idea where you live in the Bay Area."

"I've got a house in the Los Altos hills. What about you?"

"Nothing quite that upscale, I'm afraid. I have a two-bedroom apartment in Santa Clara that costs the same as some people's mortgages."

"Do you have a roommate?"

"No. But I tend to work a lot from home and late at night, so I wanted a separate space for that. Believe me, they are two very small rooms."

"Maybe your sister will come to visit once in a while."

"I hope so."

"Come check out my place on Sunday. We'll both be back from the wedding. We can spend the day together before we go back to work on Monday." He pulled into the driveway at her mom's house.

"I'd love that."

"I'll barbecue. We'll relax and hang out. Bring a suit, or don't, and we'll go for a swim." The smirk on his face and hope in his eyes said he didn't want her to bring a swimsuit.

"Sounds like a lovely way to spend a Sunday afternoon."

"Any day I spend with you is a good day."

"Then you can have as many as you'd like because I really like being with you, too." She leaned over and kissed him. "Thank you again for tonight. I don't think I'll ever think of the beach or the sound of the ocean and not think about you."

He brushed the hair back from her face. "All I think about is you."

He kissed her one last time and she fell back in her seat.

"Don't get out."

He smirked. "But then I won't get one last chance to kiss you good night."

She leaned in and kissed him again. "You don't need an excuse to kiss me one more time."

"Oh, good." He pulled her in for another steamy kiss that spun out until the windows started to fog over.

He tried to pull her closer, but she ended up gouging her ribs on the console and pulled back, bracing her arm against her side. "Ow." She laughed, because trying to get it on in a car never gave anyone enough room to move.

"I'm sorry." Gray raked his hand over his hair. "This is crazy. Go before I can't let you go."

"Well, that sounds perfect."

Gray groaned. "You should not be so accommodating of my desire to hold on to you."

"Knowing that you feel that way . . . It means everything to me. Especially since I'm about to go and talk to my sister about our father. We never mattered to him."

Gray hooked his hand at the back of her neck and drew her close. "You matter, Rose. More than you know."

"I do know, Gray. I feel it from you every time we're together. So thank you again for a wonderful night and for how you care about me." She gave him a lovingly soft kiss, smiled at him because her heart felt so full of joy because of him, then slipped out of the car and closed the door.

She knew he would but it still made her feel good to know he waited for her to walk into the house, safe and sound, before he pulled out of the driveway.

The second she walked in the door, Poppy poked her head out of the kitchen, a plea and unease in her eyes. "Want some hot chocolate?"

Mom used to sneak them hot chocolate on those few nights Dad passed out drunk early and there was no way he'd catch them. It did her heart good to see Poppy remembering the good things they'd shared as kids. "I'd love some." And a chance to connect with Poppy on a much deeper level now that all the secrets and resentments were out in the open.

Chapter Nineteen

*P*oppy didn't know how Rose really felt after their encounter earlier. But Rose looked happy, and eager to sit across from her and drink hot chocolate in the quiet kitchen.

"How was the double date?"

"Awkward." Rose frowned and stared at the tabletop. "But also really great because I was with Gray."

"I put the flowers he gave you upstairs in your room."

"Thank you. But that's not what you waited up to talk to me about, is it?"

Poppy wrapped her hands around the warm mug and stared at the floating marshmallows. "Are you mad about what I told you?"

Rose reached across the table and put her hand over Poppy's. "No. Not even a little bit. It's okay to feel the way you feel. It's okay to not miss him. He made his choices that night. He suffered the consequences. Whether you could have stopped his fall down the stairs or not . . . You are here, safe and sound, and finally free to live your life. Stop punishing yourself, Poppy, for not doing something that could have hurt or killed you, too.

Stop beating yourself up for feeling free of him. Accept that part of your life is over. He can't hurt you anymore. Unless you let him, by not moving on and living the life you want to live. Go back to school. Find a job you actually like doing. Be with someone who treats you like you matter and like loving you is important."

"Is that what you've found with Gray?"

"Yes." Rose didn't hesitate. "I mean, I hope so. We haven't known each other that long, but I can tell you this: it took me a long time and a few mistakes to know in my heart that I'm worth loving. I deserve to be loved and treated with respect and kindness. I didn't know a man like Gray existed. I didn't know someone could feel that way about me. The way he expresses how he feels so easily . . . It both surprises me and feels so right all at the same time."

"But you slept with his cousin. Is he upset about that?"

"Naturally it bothers him. But he realizes that it happened long before we met. It was one night with a guy I barely knew. It's not like we dated. Gray and Maggie both know I want a relationship with Gray. I want something that will last. And right now, it feels like it will. I'm hoping we can spend a lot more time together away from Marc and Maggie, so that we can solidify the bond we already share, so that when we are together with them, there's no doubt who I care about and want to be with."

Poppy tilted her head. "Is Gray unsure of your feelings for him? Or Marc?"

"After tonight, I hope not." Rose's cheeks turned pink.

Poppy put her elbow on the table, her chin in her palm, and smiled at her sister. "What happened tonight? I bet I can guess," she teased, feeling lighter, and thinking this was how things should have been between them the last many years that Rose had been away. This is how she wanted things to be going forward, them sharing their lives and confiding the good and the bad to each other.

"Please don't." Rose sipped her cocoa. "As for Gray . . . It may seem like things are moving fast between us, but then again, it feels like I've known him forever. It feels like I've been looking for him all this time and now that I have him I don't want to ever lose him."

"You're in love with him."

Rose tried to hide her smile behind the mug as she took another sip. "Maybe I am."

"I'm happy for you." Poppy meant it. In fact, she wanted to take all of Rose's advice and start living her life. She didn't want to just escape her father's memory and the nightmare he'd left her in but actually be happy like her sister.

It wouldn't be easy. She had so much trauma to work on, but if Rose could get through it, mistakes and all, and come out the other side able to love herself and someone else, then Poppy at least had to try.

Rose took Poppy's hand across the table. "It is so good to see some of the old Poppy back. I love the new hairstyle. It suits you. You were always edgier than me."

Poppy raked her fingers through the shorter locks. "There's been this thing inside me that wanted to break free, but I didn't know what it was or how it would manifest. Cutting my hair, changing the color, it felt like . . . changing into someone I could grow into."

Rose squeezed her hand and smiled. "What do you want to do first?"

"I'm going to go back to school."

"What do you want to study?"

"Business. Maybe marketing."

"You should talk to Maggie about marketing. That's what she does. She loves it. I'm sure she can give you some insight into the day-to-day of her job."

Nervous butterflies fluttered in her belly. "Do you think she'd mind?"

"She'd love to help you. She thinks of you as a little sister, too."

"Really?" Poppy had lost touch with most of her close friends.

"Of course. Maggie loves you. Maybe you can come stay with me for a few days and you can shadow Maggie at work, so you can get a feel for working in her field."

"That would be awesome."

"You know, you were always great at math. Gray is the chief financial officer at his company. They're getting ready to go public. I bet he'd be happy to talk to you about business finance."

"I actually thought about going in that direction but thought maybe that was too . . . aspirational."

"Why? Because dad told you you weren't smart enough to do it, that you couldn't possibly succeed at it because you were too lazy or stupid or a woman who'd be overlooked by men?

None of that, or anything else he said like it, is true. I mean, yes, you'll have to work hard, but there's no reason you won't or can't find success in whatever you decide to do." Rose leaned forward. "The next time you hesitate to do something or say something or make a decision, ask yourself if the voice in your head is *his* or *yours*. Follow your own heart and mind, Poppy. The best revenge is being everything he said you weren't and knowing that you did it all on your own."

Poppy smiled. "Is that how you feel?"

"Yes. Every time it's like a big 'F you' to him. 'You said I can't, well, let me show you just how well I can.' And I did. You can, too."

Poppy found herself choked up. "I think I've been waiting for you to come back to show me and tell me that I don't have to be here anymore."

Rose held her hand firm in hers. "You do not need to be his victim anymore. You are a survivor. Live like nothing is holding you back, because nothing is, except yourself. Find a way to release it, and let it go, Poppy."

"This house used to feel like a prison. With him gone, it's better, but I still haven't been able to escape."

"There's a kind of safety in the familiar even if it is a torment. Don't be afraid of change. Be excited about all the possibilities waiting for you out there."

"You make it sound so easy. You've shown me I have options and people who will help."

"And I will be here for you no matter what you decide to do. I'm not going anywhere, Poppy. I intend for us to be the sisters we were when we were little girls drawing pictures for each other and we were the best of friends."

"I want that back, too."

"Then let this be a new beginning for both of us." Rose stood.

Poppy met her halfway. They held each other, and it felt so good to be connected to her sister again. She felt lighter and at ease, knowing that when Rose went home, it wasn't another ending, but a beginning to something new and better between them.

Rose stepped back and held Poppy by the shoulders. "I've missed you so much. I won't let time slip away from us ever again. In fact, anytime you want to stay with me, the door is always open. I'll even get you a key."

"Really? You mean it?"

"Yes." Rose hugged her again. "Who knows, maybe one day you'll be the maid of honor at my wedding."

Poppy stepped back and smiled. "Rose Pearson has a nice ring to it."

Rose hooked her arm around Poppy's shoulders and steered her out of the kitchen, flipping the light switch off on the way out. "It does. But right now I'm going to enjoy getting to know Gray better and spending time with him."

"I bet he wishes he was with you tonight. You've gotten three text messages in the last half hour."

Rose didn't bother to take out her phone as another text alert chimed, and they reached the top of the stairs. "We miss each other when we're not together."

"That's really nice." Poppy stopped outside her bedroom door and pushed it open. "Check it out." She waved her hand toward the room.

Rose stood in the doorway with her and stared at the pink poppy painting over the bed. "You hung it."

"It was a beautiful gift from my sister."

Rose bumped her shoulder to Poppy's. "And you put out some pictures of us when we were kids. A few of you and your friends in school."

Friends she hoped to reconnect with soon. "A reminder of the good things I have in my life."

"You deserve so much more, Poppy. Never doubt that again."

"If I do, I have you to remind me I'm worth it."

Rose hooked her hand at the back of Poppy's neck and pressed her forehead to Poppy's. "I love you. If you doubt everything else, always know that you are loved."

Poppy choked back the tears and pulled Rose in for a fierce hug. "I love you, too."

Rose's phone beeped with another incoming text.

"You better answer him before he thinks you're ignoring him."

"He knows I'm with you. It's fine. But I am tired. I think I'll turn in. See you in the morning." Rose walked down the hall to her room.

Poppy stepped out into the hallway. "Rose." She waited for her sister to turn back. "I know you protected me as long as you could growing up. Thank you."

Rose nodded, wiped away a tear, and went into her room.

Poppy backed up into hers, closed the door, and turned to

the poppy painting, her heart filled with love for her sister and a sense of well-being she hardly recognized but welcomed all the same.

Possibilities. She barely slept that night imagining what her life could be, the life Rose believed she deserved. A life Poppy had finally opened her heart to living to the fullest.

Chapter Twenty

2 days to Maggie's wedding . . .

Rose pulled out her phone to read the text from Gray, but couldn't help reading the ones from last night one more time.

GRAY: My bed is cold and empty

GRAY: Do you think the hotel maid will gossip about your torn underwear and a condom in my trash?

GRAY: She's probably seen everything.

GRAY: All I can think about is that I didn't get to see you naked and laid out on the sheets

GRAY: Still sex on the beach

GRAY: Best night ever

GRAY: Wish you were here

GRAY: Also how is your sister? Good I hope

Rose smiled because although he'd been thinking about her he'd still remembered she'd left him because her sister needed her.

She'd responded last night, giving him an abbreviated accounting of her conversation with Poppy and saying that her sister would love to talk to him about business finance. Of course Gray readily agreed to answer Poppy's questions and talk about the jobs he'd held climbing the corporate ladder to CFO.

Now, though, he was as impatient to see Rose as she was to see him.

GRAY: Finished being a corporate mogul ready to get my hands on you again

ROSE: Then I can't wait to see you

A blush heated her cheeks because Maggie and the florist were only a few steps away making sure every other pew in the church would have the perfect bouquet at the end of it.

"Rose, what do you think? Is it enough to have the bouquets on the pews without the big bouquets at the altar?"

Rose stood at the back of the church looking down the aisle to the altar. "Actually, if I was the photographer taking pictures from back here as you exchange vows, all of us would block the bouquets anyway. What about lining the step up to the altar with small bouquets, leaving a wide enough section in the middle for you to walk through? That way when you head back down the aisle, the photographer can frame you in the center with the flowers spreading out on either side of you up there and as you walk by the pews."

Maggie turned to look back at the altar, then spun back with a brilliant smile on her face. "You are exactly right. That will be beautiful and perfect. The photos will look amazing."

"A memory for a lifetime," Rose confirmed as the florist typed notes into her tablet.

Rose's phone dinged with another text. Rose tried very hard not to show how much she wanted to read it.

Maggie rolled her eyes, but grinned. "That's Gray again, isn't it? The man is obsessed with you."

Rose shared Maggie's joy for her. "He finished work for the day. He's bored," she lied. He was definitely enjoying texting with her.

"Answer the man. At least he's texting you, while Marc is constantly texting everyone at work and not me."

Rose turned her back to Maggie to read the text while Maggie and the florist worked out the final details for the floral arrangements.

GRAY: Headed your way now

GRAY: Oh the plans I have for you tonight

ROSE: I look forward to every second I'm with you

Rose checked the time. The wedding rehearsal started in about half an hour. Gray would be early, which meant they'd have some time together before they ran through the ceremony.

GRAY: I can't wait to kiss you

ROSE: Can't wait to see you.

ROSE: ♥

GRAY: You definitely have mine

Maggie walked toward her after saying good-bye to the florist. "Oh, my god, you're glowing." Maggie studied her. "And you have never smiled that big ever."

Rose pressed her phone to her chest and thumping heart. "He's . . ."

"What?" Maggie looked like she'd caught Rose's excitement.

"Amazing. Wonderful. Perfect."

Maggie hugged her. "I'm so happy for you." She stepped back, a real smile on her face, but Rose still wondered if Maggie harbored any resentments about the thing with Marc.

Rose spoke before she thought better of it. "It's a strange sort of thing to meet him because you're marrying a guy I once knew."

"Maybe it was just meant to be." Maggie held her gaze and smiled. She really meant it.

"It feels exactly that way."

"Which makes me even happier for you. Marc and I, we're happy together. We're excited about starting the next chapter in our relationship. I think of the future with him, and I see us with our kids."

"I know how much you want to be a mom."

"More than anything. And our kids will be cousins." Maggie's smile brightened even more.

"Slow down. Give Gray and me time to catch up." In her mind, she didn't doubt they'd be together long after this week in Carmel. They might be moving fast, but Rose didn't want to skip ahead to a wedding and a family too quickly. She wanted to savor her time with Gray.

Maggie's smile suddenly dimmed. "I wasn't sure I'd actually make it down the aisle after . . ."

Rose understood. "After you and Joel broke up. But you and Marc want the same things. This time, it's going to be perfect."

Maggie cocked an eyebrow. "Really. You think this week has been perfect?" Maggie burst out laughing, but it sounded a little forced.

"Okay. Not perfect, but close enough because that's life. Right?"

"I don't want perfect. I just want a guy who loves me and wants to have a family and spend the rest of his life being my best friend."

"That sounds pretty damn good."

Maggie nodded, looking all too agreeable until her phone rang and she caught her breath.

"What is it?" After the cake fiasco, Rose didn't think Maggie could take another wedding glitch. Not with only two days before the big day.

"It's Joel."

Rose raised a brow and glanced at the ringing phone. "Why on earth is he calling you?"

Curiosity filled Maggie's gaze. "I don't know."

* * *

Maggie answered the call before it went to voice mail. "Hello." Her voice trembled and her heart pounded in her ears.

"Maggie, it's me. Joel." He sounded nervous, even afraid.

"Is everything okay?" She didn't know why else he'd call after they ran into each other outside the café and he took off.

"Do you have a minute to talk?"

Maggie looked at Rose, who was avidly watching her. The church was empty except for them. All of a sudden, she felt very out of place in there talking to her ex right before she was supposed to rehearse her wedding ceremony.

But she couldn't *not* hear what he had to say.

"I'd like to hear what you have to say after all this time."

"I'm sorry."

She felt all the sorrow he put into those two words. "We agreed when we ended things that no one needed to be sorry for what we wanted out of life."

"That's just it. I didn't want it to end, but I let you go because I wanted you to be happy. But all I did was make myself miserable without you. And when I heard that you were getting married barely a year after we broke up . . . If you say he's really what you want, I won't say anything more. But if there's a chance, even a small one that you still feel about me the way I will always feel about you, then I want you to know that everything *you* want is what I want for *us*. If there can be an 'us' again."

Surprise and shock zapped through her. "Joel . . ." Choked up, she barely got his name past the lump in her throat. "I . . . I don't know what to say. I'm supposed to get married in a couple of days. I'm standing in the church waiting for my fiancé to arrive for the rehearsal."

"That's why I had to call. I did come to town because I knew you were getting married here. I needed to see you to know for sure that you were happy. But I know you, Maggie. I've seen the reservation in your eyes. I saw the longing in them when you and I spoke. Tell me I'm wrong."

"I . . . I can't."

He breathed out a huge sigh of relief.

Maggie still had reservations about doing what her heart so obviously wanted when her head kept telling her that Joel had let her go because he didn't want to have kids. That was a big deal. One you didn't just change your mind about easily. One that took a lifelong commitment.

"I know I'm asking a lot."

"You're asking me to cancel my wedding and dump my fiancé two days before my wedding."

Rose gasped, her eyes so wide, Maggie feared they'd fall out of her head.

"I'm asking you to believe in us, the love we share, and that although I've been a selfish, childish idiot, I have taken the time to think about what I want, what I can't live without, and what I'm willing to *do* and *be* for the only woman I want to spend my life with."

Maggie tried to breathe and think clearly. She'd wanted this call from Joel forever but it didn't come those first few months after they broke up, so she had accepted that it would never come.

And now that it had, she didn't know what to do.

It wasn't that she didn't love him. She did.

It wasn't even the fact that she'd really put her parents out if she canceled her wedding at nearly the very last minute. They'd be upset, but they'd also want her to be happy. They'd been devastated to learn she and Joel broke up and why when they were still so much in love.

She thought of all the plans she'd made with Marc. They'd get married this Saturday, go on their honeymoon, move in together when they returned, spend a few months in marital bliss, then start working on the baby they both wanted. They'd be a family.

But am I going too fast?

Was it all going to crash and burn like the last time?

Her chest went tight, making it hard to breathe. She thought she might actually have a panic attack, or pass out.

"Maggie."

"I'm here. I just . . . don't know what to say. This really doesn't feel real."

"I shouldn't have waited so long to tell you how I feel. But

I want you to know, this isn't just because you're about to get married. I really mean it. I want you. I want us. I want the life I know we can have together. You. Me. Our children. It was stupid to be afraid of us having kids and something happening and us destroying them with a divorce. I'm not my parents. I know what it's like to feel abandoned and like a pawn in their games. I'd never do that to my kids. You'd never do that to them. And you know what I know even more than that now?"

"What?"

"I know how devastating it is to lose you and spend this past year wanting you back with every breath I take and every beat of my heart. I have been living with the loss of you when I should have been doing everything possible to get you back. So yes, Maggie, I'm sorry. Sorry for not telling you and showing you how much I love you. I'm sorry I was afraid of becoming something I'm not. And I'm sorry I denied you something we both want but I was too afraid to commit to until I realized, if anything, my parents' divorce taught me what not to do to my kids."

He'd never really given her a reason for why he didn't want children. Now it made sense. He was afraid of hurting them the way he'd been hurt.

"It seems I can't go anywhere anymore without finding myself jealous of all the happy couples I see with their little ones. All I think about is how that could be you and me and our kids. I know I said I didn't want to be a father, but that's not really what I meant, and I hope you can believe me now. I want everything, Maggie, so long as it's with you. I know you'd never let us fall apart the way my parents did because you've got a good heart. And I'm the best me when I'm with you. I promise you, I'll try to be as amazing a parent as I know you'll be to our kids."

Tears streamed down her face. "Yes" was on the tip of her tongue, but she couldn't just toss all her plans, her feelings for Marc, all of it, on impulse without considering everything. "Joel, I . . . I need time to think about this."

"Okay. Take all the time you need, just don't marry *him*. Not if you still love me. And I think you do, otherwise you wouldn't need time to think. Please, Maggie. Think about it. I know it's a lot to cancel a wedding and leave someone, but you don't have to do it alone. I'm here. All you have to do is call and I'll be right by your side. And this time, I won't leave. I'll never leave you again."

Rose wrapped her arm around Maggie's waist and hugged her to her side.

Maggie couldn't stop the tears trailing down her cheeks.

Part of her wanted to say yes right now, because Joel had always been her everything. But that wasn't fair to Marc, whom she'd planned a life with, who loved her, who over the last eight months showed her the life they could have together. A life she believed would be full of fun, laughing, great sex, and a friendship that she counted on despite how he'd acted this week.

Still, she wondered, did Marc really want to get married? She hadn't allowed herself to think too much about his father's wishes. Was he marrying her to please his dad?

Did he really love her? Or was he using her to get what he really wanted? The business.

Were her feelings real? Or did she just get caught up in how Marc pursued her and how he promised her the children and home she wanted? Had she convinced herself that this was love?

Why did everything suddenly feel more complicated than it had been just a week ago? Then, she was just looking forward to some matchmaking and the wedding. Now, Joel's reappearance made her realize one thing: she really did still love him.

She'd truly believed she'd found a good husband in Marc, but now everything was falling apart.

She'd already done this, given up one man to have that life with another. Now Joel was asking her to give up Marc for him.

Her life felt like it was on repeat.

"Maggie, all you have to do is call me back and I will help you through the rest. I promise. I hope you'll make that call soon. Otherwise, I really do wish you all the happiness in the world, because your happiness means everything to me. I just hope I'm the one you let make you happy the rest of your life, because if you say yes to me, to us, it's you and me *forever*." He paused, then whispered, "I love you," and hung up.

Maggie dropped her hand and the phone hit her thigh. She stared blankly at nothing, hearing Joel's heartfelt words echo in her head, her mind and heart at odds about what to do.

Rose hugged her close. "Maggie. Maggie. Are you okay?"

She shook her head. "No." She didn't know if she should marry Marc, the man who'd promised her everything. "Yes."

Because Joel still loved her. He wanted her. He wanted to be everything she needed him to be for her. "I don't know." *Joel wants to be a father. He wants a family with me, because he knows we can do it together and everything will be okay.*

Rose turned and took her by the shoulders. "Maggie, honey, you're not making sense. What did Joel say?"

Maggie finally met Rose's inquisitive and urgent gaze. "He wants to marry me and have kids. He still loves me."

Rose gaped at her. "Oh, my god!" She fidgeted, then repeated, "Oh, my god!"

Maggie walked to the nearest pew and sat.

Rose joined her and took her hand. "Talk to me. What are you thinking?"

Maggie glommed on to the one thing she knew for sure. "I love Joel. I love Marc. But I don't love them the same way. They are different men. My relationship with each of them is different from the other because of that. If you'd asked me last week if I was over-the-moon excited to marry Marc, I'd have said yes."

"But now?"

She sank in her seat. "How did things get so complicated this week? How did the man I've known for the last eight months turn into the Marc you've seen this week?"

"Maybe seeing me again threw him a curveball. Maybe he's unsure of things now. It could be that he's worried you're hiding how upset you are about it and that it will become a thing that you never get over going forward."

That actually kind of made some sense, though it appeared Rose was grasping at straws. "Maybe. But the thing is, I'm really clear on how I feel about it. What worries me is this: he was cheating on his girlfriend at the time. I didn't know that before this week. Or that he can be such an asshole. About you two. To Gray. So I'm wondering if maybe I did rush into this wedding on the rebound and I don't know him as well as I should before I say 'I do.'" Maggie blurted out the nagging question she couldn't stop thinking about. "What if Marc isn't the right man for me?"

Rose frowned. "I'm sorry, Maggie, only you can answer that question."

"If you were me, what would you do?"

"I can't answer that, either. I was there during you and Joel. I saw you two together a lot. I could see how much you two were perfect for each other and how much he loved you. I was as shocked as everyone else around you when you two split. I've only seen you and Marc together this week. I can see that he cares deeply about you and didn't want to hurt you. He seems excited about the wedding, but I really can't say that I know enough to say he's the one for you."

"He should have said something to me the second he knew you and I are friends. Instead he lied to me about you."

"Because he didn't want you to think there was more to what happened between us than there was."

"No." Maggie shook her head and frowned. "The more I think about it, the more I realize he didn't want me to know he was cheating on his ex."

"That doesn't mean he'll cheat on you. He asked you to be his wife. That means something."

Maggie pressed her fingers to her forehead and the aching headache building there. "Even before Joel called today, I was questioning if Marc's behavior this week meant he wasn't the right man for me. I still love Joel, but he didn't come to me with his change of heart until he found out I was getting married." She looked up to the ceiling and sighed. "I don't know what to make of all of this. I need time to think."

The door at the back of the church opened. She and Rose both turned and spotted Gray walking in, his gaze finding Rose and a big smile breaking out on his face.

"I've spent time with Gray at family dinners over the last many months. I've never seen him so relaxed and happy as he is around you," Maggie said.

Rose patted Maggie's knee. "Marc always looks happy when he's with you."

"Really? You thought he seemed cheerful and at ease at dinner last night?"

"Okay. Maybe not then. But I think that has everything to do with me and Gray and not you."

"Exactly."

"It will get better."

"What will?" Gray asked, stepping up behind them and leaning down to kiss Rose. "Hi."

"Hi," Rose said, blushing and gleefully smiling up at Gray.

Maggie turned to Rose. "I think if you and Gray got married on Saturday, even though you've only known each other for a week, you'd be a very happy couple forever." She stood and walked away, needing some space to sort through her thoughts and feelings. She only had two days until she said, "I do," and before she did that, she needed to be sure whose, if anyone's, wife she wanted to be.

Chapter Twenty-One

ose's heart hurt for Maggie. She couldn't believe Joel had waited until the last minute to make his move. He'd had a year.

At one time, Rose had no doubt their love had been real, and she believed love like that never disappeared entirely. But Joel had put her friend in a precarious position.

Still, if Maggie decided to call off—or postpone—the wedding, then Rose would support her. After all, Maggie's entire life's happiness was on the line.

"What's going on?" Gray asked, looking confused. "I thought we were practicing the ceremony, not swapping places with them."

She met his amused gaze. "Do you want to get married and have kids someday?"

Amusement turned to sincerity. "Yes. Absolutely. We talked a little about it day one. Why? Don't you?"

"I do."

"So what does this have to do with Maggie and Marc? From

all I've heard from them, it's a wedding, honeymoon, then a baby soon."

"That's the plan. But you're not going to believe this . . . Maggie's ex, Joel, just called. He wants her back, children are on the table, *and* he asked her to call off the wedding so she could think about what she wants to do."

"Shit." Gray rubbed his hand over the back of his neck. "Does Marc know about this?

"No. But from what I've gathered, Joel just made a damn good case for her to cancel the wedding and marry him."

"Shit," Gray repeated, leaning over with his forearms braced on the back of the pew. "What do you think she'll do?"

"I don't know for sure. But I can tell you, what she had with Joel, before the kids thing got in the way, it was epic."

"I don't envy Maggie having to make this kind of decision between two men she obviously loves. And this late in the game. Marc . . . He'll be . . ."

"What?" Marc asked, walking in behind Gray with the other two groomsmen.

Gray turned to him. "I was just telling Rose you'd be here soon."

Rose appreciated that Gray kept their conversation private.

"Miss me, gorgeous?"

"Not at all," she teased and smiled, keeping things light and friendly.

Marc eyed her, but kept smiling, too. "Where's my beautiful bride?"

Rose covered for Maggie. "She stepped out for a minute, but I'm sure she'll be back soon." Or not. At this point, Rose wasn't sure Maggie hadn't called Joel back and asked him to come and whisk her away.

Marc stepped aside so the other two guys could join them. "Have you met Rick and Frankie?"

"No." Rose held her hand out to Rick. "I'm Rose. I'm the maid of honor. And Gray's girlfriend," she added, loving the wide grin on Gray's face. She shook Frankie's hand, too, then stood and made her way out of the aisle.

Gray met her at the end of the pew. "Looks like we'll be doing the ceremony after all," he whispered in her ear, then tipped his head toward Maggie and the priest as they walked into the church.

Marc joined Maggie and they spoke with the priest for a few minutes away from everyone.

Rose got pulled away from Gray when Rachel and Jamie, Maggie's bridesmaids, showed up.

"Oh, my god, he's even more handsome in person," Rachel blurted out so loud that Gray heard her from across the church and grinned at Rose.

"How come Maggie introduced you to him first instead of one of us?" Jamie complained.

"I definitely got lucky with that one."

Rachel bumped shoulders with Rose. "I bet you did."

Rose shook her head, but couldn't hide the blush heating her cheeks.

Maggie saved her from trying to come up with something to say by calling them all over to the back of the church, so they could practice the ceremony.

Rose pulled Maggie aside for a moment and whispered, "Are you okay?"

"I don't know, and I don't have time to really think about it." She glanced over at Marc, then turned back to her. "He noticed something is off. And all I keep asking myself is, are there things I've ignored because we're engaged and it's inconvenient to look at them?"

Rose took Maggie's hand. "I can't imagine how you're feeling right now. But I'm here for you, whatever you decide to do. You have my support and understanding, and I'll help you in any way I can."

Maggie hugged her. "I know you will." She stepped back. "You were right. No one can help me make this decision. I have to decide what and who I want. I'd like to go away somewhere and think, but I can't just walk out of here. I'm actually hoping going through the ceremony rehearsal, standing up there with Marc, will give me some epiphany or glimpse of the future to tell me what the right thing to do is."

"I believe you know what's right for you. But maybe saying it out loud, committing to it, is still a hard thing to do because you'll hurt someone."

Maggie pressed her hand to her heart. "I know what it feels like to be hurt like that. I don't want to do that to Marc or Joel. They're good men. I'd be lucky to have either one of them."

"Then you have to ask yourself, who can't you live without?"

Maggie opened her mouth, looking as though she wasn't sure what to say, but got cut off.

"Babe! Are you going to keep me waiting on Saturday, too?" Marc called out from the front of the church.

All the groomsmen laughed with him.

Gray laughed along with them but looked at Rose with a question in his eyes.

"Let's do this," Maggie said for all to hear, and took her place behind Rose. Gray stood up front with Marc while the other groomsmen joined her and Maggie at the back. Rachel and Frankie took the lead, followed by Jamie and Rick, then Rose went ahead of Maggie. Maggie's dad would walk her down the aisle on the day, but he and Brenda had skipped the rehearsal to make sure the restaurant was set up for their dinner tonight.

It didn't take long for the priest to help them walk through the ceremony. Marc pretended to faint the second he saw Maggie walking up the aisle, Gray pretended he lost the rings—which he didn't have on him in the first place—and all the while Maggie wore a plastic smile until Marc took her in his arms and kissed her with a tenderness that made all the women sigh.

Marc held her face, ended the romantic kiss, and said, "I can't wait for you to be my wife."

Maggie's eyes teared up and she hugged him tight.

"And that's all there is to it," the priest announced.

Rose knew better. For Maggie, there was a lot more going on here than the simple ceremony. It shone in her eyes and the false smile.

Gray shared a sympathetic and concerned look with Rose.

No one else seemed the wiser about the dilemma making Maggie less than her normally vibrant self.

Everyone followed the priest toward the back of the church so they could head over to the restaurant for the rehearsal dinner.

Gray took her hand and held her back. "You okay?"

"Just worried about my friend."

"Me, too. Poor Maggie."

"You're not concerned about how Marc will take it if she cancels the wedding?"

"I want Maggie to be happy."

"Very diplomatic, Mr. Pearson."

"They won't be happy together if one or both of them doesn't have their whole heart in it."

"Gray! Rose! Let's go," Maggie called from the open church door.

Rose took his hand and they walked toward the exit, his fingers linked with hers.

"This is going to be a very long evening."

She smiled, knowing he couldn't wait for this dinner to be over, so they could be alone together. Though she worried about Maggie, she couldn't wait for the drama to be over so she and Gray could focus on them.

Chapter Twenty-Two

*R*ose and Gray walked into the restaurant where the rehearsal dinner was being held, holding hands and smiling.

"You're lucky I care about Maggie and brought you inside instead of back to my hotel," he whispered in her ear.

"I don't feel lucky at all," Rose teased back.

"Is that her?" A woman rushed toward them, her dark hair threaded with gray, and a smile that looked as familiar as the one on Gray's face.

Gray smiled even wider when the woman slipped her arm around his waist and hugged him to his side. "You're as beautiful as he said."

"Thank you." She eyed Gray.

"Mom, this is Rose. Rose, my mom, Andie."

Rose tried to tamp down the wave of nerves and act normal. She had expected Maggie's and Marc's parents to be here to celebrate with the bridal party, but not Gray's. She held out her hand. "I'm so pleased to meet you, Mrs. Pearson."

She waved that away. "Andie, please. And this is my husband, Grady."

Rose shook his hand. "So Gray's name is derived from yours, just without the D."

"Andie wanted him to have his own name."

His mom hugged Gray close again. "He's his own man."

"And a very good one at that," Rose added.

Andie looked up at her son. "I like her."

Gray's intense gaze never left Rose's. "I do, too."

Andie smiled at her. "He told us all about you. He's going to steal you away from that company you work at. And I'm inviting you to our monthly family dinner. First Sunday of every month. You can't miss it. No exceptions."

"Consider that your invitation and order to be there." Gray shook his head at his mom.

Rose skipped over the part about working at Gray's company, since they hadn't talked about it since that first night. "I love that you all make a point to get together. I should do something like that with my mom and sister." It would be a wonderful way to start a new tradition.

"Gray told us you hadn't seen them in a long time. I'm sorry to hear about the troubles you had in the past. But Gray said you've reconciled with your family now."

"I have. It's been a long time coming." She eyed Gray, wondering when he'd talked to his mom about her and just how much he'd told her. A lot, by the sound of it. They'd only started dating. But it said something that he'd not only spoken about her, but didn't seem to mind introducing her to them so soon, either.

Grady tugged his wife away from Gray. "Let's join the others. Things look tense between Marc and his dad." Grady and Gray exchanged a look of foreboding. "Have you two made up?"

Rose eyed Gray, who avoided looking at her.

Gray shook his head. "I told Marc it's out of my hands. I can't make Uncle Matt do anything. It's his decision. But I did tell Marc that it's not what I want, but that doesn't seem to matter to Uncle Matt."

"He's protecting himself and his employees," Grady explained, giving Rose some insight into their conversation. "You understand that."

"I do. He has cause to be concerned."

Grady briefly glanced at her. "This is complicated."

Rose's stomach went tight. Did they know about her and Marc, too?

Maybe it was better they did. No secrets.

Gray stuffed his hands in his pockets. "I made myself clear to Marc and Uncle Matt."

Andie eyed Rose. "Don't worry, dear. Marc's always been a troublemaker, but he usually does the right thing when it comes down to it. Especially when his father lays down the law."

Rose looked up at Gray. "What does it have to do with you?"

"It shouldn't have anything to do with me."

Grady's mouth pinched into a tight line. "If Marc doesn't shape up, you'll have no choice but to step up."

"And make things worse. They need to work this out themselves and stop putting me in the middle." When Grady tried to say more, Gray stopped him with a look. "Drop it. We're here for Maggie and Marc. Let's celebrate with them, instead of talking about them."

"This wedding can't come soon enough," Grady said, taking his wife's hand and heading to the semiprivate room at the other end of the restaurant.

Rose didn't move and waited for Gray to explain, but he just stared across the room at Marc and Uncle Matt having a quiet but obviously strained conversation in the corner. Uncle Matt spotted Gray, smiled big, and waved him over.

Gray turned to her, looking like he wanted to escape.

She lightened the mood. "I can't believe you introduced me to your mom and dad and I'm not wearing underwear."

Gray burst out laughing. "I promise not to tell them that."

"It's our secret."

He hooked his arm around her neck, pulled her into his chest, and kissed her on the head. "You're really good for me."

"Why didn't you tell me your parents were going to be here?"

He leaned back and stared down at her. "I figured you knew since this is a family thing."

She'd only expected the bride's and groom's parents. Rose wanted to kick herself. "With all that's been going on, I guess I didn't think about it."

"Believe it or not, I thought Marc might tell me to leave."

That shocked her. Though maybe it shouldn't. "Because of me?"

He shook his head and brushed his fingers back and forth on the back of her neck. "Some other things I learned."

"Are you going to tell me what's going on with your family?"

"Not here. Not now. But Maggie needs to seriously consider her options."

She gripped his sides. "You can't say that to me and not explain. She's my best friend. If there's something she needs to know, you need to tell me."

Gray raked his fingers through his hair in an unusual show of frustration. "Rose, it's a complicated mess. Maybe you can help, but you also complicate things for me."

She took a step back. "What does that mean?" Before he could explain, her phone rang. She pulled it out of her purse and checked the caller ID in case it was Poppy or her mom.

The name on the caller ID surprised her, even though it shouldn't have because she often got called on her off time. "It's my boss. I have to take this."

"Take your time. Can I get you anything?"

"I definitely need a drink."

"Strawberry margarita?"

She appreciated that he remembered her and Maggie's story from last night. "I'd love it."

"I'll get Maggie one, too. She could probably use two." Gray walked over to the bar.

Rose swiped her screen to accept the call and walked back toward the entrance and into an alcove between two dining areas for some privacy. "Hi, Ben. How are you?"

"I'd be better if we didn't have a problem. I'm sorry to call you on your vacation. I know it's kind of late in the day, but I need your help."

"I'm not near a computer, but tell me what's going on and

hopefully I can work through the problem with you." She spent the next fifteen minutes looking at pieces of code on her phone, trying to see the errors and coming up with fixes on the fly, while her boss and the team back at the office tried out the various fixes until they got the program working and performing to the customer's specifications.

"You're a lifesaver, Rose. Thanks for working this out. We've been stuck on it for two days. We couldn't have done it without you."

Something about this past week, and Gray's belief in her that she was an asset his company needed, made her bold. "Did you have Thomas look at this before you called me?"

"Yes. We've had him and two others working on it."

"So what you couldn't fix in two days with three guys on the project I did on the phone and in my head with clips of emailed code in minutes."

"Yes. You're amazing."

"Remember that the next time you promote someone over me who isn't as qualified or talented as I am. Which you've done twice now."

Ben paused for a moment, finally catching on that Rose wasn't simply going to save the day, yet again, without standing up for herself. "Rose, I really appreciate everything you do. That's been reflected in your pay raises and the projects you're assigned."

"That's a nice way of saying you're trying to keep me happy by giving me standard pay raises and good projects to work on, but you promote and pay others more than me because they're men, and I've allowed it to happen. We both know this isn't the only time I've been called in to fix someone else's work. Someone who holds a higher position than me. I hope we can discuss this all next week. I'll see you when I get back to the office. Good-bye, Ben."

Rose leaned back against the wall, hung her head, and took a deep breath. She wasn't used to speaking up that way, but damnit, she deserved a promotion and a big fat pay raise. She'd earned it. And on Monday, she'd walk in prepared to tell Ben exactly why.

"Hey there, gorgeous."

She looked up and smiled at Marc, trying her best to be cordial and let the past go.

"We really need to stop meeting like this. You can't keep harassing me, begging me to meet you alone."

Blindsided by his comments, she decided he was joking— even if it wasn't funny and was really odd. But he went on. "I've told you so many times that it's over. I know what we had was something special even if it didn't end well, but you can be happy with Gray now. I love Maggie. I know that's hard for you to accept. But you've got to stop blowing up my phone. I can't keep lying to Maggie about all these texts being from work."

She felt like she'd dropped down a rabbit hole. Incredulous, she eyed him. "You can't be serious."

"I am. I love Maggie," he implored with a pleading tone. "Not you."

She came away from the wall and stood in front of him. "You're crazy."

Marc shook his head. "You're the one who can't take no for an answer." Marc tried to walk past her, but she stepped in front of him and planted her hand on his chest to stop him. He seemed to fall off balance and lunge at her, and before she knew what hit her, he kissed her, then pulled away like he was the one who didn't want it.

His angry gaze bore into her. "I said no, Rose. You need to get a grip and stop coming after me."

"What the hell is going on?" Maggie asked from behind her.

"That's what I'd like to know," Gray said from behind Marc, his words angry and clipped.

They'd come into the short hallway from opposite ends.

From where Rose stood, she couldn't see either one of them.

Rose felt like her world had gone topsy-turvy and upended itself.

Marc frowned down at her, pulled her hand from his shirt where she'd gripped it to steady herself, took two big steps back, and looked at Maggie with sympathy in his eyes. "I'm so sorry, love, that you had to find out your best friend isn't a friend at all. She's been hiding how she feels about me by hanging all over my cousin, but it's all been an excuse for her to be close to me."

"Explain," Maggie snapped at Rose.

"Me? I have no idea what he's even talking about. I've never texted him," she said, desperately hoping her friend believed her. "I never asked to meet with him. You know how much I care about Gray."

Marc shook his head, looking at her like she was pathetic.

"So much so that you told me you wanted us to have an affair right under both their noses. I could be with Maggie, you with Gray, but secretly we'd still have each other."

She openly gaped at him. "You are certifiable." Fury swirled inside her. "I would never—"

"Really? I know you would even if they think you're something you're not." He pulled out his phone and showed it to her, then Maggie. The screen had her name at the top and a string of text messages, all presumably from her, begging him to meet her, for one more chance, for him to be with her even if he married Maggie. "The texts don't lie."

Gray snatched the phone from Marc and scrolled through them. There must have been a lot because he swiped the screen over and over again.

Tears threatened as she watched his eyes turn stormy with rage. "Gray. He's lying."

Gray handed the phone back to Marc without looking at her and walked away.

She tried to go after him, but Marc planted his hand on her shoulder and held her back. "Leave my cousin alone. You've caused enough trouble."

Rose couldn't wrap her mind around what had just happened. "Why would you do this to me? To Maggie? To Gray?"

Marc's lips drew back in a sad frown. "I had to tell them, Rose. They deserved to know the truth, that I'm not the one obsessed about that night and you're the one who wants me back in your bed. I won't let you come between me and Maggie."

Rose finally understood. He was getting back at her. He

wanted her out of the way so Maggie never had any more doubts—and Rose wasn't around to influence Maggie. And he didn't want Gray to be with her, either. He enjoyed watching Gray lose something he cared about. He'd show his father that he was the better man—the family man—while Gray remained a bachelor.

And Rose guessed this somehow had something to do with the family business.

Marc stepped between her and Maggie. "Let's not forget, Rose; they saw you kiss me. If you can't accept we're over and I'm marrying Maggie, that's not my problem. Maggie and Gray both deserve better than a slut like you."

Rose saw red and screamed her rage. "I hate you! You're a lying, cheating piece of shit."

Suddenly Marc threw himself into the wall, hitting his head on a sconce, blood flowing out from a cut near his temple at his hairline. "What the fuck! You hit me," he said incredulously. He pressed the heel of his hand to the bloody cut.

Maggie walked closer, staring back and forth from her to Marc. "Rose."

"I didn't touch him." Her heart raced. "I hate him but I wouldn't hit him."

"You fucking bitch. You bashed my head into a wall." He held his hand up, making sure she and Maggie both saw the red stain.

Two waiters, a couple of customers, and the manager, who was frantically talking on the phone, stared at them from one end of the hallway.

Maggie stood there like she couldn't figure out whom to believe or yell at for ruining her night and possibly her wedding.

Rose turned to her and implored, "After what my father did to me, you know I'd never put my hands on anyone that way. He's lying. About all of it. He just wants you to hate me. But you know I would never do anything to hurt you. I would never try to steal a guy from you. I only want your happiness. You know how much I care about Gray. You've seen us together. I've told you a dozen times that Marc was a mistake I wish I could erase. In fact, I wish I never met him."

"Who's lying now? I have the texts to prove it." Marc continued to press his hand to the still-bleeding cut.

Maggie didn't say anything.

Marc wouldn't shut up. "She'll say anything now that she's been caught. I'm sorry, babe, but you had to know what kind of friend she really is to you. I love you." A waiter handed Marc a wad of paper towels to stanch the bleeding trickling down the side of his face.

Gray's father and uncle appeared behind Marc.

Grady looked at Rose holding her hands clenched in front of her. "What's going on?"

She didn't get a chance to answer. The cops showed up, ushered the bystanders away, and approached her.

"Arrest her, Officer. She assaulted me," Marc bellowed.

The officer looked at her. "Did he strike you first?"

"No!" Marc snapped. "She's crazy. Ask my fiancée."

Maggie turned and walked to her mom, who enveloped her in a tight hug.

Rose felt abandoned and left adrift. And furious at Marc. "I never touched him."

"You grabbed onto my shirt while we argued. Then you shoved me into the wall and I hit my head." Marc pulled the paper towels away to show off the deep gash.

She scoffed. "He lied about me texting him and forced a kiss on me so my boyfriend would leave me and his fiancée, my best friend," she said loudly to remind Maggie that she'd never do something like this to her, "would think I'm after him." She looked at Marc. "Gray is going to remember everything we shared. He knows it was real. And Maggie has known me forever. She knows I'd never do something like this, but you have a history of lying and cheating. The truth will come out."

The officer pulled her arms behind her back and cuffed her. "Let's take this outside where you can calm down and give me your statement."

This time she couldn't hold back the tears that slid down her cheeks.

Grady approached her, his gaze sympathetic but also angry.

"Please find Gray," she pleaded. "He's really upset. Tell him I didn't do this. I didn't do it," she sobbed, and let the officer lead her away and through the crowd to the squad car where he read her Miranda rights and questioned her. She sat in back, shackled and devastated, wondering how this happened and if Gray would ever believe her again.

Chapter Twenty-Three

Maggie left Marc in the hallway being fawned over by his mom and walked back to the dining room where all her guests were anxiously waiting at the tables. She assured her parents she could handle the situation on her own.

Gray stood away from everyone with his mother. He looked both wrecked and angry, though he kept his hands stuffed in his slacks pockets, his gaze straight ahead as his mom patted his arm and whispered something close to his ear.

Maggie felt the rage vibrating inside her. She couldn't believe this had happened or why. And she wanted answers.

Gray came away from the wall. "Maggie. Are you okay?"

"Come with me if you want the truth, because that was a total farce. There is no way in hell Rose would ever, ever," she emphasized, "hurt you like this. I know her. She's honest and loyal. You can't tell me you haven't felt that. This whole time Marc has been subtly poking at you and her. I don't know why. Maybe he doesn't like you two together."

"He doesn't want me to be happier than him." Gray rubbed

a hand over the back of his neck. "I'm sorry if that sounds bad, but it's the truth."

"Then you can't possibly believe Rose has been texting him, trying to set up some kind of tryst while dating you."

"I don't want to believe it, but explain the texts." The desperation in his voice said how much he didn't want this to be true.

"Come with me. We'll figure it out together."

"Go," Gray's mom insisted. "Marc is scheming again. You need to find out what really happened."

Maggie's stomach soured at the thought that even Marc's aunt believed him to be an unscrupulous man and she'd been blind to it.

Not anymore.

Gray followed Maggie back to the hallway where Marc stood with one of the cops, giving his statement. Gray's father stood by Marc's dad, listening.

"What are the cops doing here?" Gray's eyes turned into a tempest of rage.

Maggie hated to deliver the bad news. "Marc had Rose arrested for shoving him into a wall. He has a deep gash on his head that probably needs stitches."

"What?"

Maggie nodded. "He says she shoved him."

Gray shook his head. "I can't imagine her doing that, even though he deserved it. I didn't want to ruin your dinner," he admitted, "so I walked away to cool off before I said or did something stupid." Gray sighed. "I should have asked Rose to go with me somewhere we could talk."

"I think we were in as much shock as Rose that Marc told that ridiculous story."

Gray stopped short and eyed her. "You looked like you believed it."

Maggie stood beside him, the others several feet away. "For a second, it sounded real. But what I saw, and you couldn't see, was that Marc instigated that kiss and Rose looked fit to kill. He manipulated the situation and schemed to make her look like the one who did it all. I don't think she had a clue what he was talking about. I certainly don't believe Rose pushed him."

"How can you be so sure?" Desperation filled Gray's voice.

"I'll forgive you for doubting my friend because you don't know her like I do. But remember, Rose is a victim of abuse. The last thing she'd ever do is hit someone. She's not manipulative or a liar. She couldn't even hold back the truth about her and Marc to spare us knowing or risking us being hurt and breaking things off with her. She had to tell the truth. It's who she is. And I know when she's holding something back. I've had years of practice seeing through her tough exterior."

Gray swore under his breath. "I suspected Marc was up to something. I know him. But then he showed me the texts and I doubted everything I shared with Rose. She's got to be so hurt and angry with me for walking away."

"She won't care if she gets you back." Maggie continued through the lobby to the hall and stopped beside Marc.

Marc waved off his hovering mom and stepped toward Maggie. "Babe, where have you been? They say I need to go to the hospital for stitches."

Maggie had little sympathy for her fiancé. She simply snatched his phone from his hand. She'd seen him punch in the code dozens of times. "I have never once felt the need to spy on you or check your phone. I find it distasteful, an ugly invasion of privacy. I thought we loved and trusted each other. When you said you were taking calls and texts for work, I believed it."

Marc tried to grab the phone back.

Gray caught his hand and stopped him. "We want the truth."

Marc put his face in Gray's. "Your girlfriend isn't into you."

Maggie tapped the text message string, pulled up the contact that had Rose's name on it, hit the phone icon, and waited for the call to go through even though she could see the phone number didn't belong to Rose.

It could be a phone Maggie didn't know about that Rose used, but she didn't think so. She put the call on speaker.

Gray's and Marc's fathers, along with Marc's mom and the cop, stood close, watching and listening to everything.

It embarrassed and angered her to have to do this so publicly.

Marc swapped the bloody towels for fresh ones the restaurant manager handed him. "Don't do this, Maggie. I'm your fiancé. You should have my back."

After what he'd put her through this past week, she wanted to—

"Baby!" The woman's cheerful voice and that endearment grated on Maggie's last nerve. "Did you finish that thing? I've missed you so much. Can you sneak away and meet me at my place?"

Marc swore. "Hang up."

Maggie's sour stomach pitched. Her heart raced. She knew it. Marc had lied. He had someone else, the cheating bastard.

"What? You called me," the woman on the other end of the line pouted.

"Who is this?" Maggie asked, watching Marc's face turn red with rage and feeling no joy as everything went numb inside her.

"Um. This is Andrea. I'm Marc's ex. I take it this is Maggie." She sounded caught.

"It is. When did you and Marc break up?"

"About a year ago. After he cheated on me with some random chick he picked up in a bar."

Gray sucked in a breath and glared at Marc.

Maggie felt the inevitability of it. "I bet I can guess her name. Rose, right?"

"Yeah. *Her.*" Andrea had lost the cheerful tone. It dipped to anger and uncertainty.

Maggie dug for the truth. "I saw all the text messages you sent my *ex*-fiancé."

Marc glared at that and pressed his lips tight, but he didn't say anything.

Maggie kept digging. "He asked you to send them, didn't he?"
"Um."

"Don't answer that." Marc fiercely bit the words out.

"Come on, Andrea, woman to woman, you've been seeing Marc behind my back, haven't you."

"Actually, no. Not really."

That surprised Maggie.

Marc looked smug. For a moment.

Then Andrea went on. "Yes, he called me a couple weeks ago, you know, to reconnect. One thing led to another on the phone, then he was drunk one night and I picked him up at the strip club he went to with his friends—"

"His bachelor party, you mean." Maggie shook her head at Marc, seething on the inside.

"Well, I didn't know that."

"Stop, Maggie. Enough," Marc warned.

She ignored him. "So he called you that night all hot and bothered and looking for a ride and a good time? For old time's sake, right?"

"Yeah. You know, I was lonely and Marc's fun, so I picked him up, thinking . . . you know. But he couldn't . . . you know, because he was so drunk. I stayed the night to be sure he was okay, and man was his dad pissed when he walked in on us."

Matt eyed Marc, who looked fit to kill.

"Andrea. Shut up!"

Maggie glanced from Marc to Gray and caught his wince.

"At least you didn't lie about not having sex with her," Gray announced, revealing he knew about Marc getting caught with Andrea by Matt.

It explained why Marc's father almost didn't attend dinner tonight.

Maggie eyed Marc and raised a brow and said to Andrea, "But he asked you to send those texts because he wanted to get back at my friend for telling me that he slept with her."

"Yeah. He didn't like that. And then she went and started sleeping with his cousin and he really didn't like that. I didn't want to do it, but then I could get back at her for sleeping with my man, and he kind of made some promises, and you know . . ."

Maggie really didn't know why she'd do something like that to someone she didn't know. Or anyone, for that matter. And Marc was the only one at fault for cheating on her, not Rose.

"Thank you for your honesty, Andrea. It's more than Marc is capable of after using me all this time. Don't take his calls. Don't see him again. He cheated on you once and now he's made you lie for him. You can do better. No one is that lonely and desperate to be treated like shit."

"You're right. Fuck you, Marc." Andrea hung up.

"Fucking bitch!" Marc dropped his hand from his bloody head, fisting it at his side.

Maggie didn't know if he directed that expletive at her or Andrea. She didn't care anymore. She stared at Marc, her heart not broken but resigned that this was over. Part of her was happy it happened, because it made it so easy to know what to do. "Obviously, the wedding is off. And I never want to see you again."

Marc took a step toward her. "This is all Rose's fault. If she'd kept her mouth shut—"

Maggie stepped back. She didn't want to be near Marc ever again.

Gray closed in on Marc. "What? You wouldn't have tried to break us up some other way?"

"She was mine first."

"Grow up," Gray snapped. "You sabotage every relationship.

You could have married Maggie and tried to be the man she deserves, but instead you hurt three women, and for what? So I wouldn't have Rose. So you could blow up the wedding your father wants for you but you don't really want at all."

Marc turned his head away, but not before Maggie saw the answer so clearly in his eyes. "You are not getting what's rightfully mine."

"Rose was never yours. She was single. You had some fun, but it was never a relationship. You had something real with Maggie, though, but it's not a surprise you ruined it, because you don't care about anyone more than you care about yourself."

Marc shrugged that off. "Screw you and Rose. Keep her for all I care. But you're not getting my father's business."

Maggie shook her head. "All of this because you're petty. If you'd spent your time and energy building up those relationships instead of tearing them down, you'd have what Gray has. Instead you lose it all trying to take things away from Gray."

"Whatever." Marc dismissed her in such a careless manner, it actually got through the numbness and felt like a jab to the heart. "You don't know what it's been like living in Gray's shadow. He can do no wrong. Everything he wants, he gets."

Maggie looked at Gray, her heart sinking. "Wow. I guess I just don't measure up to Rose."

Marc sighed and pressed the ice pack the manager handed him to the goose egg on his head. "I didn't say that," he snapped, frustrated none of this was going his way. "All Rose had to was keep her mouth shut from the beginning."

"I'm glad she told the truth because in the end it made

you show me how little I matter to you." She choked out the words past her hurt and resentment. "Not because of the past but because you tried to break up a friendship that has lasted from kindergarten to now. You tried to break up a relationship between Gray and Rose because you could see the bond they shared, the love that's already there. I don't even want to know what you promised Andrea for her participation, especially after you cheated on her with Rose." She couldn't contain her disgust. "Why she'd agree to be the other woman after that, I have no idea. But whatever you promised wasn't worth the heartbreak you'd serve her later.

"I mean, who are you? What do you care about? Because it's obviously not me." Her voice cracked despite the rage. "It's not Gray."

"Yeah, well, Rose is going to pay for fucking up my life."

"Rose didn't do this! You did," Maggie snapped.

Gray rubbed at his neck again. "I need to find her." Gray couldn't contain his worry or desperation.

Gray's dad stepped in. "First we need to deal with the assault charges."

"You bet your ass," Marc sneered.

Marc's father, Matt, stepped up to them. "Grady and I have spoken. Here's what's going to happen, *son*. If you're pressing charges against her, then I've asked Grady to speak to Rose about filing charges against you."

"I never touched her."

Maggie tilted her head. "You forced a kiss on her. I saw it. Gray saw it."

Marc glared at his father. "What the hell, Dad? You can't seriously be siding with them."

"Why would I side with you when you've lied to Maggie and have acted like a spoiled brat? I overheard your whole conversation. You set Rose up. You hurt her, your cousin, the woman you supposedly love. It is going to cost me a lot of money to reimburse her parents for the canceled wedding and your selfishness. And you expect me to trust you with my business when there are hundreds of people's livelihoods at stake?" Matt shook his head. "I asked you to prove yourself, to build a life that had meaning and fulfilled you."

"That's what I did. You wanted me to settle down with a wife and kids. I met Maggie. She wanted that, too. We got along great. Everything should have gone according to plan, except Rose had to open her big mouth about me sleeping with her and cheating on my ex. Now Maggie thinks that's all I am, a cheat."

Maggie held her hands in fists at her sides. "I think you're an asshole for not taking responsibility for your past and doing better now."

"I didn't cheat on you."

"Well, not for lack of trying according to Andrea. A little less booze and you would have, happily."

Gray turned to his dad. "Where did they take Rose?"

"I'm not dropping the charges," Marc announced.

"Yes, you are, or this officer will arrest you for what you did to her. You'll have to get yourself out of the mess, which will cost you a lot of money just to plea bargain it down to a fine or something because there's no way Rose doesn't tell the DA or judge what you did, and she's a much more credible person than you," his dad pointed out.

"I will defend her." Grady eyed his nephew. "You've caused enough trouble. Drop this, or I'll start digging for dirt to use against you like I do the other people I go up against."

Marc glared at his uncle. "Why are you coming at me so hard?"

"Because you've always had it out for Gray, but this time you went too far. You didn't just take some random thing he had and you wanted. You took away a woman who means something to him. A woman who so obviously loves him."

Gray dropped his shoulders. "Where is she?"

Grady walked his son away from them.

Maggie turned to leave, too.

"Wait. Don't go. Not like this," Marc pleaded. "I do care about you. We can work this out."

Maggie pressed her lips together and knew exactly what she'd known when she stood with him in the church in front of the priest for the rehearsal. He wasn't the man she wanted standing beside her for the rest of her life.

She'd been afraid to speak up and say it out loud. She'd thought to get through dinner tonight and take the evening to really think about it because that kind of decision deserved concentrated consideration.

But Marc made the decision for her by showing her exactly who he was and what and who he cared about.

"I'm done. It's over. I want to be a wife and mom, but most

of all I want to be loved like I matter more than anything else in my partner's eyes. I want to be looked at the way Gray looks at Rose, and the way she looks back at him. That's why this scheme of yours didn't work. Everyone, including you, sees something special between them. I had that once. I know I can have it again." Because Joel was waiting for her. Their love had always felt like a forever thing. And if he truly felt the same way, and he wanted the same things she wanted for their future, then she wanted to try again, because she wasn't giving up on the kind of love she used to have with him. Never again.

Chapter Twenty-Four

*R*ose sat in the back of the police car in the restaurant parking lot, waiting to be taken to jail and wondering what was taking so long. She didn't know the exact process, but at some point a judge would arraign her and set bail. She'd figure out how to pay it and get out and go home. She probably needed to get a lawyer first, but she had no clue how to do that, either.

But right now she stewed in frustration, anger, and pain so sharp it made it feel like Marc had stabbed her right in the heart.

She sucked in a breath trying to stave off another wave of tears.

The car door abruptly opened, letting in some much needed air.

Just past the cop, she spotted Gray.

He stood there, a look of relief and apology and desperation in his eyes. He reached in, took her by the shoulders, and pulled her out of the back seat and into a fierce hug. "I'm so sorry I believed his lies even for a minute."

He was about to release her, but she leaned into him and buried her face in his chest.

"Don't let go."

He wrapped her up and held her tight.

The tears came with the wash of relief that went through her. "I didn't send those texts," she rushed to reassure him. "I hate him. You can't possibly believe I'd want to be with him when I had you."

Gray brushed his hand down her hair. "You *have* me," he assured her. "I know it was all lies, sweetheart. We sorted it all out."

"You did?"

This time Gray pulled back and held her by the shoulders. He twisted her to the side and stared at her hands cuffed behind her back, then set her straight in front of him again. Rage filled his eyes. "He will not get away with this."

"He told them I pushed him into the wall. He's bleeding. Who are they going to believe?" She couldn't believe he'd accused her of such a thing knowing what she'd been through with her father. She really couldn't believe the show he'd put on and how he'd made it look like she'd done it.

She'd wanted to lash out, but violence wasn't the answer, so she'd spewed her hate at him. That she couldn't and wouldn't take back. He deserved it.

"There's no getting out of this." She yanked on the handcuffs, clanking them behind her back, and eyed the cop watching them. She went still and felt her stomach drop with dread.

Gray cupped her face and brushed away her tears with his thumbs. "Did I ever tell you my dad is a defense attorney?"

"Um, no. You did not."

"Well, he's one of the best in the state and between him and my uncle, they backed Marc into a corner he can only get out of if he drops the charges."

She sucked in a breath and found some hope. "How did they do that?"

Gray stared down at Rose like he couldn't stand not to look at her. "Maggie saw right through the whole charade. I wish I had, too." He kissed her forehead. "Especially when I saw the devastation on your face right as I walked away." He pressed his forehead to hers and looked deep into her eyes. "I know it doesn't make up for it, but I didn't go far. I just needed a few minutes to calm down before I . . ."

"Punched Marc in the face at his wedding rehearsal dinner," Rose supplied for him. "Believe me, I know the feeling." Though it distressed her to even think it.

Gray leaned back and tried to smile, but it fell short.

Rose dropped her gaze to his chest. "Why did he do it?"

"Because he's an asshole," Gray snapped, letting some of his anger out with his words.

Rose sighed. "He wanted to get back at me for telling Maggie that I spent the night with him."

"He sensed something was off with Maggie and blamed it on that. Obviously he didn't know that Joel had come back into the picture. Maggie didn't care about what happened with you two. She knows you, Rose. You told her the truth, said you wanted to be with me, and that was the end of it for her. But Marc had another secret he was keeping from her."

"What?" She'd wondered if Gray was keeping something from her at the dinner last night when Gray and Marc had that odd exchange.

"The night of the bachelor party when I was making sure everyone got an Uber home, Marc made his own arrangements. I figured he called for his own ride, so I didn't think twice when I watched him get into a car. But then I sent his dad to his house to check on him and he found Marc in bed with a woman."

"No." Rose couldn't believe he'd do such a thing. Again.

"Turns out it was the ex he cheated on with you."

"Seriously? Why would she go back to him?"

"Because Marc can be charming and conniving at the same time. Plus it was a way to stick it to you because you slept with Marc when he was her boyfriend." Gray shook his head. "Anyway, Marc was too drunk to close the deal that night, but it really pissed his dad off. My uncle threatened to cut him out of the business and leave it all to me."

"So he wanted to get back at you, too."

"He asked the ex to send all those texts to his phone. He changed the contact information to show your name. Maggie knew you'd never hurt her or me like that, so she took his phone and called the number to confirm her suspicions that Marc had set it all up to get back at me, get you out of my life and his and Maggie's, so that he could marry Maggie to satisfy his dad."

"And have his ex on the side," Rose guessed.

Gray confirmed that with his mouth set in a firm line. "Now he's lost everything."

"But how did your dad get him to drop the charges?"

"Marc forced that kiss on you, though he made it look like you kissed him. You have every right to file charges against him. But if you agree to not press charges, neither will he, and this will be over."

"Are you sure?" Rose didn't think so. "He's a vengeful asshole."

"Right now, I'm worried about the charges against you. My father can get them pleaded down, but you don't want anything on your record. Marc doesn't want that, either, even if he isn't thinking clearly right now."

"Where is he?"

"Being held inside by another officer with my dad and uncle waiting to find out if you agree to the deal."

"Yes, if it will end this."

Gray stuffed his hands in his pockets, his shoulders went slack, and he hung his head. "I'm so sorry, Rose."

Rose stepped close and caught his eye. "None of this is your fault."

He met her gaze, his earnest and apologetic. "I should have trusted you and believed in everything we've shared."

"Those texts were damn good fake proof. If I'd been in your shoes, I might have needed a minute to figure things out, too."

"For all the past pranks and taunts, I never thought he'd do something like this. It was cruel trying to break us up and ruin your friendship with Maggie."

Rose frowned, and the pain inside her flared. She hated that Gray and Maggie were hurt because of her. "He couldn't take the chance that I'd influence Maggie, though I never said anything against him. Not even when she asked me if she should marry him."

"It had to be her decision," Gray agreed.

"Marc made it for her." Rose sighed. "I'm so grateful your father is helping me and you believe me and came out here to reassure me."

"I'm not letting go of you ever again," he assured her, and rubbed his hands up and down her arms. "I'd really like to take you back to my hotel where we can talk some more."

Rose clanked the handcuffs again. "At the moment, I'm not going anywhere."

"My dad is taking care of it. You should be released very soon. Definitely before the cops take you to booking. Then I hope you'll come with me."

Rose sighed. "I need to talk to Maggie. She must be so hurt and upset right now."

"She's busy letting everyone know the wedding is off. My uncle agreed to pay her parents back for whatever they spent. And I think she has plans to contact Joel."

Rose didn't doubt it, but Maggie would need some time. Rose would be there for her friend no matter what.

Gray cupped her face in his warm hands. "Rose, please, let me take care of you. You've got to be hungry. You look exhausted."

The fatigue weighed down her shoulders. "You're such a sweet talker."

Gray gave her a half grin. "Whatever it takes to get you to come with me."

"All you had to do was ask."

Gray's father and another officer walked out of the restaurant. The cop watching her joined his partner a few feet away at the front of the patrol car and started a discussion while Grady came over to talk to them. "Rose. How are you feeling?"

"I'll be perfect if they let me leave with Gray."

"Do you agree not to charge Marc if he drops the charges?"

"Yes."

Grady turned to the officers and gave them a nod before turning back to her. "Then it's all settled. Marc has been advised to stay away from you and Gray, not only by me but by his father as well. Truly, I'm so sorry you got caught up in our family drama."

Rose had a hard time looking at Grady, but did so because she wanted him to see how truly sorry she was. "I'm sorry if I caused even more strife between all of you."

"You didn't do anything," he assured her. "You wanted to be with Gray. Marc doesn't know how to accept that Gray's happiness doesn't mean Marc has less than him."

"Marc doesn't come close to the good and kind man Gray is. He never will."

Gray kissed her on the head as his dad smiled at her.

"I think he finally found his equal." Grady held her gaze, sincerity in his eyes.

"Thank you." She appreciated the kind words and blinked away the fresh tears gathering in her eyes.

The officer who'd arrived with Grady came to her and unlocked the handcuffs. "You're free to go." And just like that, the officers left.

Rose rubbed at her wrists and breathed a huge sigh of relief. She held out her hand to Grady, who took it and shook it. "Thank you for getting me out of trouble. Truly, I wish I could express the depth of my gratitude."

"I'm happy I could help. Because of Marc, you could have been in a lot of trouble for something you didn't do."

She acknowledged that with a nod. "I hope I never have to see him again."

Grady eyed her and Gray. "I'm not sure that's possible. We're family."

It hit Rose that he included her in their family.

She had been invited to their monthly family dinners, which meant she couldn't escape Marc's presence for long.

Grady sighed, looking as tired as she felt. "I hope Marc has learned his lesson and leaves you both alone." Grady put his hand on Gray's shoulder. "We'll talk later. I need to find your mom. She's been helping your uncle and Peg sort things out with Maggie's parents."

"I'm taking Rose with me," Gray told his dad.

"Are you heading home tonight?"

"No. Rose wants to see Maggie before we go. She needs to eat and get some rest, so we'll go to my hotel and stay there for the night." Gray spoke for her, but said exactly what she wanted him to say, that they'd be together.

She longed for some quiet time with him to just decompress

and settle back into the way things were between them before Marc tried to spoil it all.

Grady headed toward the restaurant entrance with them. "I'm so glad Marc didn't ruin things between you and Gray. My wife and I are anxious to see you again. Keep making my son happy."

"I plan on it."

Gray took her hand, squeezed, and leaned in close. "Good. Because I plan on taking very good care of you."

Ten feet from the door they stopped short when Maggie came rushing out. She didn't stop until she practically tackle-hugged Rose. "I'm so sorry he did that to you."

Grady said good-bye and walked into the restaurant, leaving her alone with Gray and Maggie.

Rose held her friend for a long moment. "I'm sorry he broke your heart. I know you know it's for the best, but it still sucks because you loved him, and it hurts because for a while it was good and you'll miss that part of it. You lost what you thought you had together. You put your whole heart into it. That's what matters. That's what counts. He blew it. He lost the best thing that ever happened to him. Because you are kind and beautiful and strong and so much more than he deserved." Rose leaned back and looked Maggie in the eye. "You deserve every happiness. I know you'll have it, even if it feels like it slipped away again."

"How do you know exactly what I need to hear?"

"Because I am and will always be your best friend." They hugged again. "And that means, when you're ready, we'll drink, trash-talk Marc, probably cry, and definitely laugh and eat a ton of ice cream, and I will be right beside you no matter what while you grieve what could have been and decide what will be your future."

"Promise?"

Rose hugged her tighter because Maggie needed it. "Promise."

"I'll buy the booze and the ice cream and not complain a bit when she's with you and not me," Gray pledged.

Both she and Maggie turned to Gray and giggled. "Deal," they said in unison.

Maggie turned to her. "I'm so happy that you and Gray found each other."

"Because of you."

Maggie's eyes filled with tears. "What are friends for?"

Rose touched her forehead to Maggie's. "You are going to be okay."

Maggie leaned back. "I know I am. But right now, I have a lot of emails and calls to make." Maggie turned to Gray. "Take care of her."

"Always," he swore, taking Rose's hand and bringing it to his lips for a soft kiss.

Maggie took Rose's other hand and squeezed it. "We'll talk tomorrow."

"Whenever you need me. Any time. Day or night. You know that, right?"

"You've always been by my side."

"I always will."

Maggie swiped away a tear, turned, and headed back into

the restaurant. Rose took solace in knowing Maggie's parents were in there waiting for her. They'd shower her with love and hold her close tonight.

For the first time, Rose had someone to do that for her, too.

Gray cupped her face and made her look up at him. "We'll go back to my hotel. I'll order room service. You can take a hot shower and get some rest."

"That sounds so good."

Gray put his arm around her and they started down the path back to the parking lot. They stopped short at the sound of Marc's voice calling out to them. "Wait."

They turned and found Marc rushing toward them, his father and Peg and another woman who had to be his mom frowning behind him as they tried to catch up.

Marc reached for Rose, but Gray stepped in his way before he touched her. The deep wound on his head had stopped bleeding, but it had swelled quite a bit and definitely needed stitches. He didn't look angry like before but desperate. "Rose, you need to tell Maggie that I'm sorry. We can work this out."

Hell no!

Rose didn't even think about herself but about the hurt, embarrassment, and humiliation he'd caused Maggie. He'd stomped all over her best friend's heart without any care or thought for poor Maggie, someone he supposedly loved.

Surprisingly, it was pity that rang in her words. "You don't deserve my help or my best friend. It didn't have to be this way. You could have been the guy Maggie thought you were, the man she loved and wanted to marry. You didn't have to be the liar and cheater I met." Even more surprising, she found some compassion, though he didn't deserve it, but he was Gray's family. "I hope someday you really do change."

Marc's father and Peg arrived, and both of them nodded a greeting to her, their smiles weak but compassionate and understanding. "Leave her be, son. We need to get you to the hospital."

Gray didn't bother to say anything to his cousin. He barely spared his uncle and Peg a halfhearted good-bye nod before he turned with Rose and walked her to his car. He held the door for her. She slipped into the seat and waited for him to close the door and take the seat beside her.

"I'm really sorry everything turned out this way and your family is in turmoil."

Gray stared out the windshield and watched Marc get into his mother's car. Marc's father and Peg got into another. "Marc did this to all of us. And the sad thing is, he probably won't learn from it." He laid his head back against the seat, turned to look at her, took her hand, and interlaced their fingers. "The only thing that really matters to me is that I have you right by my side."

"Always," she assured him, because being with him felt like a perfect fit.

Chapter Twenty-Five

Maggie had the unenviable task of contacting the priest, florist, caterers, bakery, and all the wedding guests to tell them she'd called off the wedding. She felt the sorrow and support from all her friends and family, but it didn't bolster her mood or make her feel any better.

A week ago Maggie thought she and Marc were headed to wedded bliss.

Tonight, alone in her childhood bedroom in her parents' house, she felt very much like she'd been used, and none of what she'd shared with Marc for the last eight months was real.

It felt like he'd simply stopped caring about Maggie, or forgot about her altogether in his plotting to stick it to Gray and Rose. Like, how dare they be happy?

And then there was Joel. He'd come back to town at nearly the last minute because he wanted her back.

Was that real?

Maggie wanted so desperately to believe it was, so that it didn't feel like she couldn't trust her own judgment.

She really couldn't take one more lie.

She stared up at the ceiling, letting the tears fall as all her anger turned to pain and she mourned the wedding she thought she'd have, the love she thought she felt for Marc, the life they'd planned.

She thought about how badly she'd wanted it and chastised herself for not listening to her mom and taking her time. She thought about all the missed opportunities to see Rose over the many months she was with Marc. And how just one meeting could have changed everything.

Again, she thought of Joel. He'd been forthright when they ended things and again when he asked her to come back to him. But she didn't trust herself to know what was real right now.

Her family stood by her today, consoling her, telling her everything would be all right, and helping her clean up the mess Marc made.

But really the only thing that happened to her was that she'd lost a man who would have been a terrible husband. He'd saved her years of unhappiness and strife. He'd saved their kids from having a broken family and a selfish father who probably wouldn't have changed, who'd never put them first.

She picked up her phone and called Joel.

"Maggie. I'm so happy to hear from you."

She heard it in his voice and it lightened her heart. "I canceled the wedding. It's a long story. I'm not ready to talk about it. I just wanted to know if you'd like to have lunch with me tomorrow." She wasn't ready to dive right in. But she had missed him and needed to see if what they once had was still there.

If nothing else, she needed a friend.

"Yes. Absolutely. Where and when. I'll be there." His enthusiasm helped ease her heart.

She tried to think of a good place to meet and picked a casual place that had outdoor seating overlooking the ocean. "The Surf. Noon?"

"I'll make the reservation and see you there."

"Make it for four people. Rose has a new boyfriend I'd like you to meet." In addition to wanting them to all be friends, Rose and Gray would let her know if she was seeing things clearly until she trusted herself again.

"I'd love to see Rose and meet her boyfriend." Joel sighed. "Sweetheart, are you okay?"

"I will be. I just need some time."

"Take all the time you need." The gentle tenor conveyed how much he meant that.

"What if I want to spend that time with you at the same time I figure out what comes next?"

"We can do things any way you like and at whatever pace works for you." His easy manner and directness eased her even more. "No pressure, Maggie. Even if you don't want to take me back, I'd really like it if we could be friends again."

A good place to start over again. But she took a chance, even though she didn't feel as brave as her words. "I'd really like that, but I do hope in time we will be far more. And when I'm ready, I want us to go for it all."

"That's what I want, sweetheart. You and me. I want us to be happy the way we used to be and so much more. But I get this is a difficult time for you. Just know that I'm here for you. Now. Forever if you want it."

"I do." It hit her that she was supposed to say that to another man, but she'd never meant it more than she did right now. "Tomorrow."

"I'll be there. I promise. And Maggie . . ."

"Yeah."

"I still love you."

Those heartfelt words felt like a precious gift. They filled her up and eased her heart and mind and stayed with her as the quiet closed in on her and a brighter future with Joel bloomed from the hope his love gave her.

Chapter Twenty-Six

*T*he car and elevator ride up to Gray's hotel room were quiet, but Gray kept Rose's hand in his nearly the whole time. He held the door open for her. She walked in ahead of him and then stood between the bed and the sitting area, completely at a loss about what came next and what she should do.

Gray went to the desk where his laptop, briefcase, and stacks of files sat, and grabbed the restaurant menu. He handed it to her. "What do you want to eat, sweetheart?"

She stared at it, unable to decide if she was hungry or tired or what.

Gray cupped her face and brushed his thumbs over her cheeks. "You need to eat. You'll feel better."

"Will I?"

Gray studied her for a moment, looking deeper, reading her discontent and the wild emotions swirling inside her. "What's really bothering you?"

She leaned into his touch. "I thought I lost you and I couldn't bear it."

Gray touched his forehead to hers. "God, Rose, I felt the

same. It crushed me to think, even for a second, that what we had wasn't real. The loss of it felt like it tore me in two. I don't ever want to feel that way again. I don't ever want to lose you."

She put her hand at the back of his neck and looked deep into his eyes as he held her face. "I never thought something like this was possible or even real. I thought people made it up or exaggerated. But when I'm with you, I believe in fate and destiny."

"I believe you were meant for me."

The kiss they shared was slow and sensual and an extension of the connection they shared. She lost herself in the feel of him holding her close. Safe. Protected. Cherished.

But all too soon he pulled back. "Sweetheart, I need to get you some food, put you in a hot shower, and maybe we can find a movie and you can relax after all you've been through."

"I'm okay."

"Please. Let me take care of you," he implored.

"All I need right now is you." She kissed him softly and rubbed her belly against his thick, hard cock. "I think you need me, too."

"It's been a crap day. If you need time to—"

She stopped his words with another kiss. "I have no doubt you will make everything better." She kissed him again. "Remember the beach, your hands on me." She took his hand and put it over her breast and achingly tight nipple. "Let's turn this bad day into a really good night."

His thumb brushed over her nipple, but he didn't dive in for more.

"Remember how you wanted to see me lying naked on the sheets," she reminded him.

"I think about it all the time."

"Then make it a reality."

He pressed his forehead to hers. "How did I get so lucky?"

She looked him in the eye. "I'm lucky to have you."

The words seemed to unleash him. He dove in for a searing kiss, his fingers tightening on her breast and squeezing her nipple. His other hand dipped over the swell of her bottom, and he pulled her hips snug against his.

She wrapped her arms around his neck and found herself swept away by the passion building between them.

Gray broke the kiss. "Did I tell you how beautiful you look in this dress?"

"No. You were too busy trying to figure out if I had anything on under it."

He slipped his hands down her sides and curled his fingers in the material and pulled it up into his hands. "I know you didn't wear anything else besides this sexy dress to tempt me." He stepped back just enough to pull the dress up and over her head. He sent it flying onto the back of the sofa and stared down at her, his heated gaze traveling down her chest, over her heavy breasts, her belly, and down her legs, then back up to her face. "God, you're beautiful."

She blushed and rubbed her fingers in the back of his hair. "You make me feel that way." She slid her hand down his wide chest, then back up to his shoulders. "You're overdressed."

"What if I just want to lay you out on that bed and look at you?"

"You should do it naked," she suggested, making him smile.

"Whatever you want." He tugged the dress shirt out of his slacks and began to slowly undo the buttons.

Impatient, she decided not to wait to touch all that warm skin he uncovered. She hooked her arm over his shoulder, went up on tiptoes, and kissed his neck, then laid a trail of soft, openmouthed kisses down his chest until she reached the button on his slacks. That she undid herself. When she looked up that flat, well-defined six-pack and his sculpted chest, she found him staring down at her with pure desire burning in his eyes.

"Come back up here."

She kissed her way back up until he took her mouth in another mind-blowing kiss, his hands brushing down her back and over her ass. He squeezed both cheeks in his hands, brought her up to her toes again and snug against his erection. He dipped low, pulled her legs up around his waist, then turned them to the bed. He put his knee on the end of it, crawled forward, and laid her out beneath him. He kissed her one last time on the mouth, then planted kisses down her neck and chest until he found her nipple and took it into his mouth, sucking hard before he licked it with his flat tongue and then the tip, making her moan.

"That's the sound I love."

He took her other nipple into his mouth and repeated the move, eliciting a groan as she arched and offered up her breasts to him. He palmed the other one, tweaking her nipple with his fingers and sending a bolt of heat down to her core.

She slid her fingers deep into Gray's thick hair, the silky strands sliding against her skin as she held his head to her breast. The hand on her breast slid down her belly and between her legs. His fingertips teased her soft folds in light strokes that had her rocking her hips for more.

Gray looked up at her. "You're already so wet for me."

"I want you."

"You can have all you want." He slipped one finger deep inside her and stroked her in and out as she moved her hips to meet his thrusting finger, then he filled her with two and she spread her legs wider, loving the feel of him loving her. He leaned forward and took her hard nipple in his mouth again. The dual sensations made her writhe on the bed, and then he kissed his way down her belly again, slid back on the bed, and settled between her open thighs. He removed his fingers, making her beg for more. "Don't stop."

He granted her demand and licked her folds from the bottom up to her swollen clit, sending a shiver of need through her. Then he clamped his mouth over her, sucking softly and plunging his tongue into her. He loved her like that until her hips were off the bed, she was rocking against his mouth, and he slipped one finger inside her, sucked her clit, and her whole body spasmed as pure pleasure exploded through her.

Gray kissed the inside of her thigh, sat back on his heels, shed his shirt, and pushed down his pants and boxers, releasing his big cock. Then he pulled out his wallet, found the condom inside, ripped it open, and rolled it on. He quickly tore off the rest of his clothes and the sandals she still had on, then settled between her legs. The thick head of his dick nudged against her entrance, and he slid the whole length up and down against her wet folds, while he watched and so did she.

His gaze met hers as he sank inside her just an inch. "I wanted you the second we met."

"I felt the same way," she answered him.

He thrust deep and kissed her at the same time. She tasted herself and the passion they shared as his tongue swept along hers and his big body moved over hers. With every deep thrust and glide of his cock in and out of her, she felt them both letting go and coming together on a much deeper level. It wasn't just the sex, but the connection they shared, the need for them to be close until they were one.

She'd never felt anything like it.

She lost herself in his arms and in the intense emotion filling her up and tying her to him.

She heard what was in her heart. This man was hers.

"You were made for me, Rose, just like I was made for you." The words echoed the feelings in her heart.

Gray linked his fingers with hers and stared into her eyes, as their lovemaking became a joining so profound it overtook them.

He lay atop her, his face in her neck, his breath as uneven and rapid at hers. He pushed up on his forearms and stared down at her. "That was . . ."

"Amazing."

He smiled, but shook his head. "Not enough."

She rocked her hips against his, though he'd gone soft inside her. "Are you sure?"

"I'm sure I'll never get enough of you."

She smiled and brushed her fingers along his jaw. "I'm happy to help prove you right."

He slid to her side and pulled her close so her head rested on his shoulder, his arm around her. She snuggled in and savored the feel of him against her and the warm glow inside he always made her feel.

He kissed the side of her head and pressed his cheek to her hair. "You were definitely meant for me."

Chapter Twenty-Seven

Rose didn't know what woke her in the quiet hotel room. She reached out to the other side of the bed but found it cold. She rolled to her side and saw Gray sitting on the small sofa, the drapes closed at his back. He wore a dress shirt and tie and had his laptop on his thighs, and his bare knees told her he wasn't wearing pants. It made her smile.

"What time is it?"

He stared at her over his laptop, his eyes filled with a hunger she now recognized. He tapped a key, then looked at the screen. "I'll have to call you back." He closed the laptop, set it aside on the ottoman, loosened his tie, pulled it off over his head, undid his shirt, and took that off, too.

Then he stood in just his boxer briefs, muscles moving, all of him sculpted to perfection.

"I could look at you all day." She ate up every inch of him with her gaze.

He came to the bed, crawled over her, slid in beside her, pulled her close, so they were lying facing each other, and brushed his hand over the side of her face and hair. "Did you sleep well?"

"You made sure I did. And I definitely feel better after the lovely dinner in bed you ordered for us last night and getting some sleep."

"You should. It's after ten."

"What?" With the drapes drawn, she had no clue she'd slept in so late.

"I hope you don't mind, but I put your phone on mute. I did answer a text from Maggie. She wants us to meet her and Joel for lunch at twelve-thirty."

"Okay. Did she say anything else?"

"No. I didn't ask anything, just replied that we'd be there."

"I need to see her. I need to know that she's okay."

"I think she will be if she's back with Joel. Right?"

It took her a second to understand what he meant. She needed some caffeine. "Yes. Joel was . . . is the love of her life."

"That sounds a lot like how I feel about you."

"Yeah?" She slipped her hand up his chest to the back of his neck and snuggled in closer to him. "Well, you are the only one I want."

"So you're just going to keep me?"

"Yes. I plan to do just that." She smiled back at him, because his smile lit up her heart.

"Prove it."

"Well, it may take some time, but you'll see I mean it."

He brushed his fingers down the side of her face. "I already know you mean it." He kissed her softly. "I sent you an email this morning about the job you applied for last month."

She didn't expect that. "Are you serious?"

"A hundred percent. It's all the information for your phone interview with the hiring manager for the department that posted the job request."

"Gray, you didn't have to pull any strings for me."

"More than I want you to work for my company and be there with me when it goes public, I wanted to know why someone like you, with your education and talent, was overlooked. Twice."

That got her attention. "What did you find out?"

"It took some digging, but I'm glad I did it, because our CEO has two college-age daughters who are both studying engineering. When he found out what I learned, he fired the HR person in charge of hiring our engineers and programmers."

"Why?" She had a bad feeling, given the disgust on Gray's face.

"He only forwarded résumés for male candidates to the hiring managers because he believed only men are good at such high-level technical jobs."

"What?"

"Exactly. So my assistant and I contacted people in those departments, including the managers and their assistants, and asked questions without asking the big question and discovered that only seven women work in those departments. Seven. So I asked the managers who hired those women how they found them. In all cases, they searched for a wider pool of candidates online themselves."

"In other words, they went searching for a woman."

"Yes, because their departments didn't meet the diversity

criteria set by the company. They tried to do something about it but got pushback from the guy in HR when they did. It was only when they went around that guy that they got the person they wanted for the job. So he's out and there will be a companywide email about the situation and how we're going to fix things going forward. Starting with you."

"Me?"

"You weren't given a fair shot. Now you'll get the interview you deserved. As you can imagine, the director of HR was all too happy to accommodate my request that they find your résumé and forward it to Jay, who called me because I recommended you, and thanked me profusely because he desperately needs someone like you. He can't wait to talk to you about joining his team."

She raised a brow. "Because he knows I'm your girlfriend?"

"No. I didn't think that had anything to do with your qualifications."

She eyed him. "So he didn't ask for the interview because you said so?"

"He based it solely on your résumé. With my position, I meet a lot of people. You're not the first person I've recommended for a position I know is open. Just because I connect a manager to a potential hire doesn't mean they'll get the job. You are the right fit."

She raised a brow. "You don't know anything about my work history or what I do. How do you know I'm the right person for the job?"

"I know you're smart, honest, and kind, and get along with

most everyone, including my asshole cousin, even if you don't like them. You're a good problem solver. You're fair. You think about others. Your job and work are important to you, otherwise you wouldn't have taken that call from your boss last night during your vacation. You told me that you're used to working long hours to get a project done on time, which tells me you care about the bottom line and the work. Jay needs someone who is a team player, but who can get the job done. I told him that's you."

"Gray, I really don't know what to say."

"Yes is the only correct answer." He kissed her softly. "Do the interview. Talk to Jay about what you'll be doing for the company. He's prepared to make you a better than fair offer because he's desperate for someone with your qualifications. I know you're more than interested in working there or you wouldn't have applied twice." The sexy grin made her smile.

"I don't think it's possible for me to refuse you."

"I won't be your boss. If you take the job, you'll report to Jay and the people above him. No one needs to know we have a relationship, though I don't want to hide it. But if it makes you feel better . . ."

"Maybe we don't hide it, but we also don't flaunt it."

"So we can drive to the office together, talk in the office, and have lunch together?"

"I suppose we could, though it's a drive from Los Altos to Santa Clara and back to the office."

Gray raised a brow, his demeanor turning very serious. "Why would you be in Santa Clara when you could be with me?"

She almost stuttered. "I really don't have a good answer for that. And I'm sure we'll get there sooner rather than later."

"Fair enough. It's a lot all at once. And I don't want to push, but I also want you to know I'm all in."

"Me, too." She smiled and sighed her contentment. "Will we have all these life-altering conversations in bed?"

"I hope so." He slid his hand down her arm and side to her hip, then pulled her snug against him. "Now, I have one more proposal to make."

She rocked her hips against his thickening erection. "Oh, yeah? What's that?"

"We make love, then shower, then you can have the fruit and croissant I ordered for you, then we'll go meet Maggie and Joel for lunch."

"A proposal is usually a question. That sounds like a plan."

"One that starts with this." He leaned in and kissed her, and it wasn't long before she found herself straddling him, his hands and mouth on her breasts, their sighs and moans filling the room, and all thoughts of a job interview and lunch with friends were washed away by the sheer pleasure that consumed them.

Chapter Twenty-Eight

1 day after Maggie canceled her wedding . . .
Day 1 with hope for a life with Joel . . .

Maggie found Joel standing outside The Surf restaurant waiting for her. Just the sight of him eased her. When he spotted her and smiled with relief, her feet sped up of their own accord and she rushed into his open arms. He hugged her close. She locked her arms around his neck and held on as if he'd disappear if she didn't.

"Hey, sweetheart, I've got you. It's okay."

After what she went through with Marc yesterday and everyone telling her everything would be all right, it took Joel saying it for her to really start to believe it.

"If you don't want to do this today . . ."

"Don't let go. Not yet." She choked back tears and just let herself feel his strength and understanding. She focused on how right it felt to be in his arms and how it seemed like no time had passed since they were together. Like a couple really in love.

It felt like yesterday, like it would tomorrow and the day after that. It felt right.

But would all the pieces come together for them this time?

"I can stand here with you like this all day if you need me to."

She gave herself another few seconds of bliss before she stepped back.

Joel didn't completely let her go. He kept his hands at her hips and stared down at her. "We don't have to talk about it. We can just sit and be quiet, or devour a skillet of queso and chips, or drink. It's five o'clock somewhere, right?" He always knew how to make her smile. And he remembered that sometimes she needed to do one of those things or all of them when faced with an emotional situation.

"Today calls for a drink and a talk."

He held his hand out to her. "Let's do it."

She took his hand and they walked into the restaurant. The hostess grabbed some menus and led them out to the open deck overlooking the ocean, seating them in a quiet corner, somewhat secluded from the other tables.

"Thank you," Joel said to the hostess. "Our other two guests will be joining us shortly."

Maggie lost herself staring at the ocean, hearing the sound of the crashing waves, and feeling the soft breeze. She turned her face to the sun, closed her eyes, and took the first deep breath she'd taken since everything in her life fell apart yesterday. She vaguely heard Joel order margaritas and chips and queso. When she opened her eyes, she found Joel right beside her, staring at her.

"You're even more beautiful now than when we first met."

She laughed under her breath. "I barely slept last night and I look it."

"Believe me, you're a sight for sore eyes. I thought I'd never see you again. I hoped you'd call, but I wasn't sure. It's been hell waiting for you."

"Then you know how I felt when you ended things and left me drifting." She reined in her anger, because it wasn't about him. "I'm sorry. That wasn't fair. I'm upset about what happened yesterday and taking it out on you."

"I understand. You've been through a lot. I didn't make it easy coming back into your life the way I did, wanting you back when you'd promised to marry someone else."

"I still can't really believe what happened yesterday. I mean, after your call, I was confused and unsure what to do. We went through the ceremony rehearsal. It didn't feel right. Not just because of your call, but because Marc and I had been off all week because of the thing with Rose."

Joel leaned in. "What about Rose?"

Maggie told him everything that happened since last Friday. She couldn't believe so much had happened in one week.

Joel rubbed his hand across the back of her shoulders. "Damn, sweetheart, I . . . I really don't know what to say."

"It was petty, what he did, trying to break up Rose and Gray, to make me believe my best friend was going behind my back, trying to steal my fiancé."

"I'd never suspect or believe Rose would do such a thing.

I mean, I'm sure it was hard for her to tell you about her and Marc, but she did, so that there were no secrets."

"Exactly. It makes no sense. And then again, hearing about how Marc acted growing up with Gray, how he'd prank his cousin, mess up dates between him and his girlfriend, just be a dick to him because he was jealous or didn't want Gray to have something he didn't . . . I really never saw that side of him until we were all together."

"And he went out of his way to not see Rose until now. If he'd simply told you . . .'"

She waved that away. "It doesn't matter now. I'd already decided in my heart what I needed to do; I just hadn't talked to him or anyone else about it. In the end, he made the decision so much easier and validated that I'd made the right choice."

Joel squeezed her shoulder. "You were really going to cancel the wedding and come back to me?" Wonder and relief filled his voice.

She met his gaze and held it, needing so badly to see the truth in his eyes. "Do you really want to have children because you *want* to be a father? Or did you say it just to make me happy?"

"I denied myself an opportunity for real happiness with you because of the way my parents acted with each other and me. I'm not them. I have the experience to know better. I don't have to do and act the way they did with me. I can be a good father and partner to you without playing tug-of-war with our child if something I don't expect to happen to us happens. I love you, Maggie. I will be the husband and father you need me to be, because I want to be the best I can be at those things. I want it all, but most of all I want you."

He laid his heart on the line for her and kissed her to seal the promise he'd made.

That was all she needed to hear, because with Joel, she had now what they'd had before: trust, love, and honesty.

Maggie dove into the kiss knowing it was not the start of something, but the continuation of something that had always felt meant to be.

It felt right.

It felt like coming home.

When Maggie and Joel came up for air, Maggie found they had an audience.

Rose and Gray sat across the table from them. Rose was eating a chip with queso and smiling so big it lightened Maggie's heart to see her so happy. "I take it you two are back together."

Maggie leaned into Joel and smiled for the first time since everything fell apart yesterday. "Yes. I mean, I'm still dealing with the fallout from my breakup, but yes. Joel and I never stopped loving each other; we just thought we wanted different things. Now that we're in agreement . . ." She didn't know what else to say. They were moving forward. Which was perfect for her because she wanted to leave Marc in the past and chalk up her relationship with him as a mistake she wouldn't make again. She'd gone headfirst into marrying Marc without taking the time to watch for inconsistencies and incompatibilities.

She'd focused solely on the good and dismissed anything that didn't sit right with her because she wanted so much for Marc to be the one who gave her the life she wanted.

But having what you want and being happy are sometimes two very different things.

Joel took her hand. "Now that we're in agreement, we're going to spend time together, getting reacquainted. We're going to plan for the future we want but not rush things. We have time." Joel turned to her. "A lifetime."

Maggie brushed her fingers down the side of his handsome face, then turned to Rose and Gray. "I didn't realize that Marc separated me from the ones I love. We spent all our time together, but not with our friends and family." She held Rose's gaze. "I know we stayed in touch through emails, phone calls, and texts, but that's just not enough."

Rose reached across the table and took her hand. "No, it's not. I promise, we will spend more time together."

"I'm glad you feel that way, because I'd like to welcome you and Gray to the very first of our weekly double dates."

Rose lit up with a bright smile. "I love that idea." She turned to Gray. "Are you in?"

"It wouldn't be a double date if I didn't show up. You'd just be the awkward third wheel. I'd never let that happen to you."

Rose gave Gray a quick kiss. "We're in."

Maggie sighed with relief. This is what she wanted. A partner. Her friends. A family. A life filled with happiness and love. "I was thinking we'd meet for dinner once a week. Thursday, maybe." She met Gray's gaze. "Rose is a homebody. She's going to want to stay in with you all the time."

Gray turned to Rose. "I don't mind that. I eat out a lot for work with customers and business associates, so when I get home, I just want to relax. With you would be perfect." Gray faced Maggie. "But I know how much you mean to Rose and I'm looking forward to getting to know you and Joel much better." Gray held his hand out to Joel. "It's good to meet you, man. Looks like we're going to be hanging out a lot."

"Sounds good to me," Joel said. "Whatever makes Maggie happy."

Gray nodded. "I know what you mean. And Rose will be working at my company soon, so it'll be no problem for us to drive to dinner together and meet up with both of you."

Maggie eyed Rose. "When did you take a job at Gray's company?"

Rose bumped her shoulder into Gray's. "I have an interview. We'll see what happens."

"Jay is going to beg you to work for him." Gray showed total faith in Rose. "You'll take his offer because you're dying to be closer to me."

Rose chuckled and shook her head. "Don't mind him. Ever since last night he hasn't let me out of his sight."

"Because when I do you end up getting arrested," Gray teased, though it could have turned out a lot different if Gray's dad hadn't helped sort out the family drama.

Rose held up a finger. "One time. Are you sure you want to take me on?"

Gray touched his forehead to Rose's. "I know what I want. You."

Joel shook his head. "Maggie told me what happened. Marc really had it out for you two."

"Yeah, I'm not sure I'm ready for the next family dinner." Rose grimaced.

Gray stared long and hard at Rose, something possessive and loving in his eyes. "I'll never let him hurt you again."

Maggie had no doubt Gray and Rose were going to go the distance. They had something special. She bet they'd be engaged within a year. Gray wouldn't let Rose get away. Rose would be happy with Gray, a man who knew how to love, and who saw how wonderful and beautiful she was inside and out.

15 months later . . .
10 minutes before Rose and Gray's wedding . . .

Rose stared out the back windows of Gray's beautiful home and smiled at their guests, who couldn't see her because of the privacy tinting on the windows. It made her heart soar to see all of her and Gray's friends and family gathered under the huge oak trees in the backyard. They'd strung lights from tree to tree and over the two long tables where their guests sat.

They'd invited everyone for dinner over the Labor Day weekend.

Fifteen months had passed since Maggie's wedding week that had resulted in Rose's reconciliation with her mom and sister, Maggie's breakup with Marc and second chance with Joel, and, of course, Rose meeting and falling in love with Gray.

Rose visited her mom a couple of times a month down in Carmel. They'd reconnected and were closer than they'd ever been. And of course her mom loved Gray, who almost always went with her for those visits.

In the beginning, Poppy spent most weekends at Rose's apartment. They'd become the best friends they used to be. Poppy enrolled in college and moved in with Rose, though Rose spent more time at Gray's house than the apartment, which made Poppy happy, too, because she'd met a really great guy and they were almost as inseparable as Rose and Gray. Without the weight of the guilt she'd carried about their father's death, Poppy flourished. She was making straight A's and worked part-time in the finance department at Huff Tech with Rose and Gray.

Rose loved working there, too. The offer Jay made was something she couldn't pass up. The money was great. The job challenged her. But best of all, she got to see Gray even more. They never hid their relationship and no one seemed to think twice about her dating the CFO of the company because she proved herself to be an invaluable asset and finally got the recognition and rewards for her hard work. The company went public and her stock shares paid off big-time.

Maggie and Joel sat at the table next to the two empty chairs Rose and Gray had excused themselves from minutes ago. They were kissing. As always. All of them had stuck to their Thursday night double dates all this time, even if Thursday night turned into a Tuesday or Friday once in a while.

Maggie and Joel had eloped nine months after getting back together. Their parents, along with Rose and Gray, went with them for the elegant private ceremony, where Maggie walked down the aisle glowing and happier than Rose had ever seen her. Until Maggie revealed a couple of months later that they were pregnant. Her best friend was going to be a mom. Finally. All her dreams had come true. And Joel seemed completely at ease and excited about their little bundle on the way.

But someone else beat Maggie to parenthood.

Rose found Marc at the opposite table sitting beside his little girl sound asleep in her mom's arms. Marc hadn't wasted any time finding someone to console him after he blew up his life with Maggie. He brought Aimee to the first family dinner she and Gray attended with his family. She thought he tried a little too hard to show that he'd moved on and had someone special in his life. The tension between all of them had been nearly unbearable, but they maintained the peace, mostly because she and Gray simply ignored him as often as possible. Two months after the canceled wedding, he announced Aimee was pregnant with his child. Five months in he found out he was having a little girl and something changed. He treated Aimee with an affection and kindness she'd never seen him show anyone else. The hostility between Marc and his father evaporated. Marc even pulled Gray aside at one of the dinners and apologized for being an asshole to him over the years. Then, in front of everyone, he apologized to Rose. Only then did Gray ease into being friends with him again.

They were family after all.

Now Marc treated her with respect. And though he and Aimee hadn't tied the knot yet, they would someday, because there was no doubt in Rose's mind that Marc had finally found what he was looking for, a woman he wanted to make happy more than anything because he loved her and his child.

"I can't believe you finished getting ready before me." Gray stood just inside the living room in a black tux, the most handsome man she'd ever seen.

He stayed true to his word from that very first double date at The Surf. They hadn't spent a night apart. Not even when he had an overnight business trip. He asked her to go with him. Since she could code in a hotel room just as well as she could at her office, she went, because she didn't like being without him, either.

She stepped away from the window and twirled in her white gown.

"God, you're beautiful."

She held up the full skirt and showed off the sparkling high heels.

"Love the shoes, sweetheart."

She laughed because he'd teased her about her obsession with finding the perfect pair to go with her dress. Turned out the perfect pair had been in her closet the whole time: the pair Maggie gave her when they tried on their dresses that week in Carmel.

She and Gray didn't want a big wedding. Just their closest friends and family. But she wanted the dress, the shoes, the cake the caterer would bring out soon, the flowers decorating the tables and garden, and most of all Gray.

She didn't have someone to walk her down the aisle.

She wanted the only man who'd ever loved her unconditionally to be by her side.

They didn't have bridesmaids or groomsmen.

They wanted to stand in front of the ones they loved and make their vows to each other.

"Do you think anyone suspects anything?"

She'd never get tired of Gray's smile. "I'm pretty sure they think you and I snuck away for a quickie before dessert."

She laughed, and her cheeks heated with the blush that rose from her chest to her cheeks. "Probably."

Gray handed her the bouquet of pink roses she'd set on the end table. "Ready to surprise our guests?"

They had no idea they'd come for a wedding, but it would be no surprise to anyone that she and Gray were getting married.

She placed her hand on his chest next to the pink rose boutonniere he wore. "Ready to spend my life with you? Yes. Absolutely."

Gray kissed her, then held his arm out to her. She slipped her arm through his, and they walked out to a surprised gasp by their guests as the photographer they hired turned on the music they'd selected.

Poppy stood and took her place to officiate the wedding, wearing a gorgeous pink dress and sparkly shoes that matched Rose's. They'd had a grand time planning the wedding together with Gray.

Rose's mom's eyes immediately filled with tears. Gray's parents shared a smile between them before they beamed at her and Gray.

Maggie and her mom had tears in their eyes, but their smiles were bright and filled with joy.

When Rose and Gray turned to each other to begin the ceremony, they smiled at each other and both of them said at the same time, "I love you."

It wasn't the first time they'd said it. It wouldn't be the last. It was all that mattered. Because when you're with the one you want, the one you love above all else, you want them to know it and feel it.

They gave each other that every day.

And now, they'd have the rest of their lives together.

The nightmare of her past was such a distant memory she hardly ever thought about it anymore because Gray made everything in her life something to hold on to and cherish.

Most of all, she liked holding on to him.

Reading Group Guide

1. The novel opens with Rose returning to her childhood home and noticing that it looks so ordinary, and yet it held secrets. How do you remember your childhood home? Have you ever returned to visit it, and, if so, what did you discover?

2. Like many friends, Maggie and Rose were once inseparable, but life has pulled them apart. Why do you think some friendships last, even through time and great distance, and some do not? Do you think Maggie and Rose ever truly knew each other at all?

3. Poppy, Rose's sister, has a very different way of dealing with their mutual childhood. Why do you think siblings often experience their growing up years in very different ways? Are there memories your family has of you growing up that are quite different from your own?

4. Maggie has doubts about her upcoming marriage, and yet things proceed almost of their own accord. In what ways have you seen the *idea* of "a wedding" become more important than the reality of a "marriage"?

5. Marc seems to regard "getting married" as something that will change him for the better. Do you feel his intentions are honest? Why or why not?

6. Do we, as a society, place too much emphasis on the idea of "real life" beginning when you get married?

7. Do you think Rose's actions are the right ones? Why or why not?

8. Are Poppy's troubles, as an adult, of her own making or are some issues too difficult to overcome by sheer willpower? Why do you think Rose managed to do what Poppy did not?

9. How should Poppy and Rose's mother have acted differently while they were growing up? Do you feel she was stuck between a rock and a hard place or not? And why?

10. Is Marc's bachelor party just good fun, or do you think bachelor parties have gone too far?

About the Author

New York Times and *USA Today* bestselling author Jennifer Ryan writes suspenseful contemporary romances about everyday people who do extraordinary things. Her deeply emotional love stories are filled with high stakes and higher drama, family, friendship, and the happily-ever-after we all hope to find.

Jennifer lives in the San Francisco Bay Area with her husband and three children. When she finally leaves those fictional worlds, you'll find her in the garden, playing in the dirt and daydreaming about people who live only in her head, until she puts them on paper.